Captivating Beauty
Special Edition
Discreet Cover

Accardi Tactical, Book 6

K.C. Ramsey

K.C. Ramsey

ISBN ebook: 978-1-964688-02-2

ISBN print: 978-1-964688-06-0

Created with Atticus   Cover by: Furiousfotog

Book Blurb: Briggs Consulting, LLC

Developmental and Line Edits by: Olivia Kalb Editing

Proofing by: Zoe Reading

CONTENTS

Notes to my readers...

First of all, thank you for jumping into my world.

If you're a new reader of mine, *Captivating Beauty* is the sixth installment in the Accardi Tactical series. I highly recommend starting the series from the beginning with *Lethal Beauty*. The books can be read separately, but the storyline is so much stronger together. If you choose to start with *Captivating Beauty*, please be aware that, while each couple gets their happily-ever-after, there are family storylines that weave through the series as a whole. Rest assured, all questions that haven't been answered by the end of each book will be later on.

Chapter 1

XANDER

The lingering reverberation of almost fifty motorcycles fading into the distance made the room seem beyond quiet.

"Well, thank fuck they're finally gone," Wyck, a big man who looked like a half-giant, said. I was a large guy, but he could barely fit through a door without turning sideways; he was so tall and wide. Despite his appearance, including the tattoos that ran around both biceps and down one forearm, something about him put off vibes that he was a friendly giant—at least, compared to those around him. Anyone in the club was certainly not a choir boy.

"I told you, just because you're hoping for some peace and quiet around here, doesn't mean you're going to get it," a man sitting in a booth in the shadows shot back. His features were obscured by the lack of light above him, and the only identifiers I saw were his lanky but muscular build and muddy brown eyes.

"Yeah," Another one of the bikers—the few left, anyway—pointed at me. "I'm sure he alone is going to cause shit to go down. He has that look." My back tensed, but while his words weren't complementary, his tone was friendly, if not damn full of anticipation.

"At least we won't have to worry so much about someone in the bedroom next to us slitting our throat while we're sleeping," Wyck grumbled, but he eyed me with suspicion, as if he wasn't so sure about me. I didn't blame him. Not only was I an unknown, but he wasn't wrong in thinking one of his own MC members could do something like that. The Iron Wraiths motorcycle club was world-renowned for their blood-thirstiness, complete disregard for the law, and cold-blooded capability. They didn't claim to be one percenters—the MC clubs that boasted about being the one percent of clubs that weren't law-abiding citizens—but anyone who knew anything about them knew they were at the top of the list, whether they made claim to the title or not.

I raised a hand, not about to back down or appear weak, but realizing I needed to make an effort to bond with the group. These men had not only protected Vik's back when I couldn't, but some of them had even saved my Alex. "Should I recite an oath or something," I asked, putting humor into my gravelly voice. It'd been almost three months, and I still didn't recognize the sound of my own voice. I wouldn't even think about the face in the mirror that went along with it.

I was surprised, and more than a little pleased, that my practiced Texas drawl was at least on point. I'd taught myself the twang by watching old western and other classic American movies over the years in preparation, but I wasn't confident at how natural it would sound. After all, Russian's always sounded like thugs in all the American movies I'd ever seen. Though, when it came to myself, at least, the accusation was fairly accurate.

"I guess we could demand a blood sacrifice," the teasing one said with a grin, extending his hand. "Shade, I know Grimm had to throw you to the fire with those introductions, and I imagine most of the ones that stuck belonged to the men who left ... numbers and all."

I exchanged pleasantries, looking around at the remaining men with interest. I'd arrived scarcely an hour before the bulk of the men had cleared out, and while I knew better than to try to draw attention to myself, I was anxious to see Vik. I knew the remaining men around me were his brothers-in-arms, but I hadn't seen him in the throng of people, and I didn't see him now.

"He's not here," Grimm, the chapter president and leader of the group, said, knowing who I was searching for. "Everything right now was about putting on a show and doing absolutely nothing to draw suspicion to the two of y'alls connection to the branch of the MC that just left." He motioned toward the door. "Vik is well known as a surly, anti-social SOB who's always behind his bar. And if he's not behind his bar, he's behind ours." Pointing to the other side of the empty bar top in emphasis, I understood his point.

"An emotional—and crowded—sendoff isn't Vik's thing, so him being here would've been weird. And you showing up, well, it would make some even more suspicious, seeing as Vik never mentions his past, and we sure as shit don't need them to see y'alls Hallmark moment." A man I recognized as Savage added helpfully. He'd been one of the men to pick me up from the last transit point, and his looks were so close to that of Matteo—the man running the entire operation—that I assumed he was a relative. "While you're still going to have to play a role in public, you won't have to worry about being yourself with us now that the brothers have left. Don't worry, though, we're not going to leave you hanging. We'll give you a few minutes, run you through the players and what you need to know, and then head out. I'm sure your anxious to see him, and the fucker's been even more hormonal than normal—another reason Grimm made him stay away until the main membership left. Lessia's sending a text when the moment's right for us to leave. You do know how to ride a motorcycle?"

I raised an eyebrow, wondering if that was even a legitimate question. The entire room broke out in chuckles, breaking up the lingering tension.

"All right, so reintroductions." Grimm took over. "You've got Whisp over there in the shadows, Shade is the bloodthirsty one, Savage, Wyck, and Charge. Jasper is an ER doctor and works the night shift, and Raptor and Judge are out on assignment right now. Not everyone here is an operative—and there's even more support staff who aren't connected to us outright. Some work for Matteo in the field, others provide cover right here, and a few don't have anything to do with the bloodier side of things. But all of us are brothers, and we support each other the way family is *supposed* to. We might not always get along, but when it matters, we're there, no questions asked. Now, our original purpose within the club was to ensure the right people could get through the Iron Wraiths MC smuggling operation undetected, even from the rest of the MC members. That's something we're *all* involved in—and part of what you agreed to assist with once you're settled. Anything else is optional, but you mess with what we do—or fuck up—you're going to wish you'd stayed in Russia."

I nodded, believing the threat but not nearly as phased by it as I was sure he'd wanted. When you had a mother whose favorite pastime was torture and contemplated turning the tables on you pretty much your whole life, it was hard to be impressed with anyone else's attempt at intimidation.

Shoving my hands in my pockets, I clarified, "According to what I was told, the smuggling operation I'm joining is only to save victims of human trafficking or other victims who need to be moved through underground channels to ensure their safety."

Grimm smiled as if I'd just gotten a gold star in his book. "Fucking right. Not that the MC doesn't smuggle other shit in addition to money—the Iron Wraiths primary bread and butter—weapons, and other black market goods, but *our* purpose is to ensure that those who need it have a second chance at a normal life. We work with others all over the world in a ... global underground pipeline ... I guess you could call it. Paper trails can be tracked, no matter how deep they're buried, if someone's good enough and determined enough to find one."

"Unless," Savage said with a wink, "there isn't one to find."

"Nonetheless," Grimm continued, "I know there are certain risks returning to anything remotely similar to your last profession. But that doesn't mean you have to start out your new life as a law-abiding citizen if you don't want to. Though that's available if you want it." He pointed a thumb over his shoulder at Wyck. "This guy owns his own construction company—one of the best in the state. He's always looking for good, capable help."

"I see you never offer up me good labor," Shade grumbled.

Savage laughed. "As if anyone wants to assist your employees on crime scene cleanup duty, asshole. It's our job to make the mess, not clean it up."

"You clean up crime scenes?" I asked, half-fascinated, half-disgusted, thinking of some of the ways I'd killed others. Taking in what he explained, I had to readjust my understanding of expected roles within the group. I thought I'd have a similar life to the one I'd left—one with very little choice and all of it bloody. Apparently, my chance at a fresh start provided more freedom than I'd ever had.

"Own it, I don't do the work anymore," he said with a shrug as if the details didn't matter.

"He's being modest," Charge piped in. Something about his stance screamed military to me, and I wondered how long he'd been out. "He owns the company most of the law enforcement in Texas recommends for major disaster cleanup. You're up to, what, twenty branches?"

Shade still looked bored with the conversation. "Something like that. Grimm's making me expand out to

Louisiana so I have an excuse to go out to talk with Hazzard without raising suspicion."

"I'm willing to float around to whomever needs assistance until I get more settled. I'd like to spend some time with Viktor—Vik," I corrected. "And see what kind of life Xander Hawkings will have." The name still sounded foreign—almost as foreign as the body attached to it. I'd had countless surgeries on my appearance and vocal cords, along with months of coaching to change my mannerisms and teach me what living and growing up in America would have been like. Now it was time to see what my present and future would shape up to be.

"Yeah," Savage said, a wicked smile on his face. "Who knows, maybe after all this time 'incarcerated' you'll fall in love at first sight and live happily ever after as a soccer dad."

My mouth kicked up into a semblance of a smile. As far as the locals were concerned, I'd spent the last twelve years doing time for murder before being exonerated on a technicality last week. Aside from a few others, only the people in this room, and Andrie, once I told her, would know I was a Russian asset, but that was it. Only Matteo, Lessia, Vik, and possibly Grimm knew my true previous identity.

"Do I look like a soccer dad to you?" I was covered with ink before I'd left Russia—pretty par for the course being raised in the Bratva. Gangs, no matter how large or their country of origin, had a reputation for such things, Russian's more than most. But my ink had been altered along with my face, fingerprints, and damned DNA. Overkill? Probably, but when there was a remote chance of get-

ting on the radar of people who had the power—and desire—to kill you, the extra effort was appreciated, even if
the rehab had been a bitch.

The blocky black tattoos, some of which had run down
to my fingers, were gone. In their place, swirls of trib-
al-looking ink were placed over bright blues, reds, and
green sleeves that went down to my wrist on one side,
with a joker tattoo and snake running down my other arm.
My hands and neck no longer held any indication they'd
ever been tattooed, and my scalp was shaved bald, hiding
what had been pale yellow hair. I'd grown out my beard,
which, thankfully, was a much darker shade. But even if I'd
shaved and thrown on a suit instead of the simple t-shirt,
leather vest, jeans, and boots, there was no way I'd look
like I was anything other than someone kids ran away from
screaming. Some adults, too.

The guys broke out into laughter, getting another
round of ribbing in, before Charge—another biker brother—showed me the room I'd have upstairs. It was larger than I expected, with a private bathroom. The bed
was a king, with clean sheets, two pillows, and a nightstand. A dresser was against one wall, with a small closet.
"It's not much, but it's yours. Whether you crash here
or not, this room is earmarked for you. It's a good idea
to keep some supplies here regardless. You know, clothes,
weapons, go-bag, that sort of thing. If Grimm calls us all
in as a safety precaution, you'll want enough here to last a
while."

Charge tapped on the door, and I noticed the word
"Revenant" on the door. Tilting my head in silent ques-

tion, Charged looked up at where I was staring. "Your road name. As you already know, none of us actually go by our given names much."

"Revenant?" I asked, and Charge grinned.

"Revived from death to haunt the living? Seemed appropriate." He slapped me on the shoulder in a friendly manner. "Now, drop your shit off. Vik's waiting, and Lessia arranged another surprise for you."

Anticipation surged inside me, all my senses coming to full alertness. *Alex*. It had to be. Only, she no longer went by Alex. It was Andrie now. My heart warmed at that. I'd damn near cried when I'd first heard the name she'd chosen. Andrie Demming. Doctor Andrie Demming. Only she and Vik had called me Demi instead of DM. And Andrie referenced my middle name, Andrei. She's literally taken my name the only way she could. Just like I'd done with hers.

All of these years apart, and now, it would be mere minutes until I could lay eyes on her, touch her. The only catch ... she couldn't know I was me.

Chapter 2

ANDRIE

"I really think I should go," I whispered to Lessia, looking around with wide eyes. When Alessia Accardi, a colleague, sometimes-patient, and someone I thought I might even be able to be friends with, had asked me to join her and some others for dinner, I'd thought we'd be meeting at a family-style restaurant or possibly an upscale one. Lessia—as her friends called her—had been an in-demand model until her recent retirement and was still a part of one of the most wealthy and influential families in Texas.

Never in a million years would I have thought she'd bring me to Vik's Bar. Vik, my next-door neighbor, pseudo brother, and self-appointed guardian, had forbade me from going anywhere near his place of business unless I was with him. Having seen the location—and building—when he'd purchased the falling down heap, I'd readily agreed.

I really should've known better. Lessia's reputation for getting into trouble was legendary, even within the exclusive ranks of the men and women I counselled. But I just didn't think I'd get dragged into her plans. I was a professional wallflower. As a psychiatrist who specialized in trauma studies, most of my time was spent working alongside elite military personnel and their families, trying to help them work through the mental fallout that was inevitable when honorable men and women came across the horrors of what other people could do to each other in the name of money, love, hate, or God.

Due to the confidentiality of not only my patients but their very existence, I kept myself under the radar of others. After all, my files contained not only minimally altered documentation of missions, units, and other military information for the best and brightest the United States government had to offer—publicly acknowledged or not—but also patient files for those starting over, under new aliases, and trying to keep hidden themselves. Typically, I didn't even see my patients outside of the office—for both professional and safety reasons—but I'd known Lessia before I'd even *become* Andrie, and she was one of the very few who knew what had led me to the basement I'd been rescued from. Besides, all of us who knew her were well aware that Lessia Accardi didn't let rules dictate her desires. If she wanted to meet up from time to time outside of the office, she'd damn well do as she pleased. Sometimes I wished I could be like her, and at one point in my life, I was, but at times like now, I wished I wouldn't let her cross those boundaries.

Everything about my life was understated and minimalistic, from my home to my chosen dress and even the car I drove. No, Dr. Andrie Demming would never go to a biker bar in the most dangerous part of town to celebrate the engagement of a woman I'd never met. And she'd never have a beer drawn from a tap, let alone two. I frowned, looking at my nearly empty pint. Hadn't it only been two?

Lessia, who'd squeezed in next to me at my table near the bar, caught me glaring at my glass.

"Come on, Andrie, lighten up," she whispered, watching the small group of women she'd come in with dancing on an impromptu dance floor to some new hip hop song that was all the rage.

I looked over to Vik. I was surprised he'd allowed a bunch of women to invade a space that consisted solely, I was sure, of his MC brothers, the odd gang member or two, and some rough necks, if they were feeling confident. Heck, Vik owned the bar and freely admitted that his customers were some of the worst humanity had to offer. I couldn't be sure, of course, but I was confident that at least a handful of people had killed or been killed right there in the building. And I didn't want to know how many had met their end in the parking lot. Just last week I'd read in the paper that someone had been stabbed and nearly died after a fight that had started over who got to choose the next song in the jukebox. At least, that was what Vik had said it was about when I'd asked him. Seeing as the jukebox in question—and the songs it contained—was older than I was, I wasn't sure if the outlandish reason was legitimate or not. Honestly, the odds that Vik had told me the truth was probably fifty-fifty.

Vik, to my utter confusion and complete surprise, looked almost pleased at the group of dancers. That was, until he caught me staring at him. He immediately went back to looking down and polishing beer glasses. My gaze narrowed. Vik was never a man of many words, and his poker face was excellent, but he had tells, just like most people. And when he was nervous or on edge, he fidgeted. Nothing super noticeable or high energy. He wouldn't jiggle a leg or flit from one room to another. But he would keep his hands busy, and those glasses looked like they'd just come out of a brand-new box.

Lessia let out an ear splitting whistle, pulling me from my thoughts. "Y'all," she said pointedly at a few men who'd just walked in. They looked bewildered at the show on the dance floor but cocky enough to enjoy the show—or want to join. "That group of women right there"—she motioned at where her friends Paige, Kassie, and Claire danced—"belong to me." Her tone left no room for argument. "I don't care if you think they winked at you, shook their ass for you, or so much as smiled in your direction. None of them are up for grabs, and anyone who so much as bothers my best friend's celebration will answer to me. Is that clear?"

Obviously, Lessia was a regular with a well-known repu-tation because the men gulped and slunked off to a corner, well away from the women.

"I'm engaged, y'all!" Paige shouted drunkenly, raising her hand in the air to show off a stunning engagement ring, totally oblivious to Lessia's words or the men watching the group like a pack of wild dogs, debating whether or not the risk was worth the reward.

"What's going on?" I whispered, starting to get suspi-cious the more I thought about it. Lessia wasn't drinking like the rest and seemed keyed up, though it'd taken me a while to realize it. The therapist in me couldn't help but track everyone in the room, noting body language. I tried to turn it off when I wasn't working, but it was hard to do.

"Can't you just take a night off?" Lessia whispered back. "You're supposed to be living it up tonight. You know, taking a break from the straight-laced you. It's not like Vik or I would let anything happen to you. God, Andrie, you're so prim and proper all the time, I'm worried you'll turn into a robot."

I gasped, the world spinning ever so slightly as I whirled around to her. "You're the one who called me a Stepford shrink," I accused. I'd heard rumors but hadn't been able to track it back to the source.

Instead of denying it, she raised an eyebrow. "Am I wrong?"

Tilting my head to the side, I thought about her question. "No," I said finally. "But you hurt my feelings." I tried to pout but felt a little ridiculous. I wasn't drunk enough to act like a total fool, just buzzed enough to feel the effects. Maybe I'd been a little uptight lately if two glasses were hitting me that hard. At one point in my life, I could hold my own, drink for drink, against any college frat kid. *It's amazing how one can go from a free-spirited, living-large college student studying abroad to a boring, fade-into-the-woodwork woman, but I supposed being ripped away from the love of your life, stuffed into a shipping container, and forced into the life as a sex slave for a few months changes a girl.* Of course, considering what I'd gone through, I was pretty proud of just being normal ... relatively speaking. And while the abuse would always leave psychological scars, even the professional psychiatrist was amazed that the most lasting damage was being taken away from ... him.

A snort brought me back to the present. Lessia didn't apologize for the comment, not that I'd expected her to. Lessia didn't sugarcoat her words or take them back. "You're still mourning him, after all these years, Alex." Her voice was quiet enough that I could barely hear her, but I still gaped at her when she used my old name. "All the sacrifices y'all made were so you could live. Really live. Instead, you're dwelling in a prison of your own making. He wouldn't want this."

My mouth opened and shut several times as I began to speak, only to stop. Objectively, she wasn't telling me something Vik and I hadn't argued about—at length—on countless occasions. But just because I didn't have a good counterpoint didn't mean my feelings weren't valid. I'd loved Demi for almost ten years, even though our time together had been brief. As a naïve twenty-two-year-old, I'd taken one look at Demi and fallen hard and fast. But despite my age, our whirlwind romance, or the events that had led to our separation, I'd loved him with every part of me. Still did. My heartache might not be as fresh as it once had, but it was a wound that wouldn't heal. Being apart from him hadn't just torn my heart in two ... It was as if one of the halves had been surgically removed. I'd always felt as if I were missing a limb, knowing he was out there and not being able to reach him.

I hadn't seen him in years, not even looking at pictures any longer—it hurt too much. To see him age, his eyes turning harder and harder, seeing more and more scars on his body, and know he was sacrificing himself for me while I was dying by inches each and every day. When I was told he'd been killed a few months ago, the last bit of hope I'd clung to had withered away as well. I felt like a shell of a person, just going through the motions.

"What do you think I should do?" I shot back, angry at the world for putting me in the position I was in. "Have a one-night stand with the next man to walk through that door?"

Before Lessia could comment, a rumble of what sounded like thunder echoed from outside, multiplying until I couldn't count how many motorcycles had pulled up. Vik froze, turning to the door in an anticipation I didn't understand. The women stopped dancing, and someone cut off the music as the noise got even louder before the engines cut off, one by one.

The silence afterward hung in the air, and the entire room seemed frozen as they waited. Some of the men appeared apprehensive, but I noticed Vik wasn't reaching for a weapon.

The door flew open with a bang, and the shadow of a large man stood in the doorway for several long seconds, the darkness making it hard to see anything but the profile of a hulking figure made by countless hours of hard labor and a strong worth ethic. My breath caught; something about the way he stood caught my attention in a way that only one other man ever had.

"Sounds like a great idea," Lessia said with mock innocence.

He took one step inside, his leather vest, paired with the tattoos that ran down both arms to his wrists, pegged him as an MC member. And if the solid muscles and shaved head didn't scream danger, his dark blue eyes, impassive and cold, would have.

Hope I'd known better than to have, so quick to rise, was extinguished in a heartbeat. *Wrong color,* my mind whispered. His eyes—and tattoos for that matter—weren't Demi's. But even as my breath caught in inevitable disappointment, my body stirred, taking notice of a man for the first time in more years than I wanted to count.

Vik, who'd been still as a statue, threw the bar towel he'd been using over his shoulder and, as if the pass-through to the bar was too far away, put a hand on the bar top and hoisted himself over it. He landed beside an empty barstool and just stood there, taking in the stranger.

The moment stretched on as the two men assessed one another. In an instant, Vik's face stretched into a full-out grin—his happiness so apparent, I could only stare. Vik was a lot of things, but most of them centered around being grumpy, decidedly close-mouthed, and emotionally closed-off. A smile was a rare thing, but I couldn't remember ever seeing Vik this unguarded, even if it was short-lived.

The two men reached for each other, pulling in for a long bro-hug, complete with multiple back-thumps and murmured words no one could make out.

"Who?" I breathed, not wanting to break up the scene in front of me.

"Vik's brother." Lessia's words hit me hard. In all the years I'd known him, Vik had never told me he'd left a brother behind. Happiness for him surged through me before envy roared to life. How was it this man had made it out when my Demi hadn't?

Ruthlessly, I shoved back my own feelings. Vik was family to me ... the only family I had left. And this return of a sibling after all these years was surely something he'd have strong feelings he'd have to work out. And this brother, if he'd been in the same life as Vik and Demi, likely had a lifetime of trauma to work through once he had time to process everything. I needed to make sure I could be there for both.

Lessia rose, sidling up to the two men. I barely registered the rest of the Iron Wraiths as they filtered into the bar. "Xander," Lessia greeted. "I heard you got out of prison early for good behavior. Please tell me you at least have a better control over your temper—I don't want to hear about you going back for good this time."

I gulped before realizing that must have been the cover story the MC had produced to explain his absence until now. I knew more than most that the Iron Wraiths were deadly, stone-cold killers, but the one's I knew would cut off their hand before doing harm to an innocent. The group might look like they could gut someone like a fish, but I'd always felt safe with Vik's friends. Even now, as they settled in various places around the room, I felt more protected than I had with Lessia sitting next to me—and I knew what that woman was capable of.

The newcomer, Xander, pulled back from Vik to look down at her—something that didn't happen to the tall brunette often. "Just call me Revenant," he growled, the joke completely at odds with his stone-faced expression. "I should've had ten more years to go, but you have to love it when someone's fuckup is uncovered. Hell, I was doing humanity a favor, offing that asshole. It just so happens the government finally decided to agree."

Lessia, never one to miss a beat, slapped his shoulder in greeting. "Come on, then, Rev. I'll buy you a beer."

The men made their way to the counter, where Lessia, acting as if she'd bartended her entire life, stepped behind the bar and began pulling beers. In an effort to stop staring at Xander, I forced my eyes to roam the bar, wondering if I could make my escape with everyone distracted.

Charge, one of the Iron Wraiths MC members, caught my attention. He mumbled something to Grimm, the leader of the group, who nodded, then Charge caught the eye of some of the other men who'd been drinking for as long as we'd been in the bar and tilted his head to the door.

At the unspoken signal, most of the men not in the MC rose, tossed some money on their tables, and left without a word. A few of the others looked around uncomfortably, reading the room, and decided to call it an early night as well.

The door barely had time to shut behind the last of them when a new group of men came in, practically rushing into the room. In direct contrast to gang members and bikers that just left, these men looked as out of place as the women they'd come for.

"Keene!" Paige squealed, hiccupping as she stumbled her way to her fiancé.

Keene who'd come to a stop as soon as he'd gotten through the door, his brothers Boone and Royce flanking him, slowly smiled, paying attention to no one but her. "Having fun?" he asked, gathering her to him.

"So much fun," she sighed, burrowing into him.

The sight of her, cradled in his arms, twisted my gut. I wanted others to find love; I truly did. But seeing couples so certain of one another and blissfully happy only reminded me of those stolen weeks when I'd had—and lost—the same. Never again would I be that carefree and confident.

"Turn the music back on and lock the door," Lessia called out, hard at work at the tap. "We've got a double celebration and the place all to ourselves."

The MC men—and Lessia's girl crew—all cheered. Brody, who'd been closest to the door, slid the lock into place before coming around to help Lessia.

Someone traded the pop songs for country, and soon, the women had their men on the dance floor with them. The MC members settled around the room, happy to steer clear of the engagement celebration.

Deciding I'd stayed long enough, and pretty uncomfortable with the idea of hanging in the booth by myself like a lurker, I rose, pleased that my feet stayed steady under me. Maybe I wasn't as out of practice as I'd thought.

Lessia, who was setting down Vik and Xander's drinks in front of them, must've seen me stand because she said something to Vik, who rose.

"Andrie," he said, motioning me over to him. "You've got to meet Xander."

His elation at his brother's return was still easy to see. Giving him a tight smile, I let him pull me under his arm in a sideways hug. "Xander, meet Alexandria Demming. Andrie, this is my brother, Xander."

Taking a nervous breath, I extended my hand to the hulking stranger. He looked down at my hand as if the movement was foreign to him, and I wondered if maybe he'd truly been incarcerated and was unused to social niceties. Slowly, he grasped my hand in his, the calluses on his fingers rough against my skin, but he kept his touch light, as if afraid of his own strength.

Nerve endings I'd thought long dead flared to life, sending tingling warmth through me so fast I gasped at him in wonder. His eyes flared, and I wondered if he'd felt it, too. I wanted to pull back—I'd only had these feelings for one other man in my life, and he wasn't there—but Xander's hand firmed around mine as if he'd read my intentions.

"Andrie was my best friend's sister, and when he died, she became my little sister." Vik was explaining the cover story we'd fabricated before our new identities had even been finalized.

"Well," Xander's deep, raspy Texas drawl had my body shuddering. "I'd say any little sister of my brother's is kin to me, but I'd be lying. Come sit with us for a while, sweetheart. I'd love to get to know the only family my brother has had to count on while I was gone."

Feeling as if I were in a dream, I found myself sitting between the two men. Lessia slid yet another beer in front of me with a sly wink, reminding me of my flippant comment just moments before Xander walked into the bar, and I flushed.

I was Dr. Andrie Demming, professional wallflower. And conservative, boring wallflowers *did not* have wild flings with dangerous bikers.

Chapter 3

XANDER

I could hardly believe the day I'd never let myself think would be possible was here. Everything I'd done, everything I'd sacrificed for, had led to this moment. Thinking about what life would be like after the fallout of my actions was something that had sustained me in my darkest times, but never in the thousands of scenarios I'd come up with did I think I would be nervous.

The woman I'd loved with foolish abandon, the one whose life had been shattered because of my choices, who still—by all accounts—was loyal to my memory, was just beyond the door in front of me. Hope, anxiety, and dread swirled in the pit of my stomach. *Would she recognize me?* I knew if she did, I'd have no choice but to disappear again, but the elemental part, the one that laid claim to that slip of a girl all those years ago, wanted her to know I'd kept my promise. That I'd done the impossible and gotten all of us out.

Another part of me was terrified she wouldn't have a clue who I was, or worse, would reject the man I'd become in order to survive. *Damned if you do, damned if you don't. It's the story of your life, Demi. Might as well get it over with.*

I knew the men—my new family—were waiting for me to make the first move. They were a good group of honorable guys from what I could gather—but we were still feeling each other out, and the last thing I needed was for them to think I was afraid of anything this life could dish out.

Pushing the door aside with more force than intended, I allowed myself to take stock of what I was walking into. I'd already gathered—from the drug dealers blatantly selling on the street corner a half-block from here, the prostitutes across the street, and the ramshackle appearance of the buildings—that we were in a dangerous side of town. Even if we were walking into a five-star restaurant, the need to categorize my surroundings, identify possible enemies, and note exits and entry points, was so ingrained I'd likely never be able to break the habit. But lucky for me, the new me was just as paranoid of a bastard as the old one had been.

Three women were gathered in the middle of an open area, looking as if they were celebrating. Considering none of them appeared to be armed—or was Lessia—I moved on, as much as I wanted to linger over one of them. With any luck, there would be time for that another day. At the bar sat four men, and there were two groups of three at the tables at the far side of the room. Judging by their expressions and body language, they were not exactly friendly, and they were definitely carrying. Movement in a corner booth caught my eye, but before I could lock onto it, a man—the bartender—jumped over the counter, coming to stand in front of me.

For several long moments, we just stared at each other. Vik was older now, of course, with new scars on one of his arms and what looked like a bullet hole close to his bicep, but the familiar golden-brown eyes were the same. There was a sheen in them, just for a moment, that I was sure matched mine, though neither of us had cried since we were children, quick to learn, as we'd been, that tears had no purpose in life. He'd grown another inch or so, his somewhat lanky frame filled out now with the aid of good food and a healthy appreciation for manual labor. He was my friend ... my brother ... and yet not. I saw him taking in my appearance the way I was him, and I wondered if there was any part of the old me left to find.

His gaze, which had been trailing me up and down, finally rose to meet mine. As one, we stepped into each other, pulling in for a hug that was years in the making.

"I'm so glad to see you, brother," Vik whispered in Russian. "I've kept her safe for you, just as I swore I would."

I swallowed hard. "Is she here?" I asked, already knowing the answer but needing the confirmation anyway.

"Yes, but she has no idea. And there are others here we need to put on a show for. A few more minutes patience, and I promise you'll see her." He hesitated. "Did they warn you?"

I tilted my head. "What?"

"You're going to have your work cut out for you," he said simply. "She's as in love with you as she was the first day I met her. Maybe even more so since all she has are memories of a damn ghost. She's not going to welcome Xander Hawkings into her life easily."

Before I could reply, a woman rose, gliding up behind Vik in a sexy strut I recognized. "Xander," Lessia greeted me as if I were a long-lost friend. "I heard you got out of prison early for good behavior. Please tell me you at least have a better control over your temper—I don't want to hear about you going back for good this time."

I pulled back from Vik to look her over, please she seemed no worse for wear from her latest adventure. I'd heard that, despite my warning, she'd ended up in Karl Albrecht's private collection, but had held her own until she'd been extracted.

"Just call me Revenant," I growled out, letting my familiar mask fall back into place. I wouldn't have picked the nickname myself, but if I had to have one, there were certainly worse ones they could have chosen. And it did have a ring of irony to it. "I should've had ten more years to go, but you have to love it when someone's fuckup is uncovered. Hell, I was doing humanity a favor, offing that asshole. It just so happens the government finally decided to agree."

Lessia, never one to miss a beat, slapped my shoulder. "Come on, then, Rev. I'll buy you a beer."

We made our way to the counter, where Lessia waved Vik into a stool and took over for him behind the bar. She looked completely different than the way she usually did when we crossed each other—which was typically during some charity event or fancy dinner. Instead of a ball gown, high heels, and a shit-ton of makeup, she was barefaced, wearing shorts, tennis shoes, and a simple t-shirt. Sure, the shorts were an inch shorter than I was sure her brothers were comfortable with, and her shirt was practically molded to her, but that was just typical Lessia. For a former model, she wore the classic hometown girl look well.

I followed their lead, making small talk with Vik as Charge signaled to the outsiders to get out. It spoke to the MC's power that the men all took off without hesitation. I'd only been read in on the club's exploits in the broadest sense of the word, and I figured I'd learn more as I went. But Grimm seemed like a fair and well-respected leader thus far. At least, within the club. The fact that these road-hardened men left without a word at a simple gesture by an MC member cemented what I'd already gathered—the Iron Wraiths reputation was well established, brutal, and, for now, uncontested in their territory, even with the mass exoduses earlier in the night.

I, for one, wasn't ready to trust anyone outside of the man and woman in front of me—at least for now. Vik was my brother in everything but blood, and Lessia had proved herself trustworthy, even if I was under no illusions of her loyalty to me. If anything, I was beholden to her. Without her, my life would have lost all meaning a long time ago.

The front door opened, and several men—one of whom I recognized as Lessia's bodyguard—walked in.

"Keene!" one of the women cried, stumbling her way over to one of the men. Based on the ring on her finger and the look in his eye, they were either newlyweds or engaged. Keene and the other two who weren't the bodyguard looked similarly enough that I pegged them as brothers.

"Turn the music back on and lock the door," Lessia called out, pulling out more mugs. "We've got a double celebration and the place all to ourselves."

The entire bar cheered, and the bodyguard slid the lock of the door into place before coming around to help Lessia, who was serving all the men lining up for a beer. I saw her toss a small smile up at him as he placed a small kiss on her head and rested a hand on her hip—something that she would have laid a man out for if wasn't welcome—before grabbing mugs to fill. Well, well, apparently, the mighty Alessia Accardi had fallen in love.

Old country music started up on the jukebox, and the three women pulled their men onto the dance floor with them. The rest of the MC settled around the room, giving the corner booth a wide berth.

It took everything I had not to let my attention linger on the woman I knew was sitting there. She was pressed into the booth, despite having the entire bench to herself, wearing black pants, low-slung heels, and a white blouse. Not the look one typically wore coming to a place like this, but I suspected she might have come straight from the office. I couldn't see but a flash of an arm, the cross of a leg, and the flick of long black hair.

"Steady," Lessia murmured under her breath, reading me like a book, though I tried to hide my feelings. "She's going to be skittish. Let her come to you." She refilled our drinks, her eyes flicking to Vik. "She's going to try to bolt. Call her over," she directed.

Vik turned, rising as he did so. "Andrie, you've got to meet Xander."

It was all I could do not to jump out of my chair in anticipation. Lessia was correct, though. Everything about the woman in front of me screamed *runner*, even at a glance. My jaw tightened at the change. Alex had been a carefree ray of sunshine—the total opposite of me; it was one of the things I'd loved most about her. She couldn't walk into a room without drawing everyone's eye. *Solnyshkuh*, little sun, was what I'd called her.

Now, she appeared all shadows.

Her long black hair was pulled into an understated ponytail, but the loose end was wavy as if it had been up in a clip earlier in the day. *A concession to comfort*, I wondered. Her clothing wasn't baggy, but it did little to emphasize her figure, and her face was bare, save for a swipe of mascara. She wore no jewelry of any kind. Her brown eyes, while still warm, lacked the bright humor and zest they'd once had. Nothing about her stood out, even her energy level was muted. This woman could blend into the woodwork, be passed by everyone in the street, and they wouldn't even remember seeing her. Clearly, she worked at being as nondescript as possible and was good at it. Still, my breath wanted to catch as I took her in, scarcely able to believe she was standing in front of me.

"Xander, meet Alexandria Demming. Andrie, this is my brother, Xander," Vic introduced.

Alex—Andrie—extended her hand, looking nervous. I looked down, wondering if, despite all the preparation I'd gone though, it would be enough. Slowly, so as to not scare her any more than she already was, I grasped her soft hand in mine.

Heat flared, hotter and as perfect as it had always been. As if all the time apart had only stoked the flame, and our touch was the spark that set it ablaze once more. She gasped, looking up at me in wonder, and I knew she'd felt it, too. I sensed more than felt her thought of pulling back, of rejecting what was happening between us, and I couldn't help but tighten my hold. After all of these years of having only dreams and memories to sustain me, I couldn't let her go just yet.

"Andrie was my best friend's sister," Vik explained. "And when he died, she became my little sister." I could see the twinkle in his eye as he spoke, the corners of his mouth twitching when he saw Andrie's eyes widen.

"Well," I said, unable to stop the delight at seeing her body shudder delicately as I spoke. "I'd say any little sister of my brother is kin to me, but I'd be lying. Come sit with us for a while, sweetheart. I'd love to get to know the only family my brother has had to count on while I was gone."

I didn't ask, knowing she'd probably make up an excuse to go home if I let her, but I was careful to keep an eye on her body language—the last thing I wanted was for her to fear me. I slid the barstool I'd been sitting on out for her, extending my hand to help her into it, and she willingly complied. I sat on the barstool next to hers, pulling it as close as I dared. After all these years apart, I was determined to make up for lost time. Lessia might caution me to be careful with Alex—Andrie—but I'd known her better than anyone in the world. I knew how much I could push, when to cajole, and how to romance her.

We'd been separated for nine years, eight months, and sixteen days. We'd more than paid our penance, and I wasn't going to let anything stop us from living the rest of our lives ... together.

Chapter 4

ANDRIE

I woke up to nails hammering into my temples the next morning. Biting back a moan, I flung a hand over my eyes, trying to keep out the morning light peeking through the window blinds. Blowing out a slow breath as my stomach rolled, I tried to talk myself into committing to waking up. The responsible thing would be to hydrate, eat some toast, and force myself to spend the morning in misery as punishment for my bad choices last night. But the old me—Alex—the side I didn't let out often, wanted to give the morning the middle finger and go back to bed. I'd just decided that burrowing into the covers and going back to oblivion was the best choice for working through the hangover when something large moved next to me. Adrenaline kicked in immediately at the realization I wasn't alone, but I resisted the urge to scream ... or scramble out of bed.

Andrie, what did you do? I tried not to panic. In the almost eight years I'd lived there, I'd never once had a houseguest, let alone anyone in my bedroom. Vik had tried to tell me Demi would understand needing companionship if I felt the desire, but the thought had horrified me as much as it had uninterested me. At least, until now.

Taking a deep breath to steel myself, I opened one eye, then resisted the urge to squeak. Xander freakin Hawkings—Vik's brother—was in my bed ... naked.

Immediately, I looked down at myself. *Please, no, please.* No matter how much I wished otherwise, the perfectly sculpted man wasn't the only one lacking clothes. *How much did I drink last night?*

I resisted the urge to rub at my throbbing head again, trying to remember how I got from the bar to my own house. I wouldn't have put it past Lessia to continue to encourage the ridiculous one-night stand suggestion, but surely, Vik wouldn't have let me ... and his brother ... not when he knew my feelings on the matter. Add in that he knew I'd have to face this man again and again, and it just didn't make sense. Vik protected me from the world, even when I didn't need protection. It didn't matter that we weren't truly brother and sister; in his mind, I was his family, and he'd do anything to keep me safe. Letting me go home with a stranger was the exact opposite of what he'd permit. Maybe he thought his brother was the perfect man to let loose with?

I stared at the man sleeping in my bed. Most people looked more innocent in sleep, but Xander looked just as scary and deadly as he'd been walking into the bar last night. His dark blond beard was unkempt—something I distinctly remembered being responsible for—the tattoos that ran over his chest and down his torso were nothing but swirls of black on backgrounds of color, but they looked more sinister for their meaninglessness, not less.

He obviously spent his downtime lifting weights; his biceps alone were the size of my thighs. His chest was almost entirely bare of hair, save for a smattering that got more plentiful before disappearing beneath the sheet. The man had muscles on top of muscles, even in rest I bet I could bounce a quarter off his six-pack.

Curiosity got the better of me, and I carefully lifted up the cover to peer down at the rest of him. *Holy mother of pearl.* I felt my jaw drop at his impressive morning wood, even as my body heated. It had been a good long time since I'd seen a cock in person, but Xander rivaled Demi in his rather impressive girth.

Xander shifted, causing me to freeze. The last thing I needed was to have this man catching me ogling him. Carefully, I shifted off the bed, not wanting to wake the sleeping man. If I could just get some clothes on, I could probably think of a way to make this less awkward. I looked down at my hands, clenching them when I thought of the small tattoo, invisible without a black light but a part of me nonetheless. My rolling stomach had little to do with my choice of drink last night now and everything to do with my betrayal of the man I'd swore to love forever.

A shrill tone had me jumping in bed while Xander bolted upright, a wicked looking knife appearing in his hand. Recognizing the lifeline for what it was, I scrambled to answer it before it went to voicemail. "Dr. Andrie," I said, trying not to sound hungover as I swung my legs over the bed so I could sit up.

"Hey, Doc." Steve, one of my DEVGRU patients, sounded as rough as I felt. Steve had been captured during a mission and spent over three weeks being tortured for information before he was rescued. By a miracle, he'd escaped the entire ordeal without any lasting injuries, save from multiple scars, insomnia, and a huge helping of PTSD. It was his goal, with my help, to manage the PTSD enough to go back to his unit. I had to give the man huge props; if I'd gone through anything close to what he had, I'd have been a shivering mass, huddled in a corner. Steve, on the other hand, was already working on regaining his physical fitness, went out on a date with his wife for their anniversary, and was having his men over for a get-together next week. His unit was based in South Carolina, but he'd been staying in Texas to be closer to his wife's family and had gotten in touch with me at the urging of a friend the week they'd arrived. He had another few weeks left before he'd be going home and, hopefully, back to his unit.

"Bad night?" I asked, rubbing a hand over my face and trying to ignore Xander as he walked naked into my bathroom.

"Yeah. Look, I know I'm not on your books today, but I don't suppose you have an opening ..." he trailed off.

"Of course," I said, ignoring the fact it was a Saturday and I hadn't scheduled any patients today. "I can squeeze you in right away. Can you meet me in an hour?"

"Thanks, Doc." The relief in his voice was evident. "I appreciate it."

"It's never a problem," I reassured him. "That's what I'm here for."

I hung up, rushing for my closet. I longed for a shower, but the sound of the water running told me it was already occupied. If I hurried, I could use my emergency bag in my desk and at least brush my teeth and pull my hair back before Steve arrived.

I'd just jammed my feet into my shoes when I heard the water cut off. "I have to run into the office," I yelled from outside the bathroom, careful to keep my eyes averted from the half-open door. "Just lock up when you leave. I'll have my key with me."

"What?" Xander, wearing a small towel that barely covered him, came into view as he stepped out of the shower. Clearly, modesty wasn't something I needed to worry about.

"Sorry," I said, feeling guilty about not only my own actions the previous night, but that I'd wrapped this man into my issues. He'd been looking for some no-strings companionship for the night and, likely, was perfectly comfortable with a quick—and normal—goodbye. And there I was, basically abandoning him in my own home and making it awkward on top of it. "I have a patient."

"Patient?" He looked so bewildered.

"I'm a psychiatrist. I specialize in trauma studies. My patients are military, former military, and their families. Most of them, anyway," I said, not wanting to get into the rest of my patient list.

His dark blue eyes held mine as if looking into my soul. "I'm sure you have a patient," he said in his deep, rough tone, after a moment. "But I can't help but think, regardless of that phone call, you'd be looking for an excuse to get me out that door or for you to disappear on me."

I flushed, embarrassed that he'd read me like a book. "I-I'm sorry. It's not you. I'm sure you're a nice man. It's me. I know you probably won't believe me, but I'm not the kind of woman who has one-night stands."

He gave me a rueful smile. "I guess I was hoping this wasn't exactly a one-night type of scenario."

Wincing, at my own rushed judgement, I hurried to explain. "I-I didn't mean it that way. I am—I was—with someone. And ... he ... died. I'm just not ready to move on."

His gaze softened with sympathy that was neither wanted nor appreciated as he inched closer to me. "I'm sorry to hear about that. How long ago did he pass?"

Shaking my head, I took a step back. I wasn't about to get into that story. "Not long enough for me to get over him." Running a hand through my hair, I continued, "Look, I'm sure we're going to run into each other a lot, with you being Vik's brother." I raised a hand when he went to speak. "So, I'm hoping you'll agree to pretend like this night never happened. Apparently, we both needed a little companionship for the night, but it was a one-time thing."

Glancing at my watch, I cursed softly, knowing if I didn't leave right now I wouldn't have a chance to clean up before Steve arrived. "Feel free to grab a bagel from the kitchen if you want. Otherwise, I'm sure Vik has something at his house."

"You're kicking me out," he asked, looking amused.

"No, of course not." I could feel myself blushing. "But I figured Vik might be more suited than an empty house here," I explained. "He lives in the house next door. Fair warning, though, he's not a morning person."

His mouth twitched. "He never was."

"Well, being up until the wee hours of the morning doesn't bode well when it comes to any business before noon." Why I felt the need to defend Vik to his own brother, I had no idea, but my words seemed to amuse Xander even more than me rushing off this morning and leaving him here, almost naked.

"All right, sweetheart. I'll let you get to work. But I feel it's only fair to warn you."

"Warn me of what?"

He strolled up to me, predatorily, taking his time. "I understand you might still think you're grieving. But there's no way you would have taken me to your home—yours, not mine—if you weren't looking for something more than stress relief. Even if you haven't admitted it to yourself, you're ready for more."

Cupping my cheek, Xander leaned down until his lips were only a whisper away from mine, freezing me in place. "And I intend to show you just how much you're ready for." His kiss was gentle against mine, barely a whisper. "I'll wait while you think about my words, but I'm not known for being a patient man, so I'll warn you now, I'll likely push you faster than I've a right to. You just push back when I get to be too much, all right?"

I stared, too surprised to say anything, as he pulled away.

"Go on, sweetheart. You've got a patient waiting. I'll see you later." The last part sounded almost like a threat.

Unable to think of anything else to say, I turned around and walked out of the room, my head spinning for more than one reason.

Chapter 5

XANDER

"You asshole," Vik said, yawning as he poured us coffee strong enough to strip paint. "We told you not to spook her. And you didn't make it two hours before you got her into bed." He cringed. "And that's the only thing we'll ever say about that matter. Jesus, she's like my little sister, man. Not just as a cover, but truly my sister. Please be careful. I feel like I'm stuck between a rock and a hard place. You're both the only family I got."

"The only ones we've ever had that mattered," I agreed, toasting him with my coffee cup. "And I'm glad you had each other. I can never thank you enough for everything you did. For her ... for me. Hell, you gave up your entire life, became an entirely new person."

Vik settled into a chair across from me at the table. "It's not like we weren't already looking for a way out, D—Xander. Hell, I was able to actually live once I got here. I have friends—such as they are," he said affectionately—or as affectionately as he ever got. "A roof over my head, a bar that pays not only my bills but allows for me to splurge every once in a while. The MC men are involved in enough illegal shit to keep me satisfied, and every once in a while, we get to rescue people who have no hope of being saved by others."

"That reminds me," I said, my mood turning dark. "How was she? When you found her, I mean?"

He frowned. "No one ever told you?"

I grunted, looking down at my coffee. The last thing I wanted him to see was the anguish in my eyes. All these years of imagining what could have happened, what she might have endured. "You'd been dark for about a month—gone for two. I was just about ready to say to hell with it all and leave despite the consequences when Lessia showed up at a charity event my father insisted I attend."

Standing, I refilled my coffee, needing the momentary reprieve as I thought back to that time. Alex had been taken, and I'd known who'd done it and why, but I was unable to do anything about it. I'd sent my only friend—the only person in the world I trusted—to try track her down, only to end up fearing the worst had happened to him as well. Everyone I'd ever loved might have been killed, and all because of me.

"She managed to manipulate me into dancing with her. When she whispered our code word into my ear, I almost went into shock." I shook my head, remembering meeting an eighteen-year-old Alessia Accardi. She was young, cocky, but so certain in the path she'd set out for us, I couldn't help but believe her, believe *in* her.

Vik raised the coffee cup to his lips. "I bet that wasn't in the top ten things you would have thought she'd be whispering."

Shaking my head, I continued, "All she told me was that you two were safe. And that she was there on behalf of her family to make a deal to ensure you two stayed that way." I shrugged. "Passing information about my mother's operation and my grandfather's dealings at least allowed me to get small digs in at her, save those we couldn't on our side of things. I was more worried I'd get Lessia into trouble. As my contact, I was afraid I'd get her killed if my mother thought I'd started getting ... distracted ... again."

Vik stared at me as if I were an idiot. "What?" I asked.

"Dude, Lessia is the absolute last person I'd worry about when it comes to safety. Hell, she's lobbying for that assignment herself—your mother, I mean. Orders are we have to wait until the heat around your family dies down, but you can be sure that bitch's days are numbered."

Now, it was my turn to stare. The fact my mother's death was being fought over didn't surprise me in the slightest, but Lessia ...

"You didn't know she's an operative?" he asked, his voice low despite the fact I knew there were safety measures in place to prevent us from being overheard.

"I thought she was a go-between for her brothers ..." I trailed off.

He snorted. "Her brother's aren't part of the operation at all. Hell, they had no idea she was anything more than a model until right before she 'retired' and moved back to Texas. She was there when I found Alex. And, to be honest, without her and some of the men you've already met, I'm not sure if I could've gotten her and the others out without it turning into a bloodbath."

"You mean, she was an operative at eighteen? I know she grew up with all the resources Accardi Tactical had to offer, but still." God, that was young. Though, had I been so different? By that age, I'd seen more, done more, than most hardcore criminals ever dreamed about.

Vik shook his head. "I'm not sure about all the details, but I know she was sent to Europe with that job description in mind."

"I can't believe it. All these years, I thought she was just a middleman," I said in wonder.

"No, brother. She's likely the deadliest operative currently active. She's not just trained; her mind is like a steel trap. And whatever you do, don't piss her off. Her ways of getting back at you are inventive and vicious."

"I have no intention of getting on her bad side. Hell, she's the one who got you both here and kept me sane all these years."

"She's also the one who came up with the plan to get your sorry ass out. Though, I can bet she's a little peeved at you right now. She's got a soft spot for your girl."

Wincing, I took another sip from my mug. "She'll get over it. I know Al—Andrie better than anyone."

"No, you *used to* know Andrie better than anyone. She's not the same girl from all those years ago." Vik's eyes were sober.

"I noticed," I said grimly, remembering the shadows in her expression. Even last night, I couldn't tease her out of her seriousness. She'd come after me like she was desperate, but not in a fun way. It was almost like she was using me to exorcize demons. "What happened?"

"She never said. Not to me. But ..." He hesitated, and I steeled myself before he continued, "When we rescued her, she was shackled to a wall in the basement, naked. The other ones we got out had been held in dog cages."

I set my mug on the table hard, causing some of the liquid to splash over the rim, and pushed back from my chair, cursing in my native Russian. The thought of what she might have suffered, all because of me.

"I can read your face. This isn't your fault. None of it. And even knowing what would come, you can bet Andrie and I would do it again. We've talked about it more than a few times, even if she won't give me the particulars. She's told me more than once whatever she went through was more than worth the price of getting to fall in love with you."

Blowing out a breath, I sat back down, knowing I'd never believe her ending up on a boat to be sold as a sex slave wasn't my fault. "So, since getting to know my girl isn't on the agenda today, did you have plans?"

"Well, knowing you—and the fact you were likely cooped up like a lab rat most of your trip, I figured a ride might be a nice way to show you around."

The rumble of several motorcycles coming up the street made me smile. It was time to see what all the fuss was about when it came to two wheels and the open road.

Chapter 6

ANDRIE

After Steve left, much more at ease about seeing the men from his unit that weekend and promising to come back Monday, I decided to tackle cleaning my office. I kept everything ruthlessly organized, both out of necessity as well as personal preference. Because most of my clients were military, it was reassuring to them that everything had a proper place as well.

I unplugged my external hard drive, putting my laptop in the floor safe before I put the hard drive in its own hiding place in the bookshelf. Other than a few pens, a notepad I used for doodling more than actual note taking, and a desk phone, nothing else remained. Even the bookshelf behind me held few books in favor of some knick-knacks that were easy to clean. The only sign of personality in the space was a few drawings some of my youngest patients had presented to me over the years. I'd framed them myself and hung them above the couch. It was cliché—a couch in a therapist's office—but after a few sessions when new patients began to relax in my company, most preferred it to the two oversized chairs across from it.

Pulling out the cleaning supplies from my small closet, I got to work dusting, taking my time to even do the walls and wash and dry most of the items on the bookshelf. I was stalling, and I knew it. Still, I couldn't help but keep my hands busy while my mind whirled. Steve and his nervousness at seeing the rest of his unit this weekend—a unit he'd led and who'd come back to rescue him—had kept me focused off of my own problems, even if it was for a short time.

But now, alone and with nothing to occupy me, I let the freak-out I'd staved off that morning come. How could I have been so stupid? Regardless of who the bartender was, I was responsible for knowing when I'd had enough to drink. Why hadn't I stopped earlier? Even if I hadn't wanted to break up the brotherly reunion and ask Vik to take me home, it wasn't like I didn't have choices. Car services might not brave coming into that side of town, but I knew any of the MC members would have given me a ride—any of the Accardi's as well, even though they only knew me professionally. I was temporarily mortified at the thought they'd seen me that drunk but vaguely remembered them leaving before I had.

Had Xander been right? Was I subconsciously looking for a relationship? He'd had a point about me taking him back to my house. I remembered him asking where we should go, and when we'd gotten to my house, he'd asked again if it was all right if he stayed. Had I wanted the safety of my home, knowing he was a stranger and wanting the familiarity, or was it because I wanted him there so I could pretend he belonged with me?

I shook my head, putting away the cleaning supplies in favor of the vacuum. The building had a cleaning service, one carefully vetted as several of the companies in the building had government contracts that required clearance levels. Still, I didn't feel comfortable letting anyone aside from my patients into my office. I didn't even let them into the sitting room.

After my office was clean and smelling of the lemon polish I used on the furniture, I moved onto the front room. The sitting room was supposed to hold a secretary's desk and a small waiting area for patients, but since I was a one-woman operation, I'd turned the entire room into two sitting areas. Decorative screens—lightweight but solid fabric—were placed just inside the door so no one from the hall could get a glimpse of the room or anyone else in it. Another section of screens was placed to separate the two areas, one purposefully light and airy, while the other was not as well-lit and held darker chairs and décor.

Most of my patients had experienced trauma, whether it be through war, torture, rape, or kidnapping. Some found comfort in the dim, while others feared it. On paper, my patients were military—active or former Tier-One operatives—there to talk about and process their fears and worries for their loved ones. And soldiers, especially elite soldiers such as SEALS, DEVGRU, Delta Force, Raiders, and the like, needed someone they could come to in order to keep their heads on straight, balancing what they had to do in the name of protecting their country with what their human psyche could deal with.

They had my counterparts in the military, of course, but knowing those they talked to ultimately had to submit reports to their superiors about each soldier's mental status didn't exactly allow for free conversation. Fortunately, the military realized it as well, and I was their solution. In addition to counseling military members, I counseled their families. Plus, I was available for the people the MC rescued from human trafficking—those who'd been taken as POWs in war, along with other men, women, and children who'd had to face the horrors mankind inflicted on one another.

I put the vacuum away with a sigh, then looked around the room, at a loss as to what I should do for the rest of the day. If I went home, I was sure to run into Vik at best, Xander again at worst. Not that I wasn't going to have to face the music at some point, but I didn't want it to be now.

A soft knock at the door startled me out of my thoughts. "Andrie, it's Lessia. Open up!"

I hurried to open it, surprised to find Gideon Accardi with his sister. "Is Gia all right?" I asked in alarm, waving them in. I'd been working with Gia and Gideon ever since the little girl's abduction. Gia was getting better each and every day—one of the benefits of children was their incredible resilience—but her father was actually the one I was most concerned about. He'd been so focused on his daughter that he hadn't really processed his own feelings.

"She's fine. At a friend's house, in fact," Lessia said with a knowing look at Gideon. "We're here to talk to you."

I blinked. "I kinda figured that, seeing as you're in my office. How did you know I'd be here?"

"Well, seeing as you went home with Xander last night, I played the odds and thought you'd likely bolt to your office as soon as you could sneak out of the house."

"Lessia," I gasped, looking to Gideon with wide eyes.

"What? You asked?" she said, acting as if she couldn't understand why I was upset at her commentary in front of another patient.

Gideon frowned at his sister, then turned to me. "I'd apologize for my sister, but we all know if I did that, I wouldn't have time for anything else in my day. I promise not to hold the fact that you're human and have a private life against you."

Lessia just rolled her eyes and waved a hand at one of the couches, indicating we should sit. "We're here with a job offer."

"I think you know more than anyone that I already have plenty on my plate as it is," I answered wryly.

"Actually, that's part of it," she began to explain. "This office is secure, the military made sure of that when they provided you the space. But I know I'm not the only one who feels a little … exposed … coming here. It's not like someone couldn't set up surveillance down the street. I'm sure your military personnel have mentioned something similar."

I froze. "No, actually. What do you mean?"

She shared a knowing look with Gideon. "The underground parking garage is secure, but anyone tailing a car or watching the building will know who's coming in and out. There are only a handful of offices in this building, and all have to have some sort of clearance. But most are low-level office jobs. The people going in and out don't exactly look like military types."

"Is that why you always look like you're coming from the office when you meet me here?" I asked Lessia. "To blend in with the rest of the building?"

She nodded. "But others can't exactly go unnoticed, and I don't have to tell you that your active military often have body language that screams Special Forces."

I ran that over in my mind, realizing that most of the operatives—military and black-ops alike—did seem to take longer than I'd expect to settle into sessions. They often arrived on edge, though I'd always attributed that to their current mental status, not the trip into my office. I looked at Lessia with a critical—and expert—eye. "Are you just saying that for some hidden agenda or because you have legitimate concern over the safety and comfort of the men and women who come and see me?"

"I wouldn't say hidden," Lessia hedged.

I narrowed my eyes at her. But before I could speak, Gideon beat me to it. "It's more of a two-for-one. At least, for us."

Turning my attention to the oldest brother, I settled back in my seat. "I'm listening."

Twenty minutes later I was staring at them, slack-jawed. "You can't be serious?" I asked Lessia.

Gideon's lips twisted into a rare smile. "I'm pretty sure I said something similar when she filled me in on her plans."

"How did you even accomplish all of that?" My eyes darted to Gideon, but he still looked amused more than upset.

"Oh, well. When you have the right access, connections, and brothers who let you do almost anything you want without looking too deep, it's actually pretty easy. Ow!" Lessia said, rubbing her side where her brother had poked her in the ribs. I bit back a smile at the teasing, especially from the oldest and most serious of them all.

"What do you want from me in exchange?" I asked, still suspicious of Lessia's motives.

Gideon spoke up now. "Actually, it's yours regardless. Unlike my sister, I'm not nearly as devious. But we were hoping you'd set aside some hours for our staff, maybe even go through some files of prospective personnel HR is vetting? We'll get you an office in the regular part of the building so A.T. employees will have a place to see you, and so you have a cover for being in the office. Most of our employees are former military. If they see you coming and going but can't track down an office or position for you, someone will notice eventually," he explained. "And if you could possibly teach a class or two in the future for others looking to expand their education so they can better help their own patients."

I leaned forward, resting my forearms on my knees and ignored his last sentence. "You caught Michael Tomelson before he was hired," I began, reading Gideon Accardi like a book. His words might be casual, but the intensity of his stare belayed his desire for a separate review of applicants' mental states prior to, and after, being hired by A.T.

He shook his head. "But we would have missed it. His not being hired had nothing to do with a red flag of his mental state and everything to do with the former HR director cutting corners. We've always assumed that clean psych reviews from their departments were sufficient, but that's not always the case."

I swallowed hard, remembering Gia's retelling of her abduction. "No. No, it's not."

"Especially when we're in charge of training the next generation of badass soldiers," Lessia said, injecting just a slight amount of humor into the situation.

"I've got to admit, it sounds like a good idea. At least, in theory," I admitted. "Have you talked to, uh, upper management yet?" No matter how good the security, I never felt like I could utter their names without whispering.

"Not exactly. I mean, not about you specifically. I didn't want to presume. But the triplet's digs are being set up there, too. You know, among others," she said pointedly.

"So, you did this entire project just so you could keep us close?"

She sniffed. "I prefer the word safe, thank you very much. I got the idea from the bank over in Italy. Some of the bank tellers aren't actually bank tellers. They're account managers who help clean donated and confiscated money for victims starting over. Here, our operatives will be able to hide in plain sight, right in the middle of other military and former military employees."

A slow smile crossed my face. "You can't pick out operatives in a building full of operatives."

"Exactly." She beamed. "Plus, the security around the entire building is pretty much iron tight. At least, from a surveillance perspective. No one's getting into what's ours. Not unless they have an RPG or tank."

"And you're alright with me taking outside patients?" I was a little skeptical on that front.

"Well, the ones with the right military clearances will be no problem. We still have to work out logistics for the rest, and that's why I thought you might want to keep this office. Your human trafficking patients wouldn't be comfortable coming to an office filled with meat-heads, and families wouldn't feel as comfortable there as they do here, either. But your active duty military will probably jump at the chance to switch."

I nodded, thinking it over. "Not a bad idea. At least for now."

"It's settled then." Gideon rose. "We can reach out to ... upper management ... and finalize the details."

"When do you think you'll be able to organize an office move?" Lessia looked around. "Or partial move? I guess you really don't need to move anything since this one is staying. You just need time to tell the patients who are moving to the new address and decorate a new office. Well, two, really."

"Yes, but I can't tell patients until I know which ones are cleared to transfer. And I can't send over patient names for vetting until I get the all-clear from my superiors," I reminded her, not bringing up my thoughts on a total dispersal of my patients and moving from this office as well. It was something I'd have to think about at length before deciding anything. But Lessia had been right last night when she'd tried, in her own way, to shake me up. Maybe I was getting too settled into my routine ... too boring. And while I wasn't about to go light up the town—one one-night stand was more than enough excitement—perhaps a small change would be good. If I was already moving patients around, why not move the rest to a building more suited for the ones staying with me outside the A.T. office?

The spark of spontaneity was so reminiscent of my choice to spend a semester abroad—something I'd gone from never thinking about to totally committing to in a ten-minute conversation—had me swallowing hard. "Until I get clearances, I can't do much, I'm afraid," I said, getting back to the matter at hand.

Gideon nodded in understanding, but Lessia rolled her eyes, muttering something about rules and what I should do with protocols, but we both ignored her.

"We'll get out of your hair," Gideon said, half-guiding, half-pushing his sister toward the door. "As soon as everything is in place, I'll let you know."

"I supposed you would feel more comfortable continuing our sessions at Accardi Tactical?" I asked. "We could do them after hours, if you'd like?"

"Not a bad idea," Lessia mused. "We can at least start transferring family members' appointments. Why don't you come back with us? You can decide what office you'd like. At least, the office in the building. It'll be a few more weeks before we can safely go to the one down there."

Thinking about my day, I knew I needed a distraction, and one couldn't find a better one than Lessia Accardi.

Chapter 7

XANDER

I t took everything I had not to grin like a schoolgirl. The feel of the engine humming under me, the wind on my face, and the men moving with me, almost as if we were one, was an experience I'd never forget. We were flying down the empty stretch of road, well above the posted speed limit without a care in the world.

Vik was next to me, his expression mirroring mine. We'd been riding for hours. I wasn't even sure where we were any longer, but I didn't care. He'd been right, I'd been cooped up way too long. I was a man of action, and while this wasn't exactly exciting, it was fucking fun.

Grimm, who was in front, abruptly pulled off the black-top and onto a path that led into a patch of trees. We all followed, slowing our bikes as he led us deeper into the woods. I looked around, uncertain as the path narrowed into what could only generously be called a trail. Maybe I was about to perform a blood oath or participate in some sort of hazing after all.

We finally stopped under a particularly large oak, all of us cutting our engines and getting off our bikes. Walking a few feet, Grimm leaned down and pulled up a door in the ground covered in grass and debris. A darkened set of steps appeared, and Charge led the way, while the rest of us followed. The uneven steps were hard to traverse in the dim light, made worse when Grimm shut the trap door above us, but a few seconds later, I saw the glow of man-made light up ahead.

"Can someone tell me why all of our meeting places seem to be underground?" Charge grumbled.

"Still afraid of the dark?" Savage teased from behind me. "Seriously, bro, you need to get over it. No heat signatures, listening devices, or bitches with big ears and loose lips can reach this far down. Not with the way we have it shielded."

"You know what else is this far down? Rats," Charge said with disgust.

"As if Raptor would allow that," Shade called out from somewhere in the back of the line.

We stepped into a room bathed in white light. It was a complete contrast to the dark, damp dirt tunnel we'd just been in. The entire room appeared to be sealed concrete. There was a single table pushed against one wall, with two metal chairs facing each other in the middle of the room. Sitting on one of the chairs was a man I'd met once before.

Before I could begin assessing options—all of which started with reaching for my guns—Matteo smiled and gestured to the remaining chair. The men fanned out behind me, and I felt Vik stand at my back. "No need to worry. We just need to get to know you better. I promise, we'll keep the rubber hoses stashed away. Someone break out the beer."

Several hours later, I felt like I'd been worked over without a single broken bone or bruise to show for it. Sure, the inquisition was under the guise of male bonding, but I was under no illusion about what it was—an interrogation.

Knowing that no matter how much they joked, I was under a microscope and my entire new existence would depend on their acceptance of me, I answered everything as truthfully as possible, keeping details vague unless pushed. Which they did—a lot. For someone who just wanted to bury their past with the supposed body my family had buried, talking about it was as much fun as a root canal without Novocain, but not as bad as a battery-acid enema my mother had once had me watch her give a man who'd tried to kill her. One thing was for certain, if the men who were my new brothers-in-arms hadn't known who I was and what I'd come from, they did now. For some reason, the idea didn't bother me nearly as much as it would have before I'd met them. We might still be feeling each other out and trying to figure out how I would fit in, but I was starting to trust these men—and not just because Vik and Lessia did.

Finally, Matteo leaned back in his seat. "I'd say sorry for all of this, but even after those months in transition and a few members vouching for you, we had to get a read on you ourselves. This is home, you understand."

I nodded, relaxing into mine. I'd taken the remaining seat, figuring it was the least I was owed, being the center of the interrogation. The rest of the men sat on the floor or leaned against the walls. "I can't help but wonder why you didn't break out a polygraph machine and do things right?"

The men broke out in chuckles. "If you can't beat one of those, you're in the wrong MC. Hell, there's not an Iron Wraith—operative or not—who blinks an eye at being hooked up to one."

I shrugged, acknowledging the skill.

"Besides, we're all better than a poly," Whisp, the man who always seemed to be in the shadows, said.

"And you can bet we know more about you than anyone, save your boy there," Shade pointed a thumb at Vik, who shot him the bird.

"Hey, man, I know you're a little pissed," Shade told him, "but we don't know him like you do. And, honestly, after almost ten years, *you* don't know him like you used to either."

"Blood or not, he's my brother, you asshole. What would you do if someone questioned your fucking family?" Vik grumbled.

"Punch them in the face," Savage answered cheerfully. It was then I noticed the faint bruise Shade had along his jaw.

I raised an eyebrow at Vik in question, but he avoided my gaze.

"Well," Matteo said, taking another swig of beer and rising. "I've got to get home. But before I do, I have one more question."

I waited, sensing the shoe was about to drop.

"Why would your father come here and risk being arrested solely so he could question your sister about whether or not she received something from you?"

I froze. "What?" I'd seen Kassie at the bar the night before but didn't have the opportunity to approach her—Andrie was my only focus. However, I'd noticed the way she'd cuddled up to one of the Accardi clan. I fully intended on getting an entire run-down from Lessia at the first opportunity.

Matteo crossed his arms. "All the information you've passed to us has always been about the Bratva's trafficking ring, except for the abduction attempt on Lessia. Why would you risk stealing anything from Senior right when you were about to get everything you ever wanted? You have to know the timing alone would make him more suspicious. Hell, that's why we had to scramble with your exit strategy last minute and make it a lot more convoluted."

Staring at him in surprise, I asked, "Why would I? I mean, as an international arms dealer, the information would be valuable. But as you said, it isn't exactly my target area and would only bring heat on me."

"You're saying someone else took something from him? Who? And why?" He didn't appear convinced, but at least he looked like he was considering my words.

"I think the why's self-evident. You said it yourself, his client list is like the who's-who of the top of the bunch when it comes to scumbags," Shade pointed out. "Even we would have liked a peek under the man's skirt, and that's not even our area of expertise. Not directly, anyway. And it's not like we have the market cornered when it comes to spies, operatives, or stealing intel from others."

"And the timing?" Matteo asked.

Vik shuffled his feet. "I hate to say coincidence, but ..." he trailed off.

I rubbed a hand over my beard, thinking back. "Senior was distracted the last few days before I left. Suspicious and paranoid, even. I started to get the feeling he didn't trust me as much as I'd thought. We'd always believed he was under the impression I was some lapdog of him and my mother. But the way he was looking at me ... That's why I put in the call for extract. But when I came home and found my apartment had been searched and there was a hired gun waiting for me, I knew it was time to go. I stayed long enough after I'd killed him to lay a false trail, then bolted. I figured Senior had a leak in his camp, and I was the easy target. After all, it's not like he wasn't fully aware I'd have killed my mother a long time ago, and while he certainly had affection for me, it wasn't reciprocated."

"Any idea who?" Grimm asked from his place near the door.

I shook my head. "I might have been trusted in my father's home and done his bidding when it came to making public appearances, but he was under no illusions of having me take over his business, even if he played that part at times to buyers. I don't know the ins and outs of his operation. I was always expected to follow in my mother's path."

Vik snorted. "Hell of a way to keep you on the straight and narrow. Do what we want you to or else. Want proof?

Let's kidnap your fucking girlfriend from your bed and sell her into the skin trade. And if you give us any grief over it, we'll just slit your throat and be done with it. After all, think of the statement it'll make—killing your only son just because he didn't want to be involved in all your illegal activities."

Even I cracked a smile at Vik's tone. "Yeah, family dinners were always full of warm, fuzzy feelings," I quipped.

"How did they get together anyway?" Savage asked. "Your parents?"

"Scratching an itch," I explained with a shrug. "Back when he was still rising to the top, he supplied to her father and ended up sleeping with her a few times during business dealings. I was the result."

"And your grandfather didn't skin him alive for touching his daughter?" Shade asked.

"You've obviously never met his mother. Or grandfather." Vik rolled his beer bottle between his palms. "She's a stone-cold bitch who takes what she wants, when she wants, how she wants. I'm not saying her father put up a fight, mind you, but if Demetri Melnikoff was what she wanted, she'd slit her own fathers' throat if he got in the way. And he's one of the most feared people in all of Russia. The power the two of them wield is absolute."

"Tell me about it," Matteo mumbled. "That's by far the hardest extraction we've ever had. Not to mention the hoops we had to go through to make you ... you."

"There's a reason it took so many years to get him out." Grimm looked at his watch. "And speaking of time, we've got to get going. We've been here long enough, and I'm sure your woman will be wondering where you are if you aren't home soon."

Matteo smiled, took a final sip of beer, and rose. "True enough." He looked over at Savage. "Tristan, you coming to dinner tonight? We're having roasted chicken, mashed potatoes, and cornbread."

"Hell, yeah. Anytime G is offering up a home-cooked meal for a poor, single guy, I'm game." Savage, apparently serious about his food, turned, motioning Grimm to get the door.

"By the way," I asked as we traversed the dark tunnel again. "What is this place?"

"We—the Iron Wraiths—use it when we need to interrogate someone and don't want a connection back to the club. It's remote, easy to clean, and soundproof. When it comes to the shadier MC things, it's handy to have something ready to go where we can … let loose."

As we walked out into the soft daylight, I slowed, watching the men get back on their bikes, ribbing each other good-naturedly as they did so. Shade said something to Vik, who only nodded before giving the man a friendly shove and turning to his own bike. How many years would it take for them to accept me into their group? How long had it taken Vik?

A hand came to rest on my shoulders. "Come on," Grimm said, squeezing reassuringly before walking around me. "We've got another hour before we've got to split. Let's show you more of your new home."

The pang of loneliness left almost as soon as it had appeared. I had a new home, new friendships, and a whole new me. With any luck, after leading me on a merry chase, I'd have my woman to go along with it.

Chapter 8

ANDRIE

"You're being stupid, Andrie," I whispered as I crept into my own house. "He's not even here."

With the goal of making sure Xander couldn't find me at home—I was sure he was staying at Vik's, and our houses were right next door, giving him a prime view of my comings and goings—I'd decided to run errands. I'd cleaned my car until it looked like I was trying to get it ready to sell, picked up paint samples for my new office, and spent three times my normal amount of time in the grocery store, walking each aisle as if committing every single item on the shelf to memory.

It was a good plan until I pulled up to the house and realized, with Vik's latest project still in my garage, I'd have to walk from the car to the house and back in multiple trips and leave my car in the driveway for the entire street to see. So much for staying out of sight.

I'd only managed one load when I heard Vik's front door open.

"Hey, stranger," Xander said, that raspy voice sending a bolt of lust through me.

Down girl, I chided, forcing a friendly but distant tone. "Hey, neighbor. Where's Vik?"

He chuckled. "You think we need a chaperone? In broad daylight?" He gestured to the neighborhood. It wasn't the most exclusive area, but it was clean-cut enough to raise eyebrows when people noticed Xander. He waved at Mrs. Johnson, smiling as she openly gawked as she drove by.

"Besides," he continued, "it's not like Vik did much last night to prevent what happened."

Not waiting for a response, he grabbed a few of the heavier bags before walking into the house, not bothering to wait on me to follow.

Sputtering, I stood at the trunk for a few seconds before grabbing some bags of my own and hurrying inside.

"What do you think you're doing, Xander?" I asked, ignoring the thrill of saying his name.

"Helping you take in groceries," he said, too rough around the edges to pull off the innocent look he was going for.

"I didn't ask for your help." I began to pull out items from the bags, putting them away neatly even as I fumed.

"I'm pretty sure my mother would have wanted me to be a gentleman."

"Bull. I don't know much about your *mother*, but I'm pretty certain—"

"Vik, then. He'd want me to look after his little sister. And from what I understand, carrying bags for a woman is the epitome of southern manners. Thank you for giving me the opportunity to blend in," he said pleasantly, almost cheerfully.

I rolled my eyes as he left for another load, unable to come up with a retort.

"Besides," he said as he walked back in. "You can relax. I promised Vik I'd help him at the bar tonight. Brotherly bonding."

He passed by me at the kitchen counter, and I could've sworn I felt him kiss the top of my head. "I just wanted to see you for a minute before we left."

"Why?" I was starting to feel like I was in the middle of a whirlwind. On paper, this man was supposed to be a member of one of the deadliest motorcycle clubs in the country and certainly not someone I should be associating with any more than I did any of the other operatives within that cell—assuming he was going to even be an operative. In reality, other than our connection to Vik, we had nothing in common, and I couldn't understand why I not only seemed to go weak at the knees around him, but why he had anything more than a passing interest in me.

"Because seeing you makes me happy."

He was so matter of fact that I could only blink.

"You should take a bubble bath. Have a glass of wine. You know, relax," he said as he handed me a carton of strawberries.

"I-I don't take baths," was all I could get out. Not ever again. Not after ...

Xander stopped and turned to face me as if I'd said something totally foreign. "You don't take baths?"

Slowly, I shook my head. "Umm ... no?"

"Then, what the hell do you do to unwind?"

I couldn't help but smile at how flabbergasted he was. "I read, listen to music, and garden. Work out, if I'm feeling antsy," I answered, trying to remember the last time I'd done, well, any of that, with the purpose of relaxing. I worked out three times a week for an hour and read pertinent journals to my field. I listened to classical music when driving to and from work and only weeded mine and Vik's flower gardens to ensure our houses didn't stand out as unkempt or out of place. When was the last time I'd read a book for pleasure or listened to my favorite band? Hell, I hadn't even planted a garden in all the years I'd lived in Texas, despite the fact that, even in Russia, I'd had flowers in pots all over our apartment and always had my own flower garden growing up.

"That's ... huh. Well, then, I guess ... do whatever you do to relax tonight, all right?" Xander said, pulling me from my thoughts, his expression skeptical.

"All right," I said slowly, still mystified as to why a man I'd met less than a day ago was giving me orders, and worse, why I was entertaining the idea that he was right.

He held up his hand as if reading my thoughts. "I'm not saying you need a keeper when it's perfectly clear you're a capable, independent woman. All I'm saying is you seem like a person who spends her time looking after others and doesn't take a lot of time to think of yourself. It's Saturday night. If you're not going to cut loose and go wild on the town—"

"Did that last night, thank you very much," I grumbled softly.

"You're welcome," he said, not missing a beat, before continuing, "Then, at least take some time out to pamper yourself here at home."

He left after helping me put away the last of the groceries, promising he'd see me tomorrow, then walking out the door before I could tell him no.

I stood, stunned, for a few minutes, unsure what to make of him before slowly shaking my head. As much as I would have protested at the top of my lungs that I didn't want a man—and I didn't, not unless they were Demi—there was something about Xander that intrigued me. With his wide shouldered, well-muscled frame that strained his shirt seemingly to the point of breaking, array of tattoos, shaved head, and grim expression, you'd think you were looking at a killer. And I had no doubt—knowing what Vik and Demi's lives consisted of in Russia—that Xander was indeed capable of killing, but there was a sweet side to him, too. He'd come over just to help with the groceries, and this morning, he hadn't batted an eye when I'd told him I needed to run out the door to see a patient. Maybe that was why I was attracted to him? Demi himself was a hard man, feared by many—even those who were around him the most. But with me, when he knew we weren't being monitored anyway, he'd been loving and affectionate.

I bit my lip, thinking about Xander's question about taking a bath. Demi and I had fallen into a routine of taking one together whenever we had time to ourselves. He'd hated his life—hated what his family had made him do—and bathing away the sins of the day, purging what little he could talk to me about from his system, before focusing on solely each other were some of my most cherished memories. That we could share as much as we did with each other, lightening each other's load, and then stay in a bubble bath, feeling like the only two people in the world, meant everything to me. Those were the few times I'd seen the real Demi—not the Bratva member or son of a weapons dealer or even the dangerous man who killed without remorse—but the sweet and even playful soul he would've been had he been raised by different people. And he'd been careful to keep that side of himself hidden and protected from the world he'd been born into.

No, I wouldn't take a bath. But Xander was right that I needed some time to unwind. I hadn't taken time to just ... be ... in too long. Maybe a nap, novel, and some music out on the back porch was just what I needed to get my head back on straight.

Grabbing my phone, a speaker, book, and a glass of sweet tea, I settled into my lawn chair and queued up my favorite playlist, keeping the volume down low enough to hear the familiar sounds of the neighborhood around me as I snuggled into the worn seat.

Cars cruised slowly through the street out front, and the familiar sounds of the neighborhood kids playing basketball a few houses down mixed with the music. The Texas heat, slightly mitigated by a cool breeze coming off the Gulf, quickly had my eyes drooping. While last night had certainly been a lot of things, restful wasn't one of them. Letting out a sigh, I tried to blink away my malaise and reached for my book. I'd bought it six months ago when it had come out but hadn't even opened the cover since I'd brought it home.

I barely got through the first chapter before drifting off.

Chapter 9

XANDER

"How do you stop yourself from shooting every last one of them?" I asked Vik softly, watching two dumb-as-fuck assholes come to blows near the dartboard. Vik had already warned them once, so no one was surprised when, with a grunt and jerk of his head, a few of the other men grabbed them, tossing them out the door with more force than necessary.

Half-hearted cheers broke out, but I had a feeling it was because the dartboard was now open rather than about the fight, seeing as it was the third one that night, and it was barely midnight.

"By reminding myself I have to clean up the blood and pay the increase in premium if my insurance gets wind of another shooting on my property," Vik replied under his breath.

"I have stuff that gets the blood out without a trace," Shade said from where he sat at the bar, clearly overhearing our conversation. I blinked, then remembered he owned a crime scene cleanup business.

"How did you get into that line of business, anyway?" I asked, curiosity overriding my mouth as Vik moved down the bar. Another part of the "who is Xander" puzzle was falling into place. Apparently, I was a bit nosy. *Or just cared about those around you.*

Shade smirked. "Let's just say you do what you're good at," he said before taking a sip of his drink.

"Tell me, have you ever cleaned up a scene you caused?" I wanted to know.

He didn't answer, but his grin widened and he winked.

I chuckled, not able to help myself from liking the man. "How the hell are you at the top of law enforcement's list when they have to know the entire MC is a suspect in at least half the crime that goes on around here?"

He shrugged. "Suspect, not prove. On paper, I'm as white as snow and so are the rest of us. In fact, you're the only one left here in Texas that has anything hardcore on their rap sheet, you killer, you." The fact remained that while my conviction for manslaughter had been overturned, my record still stated that I'd killed a man.

It was an added hassle, but if anyone from my past suspected I was somehow connected to Demitri Melnikoff, they could easily pull my DNA from several government databases—DNA that would match Xander Hawkings but not DM. I didn't want to know how much it had cost to arrange that—especially considering the genome editing hadn't changed anything significant. Still, it was another layer of protection and insurance just in case someone came sniffing.

The time in prison also explained why I hadn't been around before. And the exoneration ensured I wouldn't cause more than a hard look with Andrie's government contacts if—*when*—she and I officially had a relationship strong enough for her to have to disclose to her superiors. It had to have been a bitch to create my new identity, especially since I've be connected to a woman who required special security clearances.

Now, it was my turn to smirk. "Jealous? At least I have proof I'm someone they won't want to mess with." I pointed a thumb to the crowd.

Savage, walking up at the tail end of our exchange, chuckled. "I see you're getting to know us," he teased, slapping Shade on the back as he took a seat next to him.

Shade looked like he wanted to pout at my words, but then he grinned. "Yeah, but the major players all know better. After all, the good ones never get caught."

I tipped my beer at him before taking my own sip. Shade wasn't wrong. I'd never been caught or even officially questioned in Russia despite all my crimes. I'd have to try for the same here. After all, Alex couldn't afford for her security clearances to be put in jeopardy because of me. Too many of her clients were Special Forces or black ops. My "past" would cause enough issues as it were. That was also something to think about as I gave serious consideration to what my new day job would be.

Vik came up beside me. "Feel like letting off some steam?" he asked, his voice low.

I raised an eyebrow, wondering what was brewing that I'd missed.

"There's a surveillance van in the back parking lot. Cameras just caught it, so they either just arrived or were farther down and couldn't get a good view from where they were."

Savage grinned. "Hell, yeah. It's been a while since the local PD tried pinning you down for anything. You think it's a raid or just a watch-and-see?"

"Just surveillance. They don't have enough for a warrant," Vik said with certainty.

"What are they looking for?" I asked.

Savage snorted. "Anything illegal. It pisses them off that this place is at the epicenter of the absolute worst part of the city and the home-away-from-home for the Iron Wraiths, but other than a few stabbings and the odd parking lot quarrel gone wrong, they haven't been able to get anything on us. No drug or weapons deals, no shakedowns, and none of the fights have ever been started by an MC member. We haven't been responsible for any of the serious bodily harm or deaths that have happened here either. They know it's happening right under their noses, but they can't figure out how we're making deals and keeping our position as top dogs when we never seem to do anything but throw darts, play pool, and drink."

"Other than a few building code violations, they don't have anything on the property or the business," Shade added. "Hell, Vik's even won some fancy award for one of his handcrafted beers. Fuck, for all we know, they aren't even here for us this time. It's not like every son of a bitch here isn't pedigreed with a rap sheet as long as they are tall," he said, motioning to the room at large.

Vik shot him the bird but didn't comment, just continued to wipe down the counter.

"So, what did you have in mind for getting rid of them?" I asked, going back to Vik's original question.

He glanced at Savage, who shared a look with Shade, the two of them with matching grins on their faces before turning to me. "What's your stance on rodent control?"

An hour later, I was in the middle of the craziest—and most fun—scheme I'd ever been a part of, watching three men burst out of the back of the undercover van, screaming as if they were on fire.

A pack of super-sized rats Savage had called nutria were pouring out of the vehicle behind them. The lone woman in the van stood there, glaring at the other officers, ignoring the vermin scurrying around her feet. "You wusses! And you gave me shit about being a woman. Who's acting like a girl now?"

Savage hooted from where the three of us were gathered around a motorcycle in the parking lot. We'd been pretending to work on it, none of us wanting to miss the show.

Turning her attention to us, she pointed at Savage. "Don't you think for one moment I don't know you did this," she snapped.

Savage gave her a shit-eating grin. "How could we be behind anything? We've been here all night—likely before you—and why would we want to play a prank on ... Right as Rain Plumbing? Who the hell came up with that?" he asked, reading the detail on the side of the van. "After all, you four are only here to fix a blocked toilet or sewer or something. That doesn't have anything to do with us. Besides, between the two of us, who do you think would have a better reason to attract rodents?"

"Now, Savage, that's not fair," Shade said, still grinning. "Just because rats are known to live in shit down in the sewers, doesn't mean those hard-working men and woman are attracting them."

The dirty blonde, looking mad enough to spit, was about to retort when I spoke up. "Do you need some help, ma'am? We'd better make sure they're all out of there, especially since it's clear those men with you are certainly not up to the task."

Her eyes widened, and I knew she didn't want us to see the surveillance equipment barely hidden behind the flapping doors. She knew as well as we did that we were onto them, but without proof, she wouldn't be in as much trouble with her bosses as she would if we got a full view of the inside of the truck.

"Oh, no. I'm fine. We're fine. Aren't we, y'all?" she said, trying to muster up some sweetness as the three of us stepped forward.

"Nonsense," Savage waved a hand at the men still nervously eyeing the van from several feet away. "A true Texan gentleman would never leave anyone that's obviously needing assistance—man or woman."

Her mouth snapped shut, and I knew she'd been prepared to go off on him for gender equality as a way to get rid of us.

"Unless, of course," Shade said innocently. "There's something y'all are trying to hide. After all, a plumbing van, parked just outside the restaurant lot in the middle of the night in this part of town doesn't really seem legit."

I rubbed my jaw, as if thinking. "And shouldn't they be wearing overalls or something?" I asked, getting into the action.

The woman muttered under her breath something about her boss and an electric company, but when she spoke, it was only another reassurance that everything was fine. And after a look that could have killed the men with her on the spot, they quickly stepped back to the van.

"You'd better get that inspected by a pest control company before bringing it out on the roads again," Savage couldn't seem to help but get the last dig in. "After all, you wouldn't want to be responsible for bringing rodents into a client's home. Especially if they carry some sort of disease."

Shade nodded. "Talk about a PR nightmare. Imagine if one of those motherfuckers has rabies and bites someone."

One of the men froze from where he'd been half-in, half-out of the van, giving the area around him a fearful look.

"You've got to be shitting me," I heard the woman say under her breath, then plastered on that fake as plastic smile again. "You're absolutely right. We'd better get this vehicle back right away so the boss can get it looked at."

Savage raised a hand in a wave. "Y'all have a good night now. And be careful driving. This isn't exactly a safe neighborhood this time of night. Or during the day."

Shade looked over at me, keeping his voice loud enough for the group to overhear but not so loud as to make it obvious he was doing it on purpose. "Considering the crime rate around here, we really should organize a neighborhood watch. You know, keep a better eye on what's going on around us."

The dismay on the officers' faces was priceless, and it was all I could do to keep a straight face.

"You need to bring that up to Grimm. I'm sure he'd agree it's our civic duty to help the police in their efforts to cut down on crime."

Before we could say more, the officers got into the van and sped off. Exhaust was still heavy in the air as the two other men broke out in laughter. Even I chuckled, feeling lighter than I could ever remember. My entire life, I'd known one wrong move, one wrong action, could result in my death. After Alex's kidnapping, I'd felt the weight of the universe on my shoulders. Alex's future, her very life, had changed in the most horrible of ways, and Viktor had had to leave everything he'd known because of me. Everything had been my fault, and it had been illustrated to me that every word, tone, and movement needed to be carefully chosen and thought-out.

If anyone had ever told me I'd one day be laughing with strangers who were rapidly becoming friends about a childish prank, I'd never have believed it.

As if reading my mind, Savage clasped me on my shoulder. "Come on. That should keep them out of our hair for a while, and the night's still young. With any luck, Vik will let you toss the next group of drunk assholes out through the window instead of the door."

Chapter 10

ANDRIE

I woke with a start, bolting upright and huffing as if I'd been running a marathon. Or had been unable to breathe. Pushing back the memory, I ran a hand through my messy hair, using the same breathing techniques I taught my patients to bring down my heart rate. Ignoring my shaking hands, I swung my legs out of bed, needing more air than my bedroom allowed.

Not bothering to even throw on shoes, I flung the back door open and practically bolted to my comfy outdoor lounge chair. It wasn't the first time my nightmares had sent me running into the night, and I knew it wouldn't be the last. But as much as I told my patients to expect long-term ramifications of what they'd been through and that nightmares were a normal by-product of their experiences, it aggravated me to no end that I still had to go through them from time to time.

Frustration warred with lingering fear, making it harder for me to come down. I was still counting down when strong arms scooped me up. I screamed, having been so focused on looking at my feet that I hadn't realized anyone else was there.

"Dumbass," I heard Vik's voice next to me. "You scared her even worse."

I stopped flailing, knowing I was safe with Vik there.

"I could hardly leave her here by herself. She's clearly upset." Xander's raspy baritone vibrated in my ear from where my head rested against his chest. I could feel his heartbeat pounding almost as fast as mine.

"I-I'm fine," I managed to get out, putting a hand on his arm, trying to get him to put me down. "I just needed some air."

"You're trembling, sweetheart." The almost crooning tone, paired with his warm hand slowly rubbing up and down my arm and back, had me biting my lip to prevent from tearing up.

I felt him look at Vik, and I stiffened, not wanting to be alone with Xander right now, knowing I was weak and would likely give in to companionship if he pushed.

But instead of leaving, Vik dragged the lounger against the house, turning it into a bench. I smiled as the men sat, our combined weight causing it to groan, and I wondered briefly if we were going to end up going through it and onto the porch, but it held.

Xander still held me, but he'd shifted me enough so I was almost between the two men, his arm still wrapped around me supportively. I marveled at his strength. He handled my weight as if I were a small child, despite the fact that I wasn't a petite woman.

Vik, knowing my preferences in working through a nightmare just as well as I knew his, stayed silent as I pulled myself together. Xander followed suit, though both men's touch let me know they were there for me. Vik's hand was on my knee, rubbing gently, while Xander's was on my midriff, the slow circles becoming more of a distraction as time went on.

"How did you know I was out here?" I asked, trying to ignore my nerve endings coming online as my breathing finally returned to normal.

Vik raised an eyebrow. "We'd just parked and were about to go inside my house when you came running out the back—we heard the door slam. When we called out and you didn't answer, we wanted to make sure you were all right."

"You're home early," I commented, uncomfortable in the silence and noting it was close to three.

He shrugged. "It was a quiet night. Plus, Xander helped with the cleanup."

Xander gave me a boyish grin that made him look ten years younger. "Vik let me throw someone out the window. The others were jealous."

I barked out a laugh despite myself, shaking my head at their antics. "Yeah, Lessia complains often that he ruins her fun. He put in a no-throwing-out-the-window rule."

Vik grumbled about cost of glass, crazy-ass games, and clean-up.

"You're getting uptight in your old age," Xander teased, chuckling. "I remember a time when you'd have come up with something along those lines."

"Yeah, when I was twelve," Vik retorted dryly. "It's not like we would've done it. Hell, the trouble we'd have been in for doing something like that ..."

"Then I guess we should be making up for lost time," Xander covered when Vik trailed off with a frown.

Vik only grunted, and I smiled at the two men's banter, realizing I was no longer shaking.

"Want to talk about it?" Xander asked as if reading my mind.

"No, thank you," I said primly. I felt Vik shift next to me. When it was just the two of us, in the dark of night, we sometimes purged our demons. But with Xander, I didn't feel as comfortable sharing my experiences.

Neither man commented, just sat with me in companionable silence for a long time, listening to the occasional sounds of a car passing by, crickets chirping and, in the distance, a coyote howling. I wasn't sure how much time had passed, but I found myself relaxing against Xander, snuggling into his warmth.

"Sorry I worried y'all," I said, finally feeling back to normal.

"No worries," Vik said behind me, patting my knee. "It'll never beat that time I almost shot you."

I smiled, though I felt Xander's muscles bunch beneath me. "Yeah, well, I probably shouldn't have come bursting into your bedroom. Though, at least, it wasn't the middle of the night."

"It was barely nine in the morning. For those of us who work nights, that's practically pre-dawn." Vik's smile could be heard in his words.

"There was a rattlesnake in the garage. You can't fault me for panicking," I protested before turning to Xander to explain. "I was just minding my business, getting ready to go to work, when the little guy came out of nowhere." I turned back to Vik as I continued to reminisce. "As it was, I had to change after you removed it because I'd dropped my coffee cup, and it'd splashed everywhere, making me late to work that day and coffee-less until the afternoon. And you cursed a blue streak when our neighbor—the eighty-year-old who kept trying to get into your pants—saw you up bare-chested and came over to visit. By the time you managed to get rid of her, you'd decided it was time to stop renting and find our own places."

Xander's amusement laced his words. "Please tell me more about this old neighbor of yours."

Vik swore, and I giggled as I explained, "She used to pinch his butt anytime she could get her hands near it."

"That was bad enough, but I had to draw the line when she started reaching for other parts of my anatomy."

Xander's body shook, moving me with him, as Vik told him about some of her more blatant exploits. I still remembered coming home that day, finding Vik a little wide-eyed, going through real estate listings for us both. We'd been sharing a house back then and already talking through the idea of living close to, but not on top of, each other. That day—between the snake and the neighbor—sealed the move for us both.

I never realized my eyes had drifted closed as I listened to Vik and Xander talking, their voices lulling me to sleep, my nightmare long forgotten, and I soaked up the feeling of safety and warmth from the two men.

Chapter 11

XANDER

I knew the second Andrie fell asleep, going slack in my arms, but continued my low teasing with Vik for a while longer, cherishing my girl in my arms and my brother at my side.

"You look like you're going to burst," Vik murmured, catching my mood.

"If you'd have told me, even six months ago, that I'd be sitting here right now, I would've called bullshit," I said just as quietly. "I'd all but given up hope. Not for y'all, but for me. It's like everything I've ever hoped for is coming true."

"You still have to get her on board," Vik cautioned, but his words were light. "You're getting under her defenses, but you still have a long way to go to get her to forget her promise to—"

I cut him off. "We'll get there. After all, she fell in love with him in weeks. I have as long as she needs to fall in love with me, too."

He snorted. "Yeah, because you're such a patient person. The fact you took her to bed last night—and haven't set her down since you swept her into your arms, Romeo—tells me you have all the patience in the world."

Not able to come up with a reply that didn't start with, "I know ..." I flipped him off before carefully rising, cradling Andrie gently in my arms.

"Should I ask if you're staying here or coming back to my house tonight?" he asked innocently, getting up to grab the door for me.

Ignoring him, I strolled down the hall and into the bedroom. Demi might have been forced to become a patient person, able to wait nearly a decade until the timing fell into place, but I was learning Xander Hawkings might just be a bit of a stream roller. I could only hope Andrie could love this new version of me as much as Alex had fallen in love with her Demi.

I was the first to wake the next day, my face buried in Andrie's long black hair. How was it she still felt the same in my arms yet different at the same time? Her body, like mine, had matured over the years. Her girlish figure had softened into womanly curves instead of sharp angles, but she still felt like she belonged there right next to my heart.

I cuddled her closer, placing a kiss on top of her head. I'd always found solace in her arms, and today was no different. When I was with her like this, nothing seemed impossible.

Her nose wrinkled adorably as she started to wake, fighting for every last bit of sleep she could get, before one brown eye opened in a bleary slit then closed again.

"Is it morning?" she asked, her voice muffled as she burrowed into my chest.

"Yes, sweetheart. But it's Sunday. You can go back to sleep if you want." I kept my voice low. She'd never liked mornings and was often half-awake for the first hour or better. Though, she'd been pretty darn wide-eyed yesterday. I wondered if that was due to waking up with me or the phone call she'd gotten.

Groaning, she stretched languidly, still mostly on top of me. "Easy," I said, catching her before she rubbed against my hard erection. "Or you're going to get more than you bargained for first thing in the morning."

She paused, considering my words for several long seconds, before her eye opened again, looking slightly more alert. Following my gaze, she trailed down to look at the tented sheet a few inches from her bent knee. "Oh." Instead of blushing, as I'd expected of this prim-and-proper version of my Alex, she almost looked like the mischievous imp she'd been in Russia, staring without pretense.

"You keep staring, sweetheart, and I'm going to forget my promise to myself not to take advantage of being in your bed and take you hard and fast right here," I rumbled as my cock grew under her gaze.

The threat took time to register, but she reluctantly turned her attention back to my face, still looking like she was debating her choices.

I growled, which seemed to break her out of her thoughts. "What are you doing here anyway?" she asked, sitting up in bed.

"When I brought you in to put you to bed, you wouldn't turn me loose, so I figured I could sleep here just as easy as in Vik's spare room," I lied without blinking an eye. She flushed, but before she could say anything, I asked, "Do you have plans today?" Playing dirty, I slid out of bed, wearing nothing but my boxers, and stood, letting her eyes roam over me as I stretched.

"Umm ... no, I don't have anything going on today," she said finally, her eyes never making it to my face. If I had to get her lust-drunk first in order to make her fall in love with me, I'd use every tool in my arsenal and not feel a sliver of guilt.

"Good. I was hoping to commandeer you to show me around the city. You know, the best places to eat, common landmarks, important places to know."

"And Vik can't do it?" she asked in disbelief, but I saw the small smile she was trying to hide.

"You're prettier to look at," I said, not missing a beat.

"Despite what happened last night, I'm not looking for a boyfriend," Andrie warned, her eyes turning serious. "Why are you here?"

I knew what she meant and decided not to play dumb. "Because something about you calls to me so strongly that I couldn't dream of ignoring it. Very little in my life has been good, and I learned early that when life gives you any ounce of goodness, you grasp it quickly and hold onto it as strongly as you can. Because it's more precious than fucking gold. You don't want a boyfriend; I'll respect it." Or attempt to for as long as I was able to hold myself back. I didn't hold much hope it would last long. "But don't lie to me or yourself either, Andrie. Because this 'thing' isn't one-sided. And you're not stupid enough to let it go, either. You want to stay loyal to a memory, I understand, more than almost anyone else can because you aren't the only one to lose someone you care about. Maybe that's why we feel it—we understand each other. And this"—I motioned between us— "doesn't have to be sexual."

She scoffed and even I couldn't resist smirking.

"Okay, not only sex. My point is, people come in and out of our lives for a reason. Whatever else you can say about your man, the aftermath brought you a hell of a lot of sadness. Maybe my purpose is to restore some of the fun. We only have one life, babe. And wouldn't those who are gone want us to live it to the fullest—not just for ourselves but for them, too?"

I waited for a beat, hating that I'd gone all philosophical, then continued with more humor, "So, to rephrase: You owe me for having me sleep in your bed twice without feeding me. After all, those aren't Texan manners." I shook my head in mock disappointment. "In trade for you not making me breakfast, I'll let you show me around instead." I threw my hands up, dramatically pointing at my cock, glaring at it. "No sex for you."

Andrie laughed, sounding a little stunned at my ridiculous antics, but she was worth my pride. "I guess I can spare a few hours."

Relieved at her easy acceptance, I closed the distance between us, tipping her head up to give her a kiss. I'd intended to keep our interaction light but quickly lost myself in her, almost forgetting my promise less than a minute after I'd made it. If I weren't careful, I'd ruin what little headway I'd made. Still ...

By the time I pulled back, her lips were red and swollen and her eyes hazy.

"I'll give you some time to get ready," I said, reluctant to leave but knowing I needed to make a quick retreat. I was already pushing my way into her space, literally and figuratively, and I didn't want to end up back into bed too soon for fear of scaring her to the point of pushing me away.

Because I didn't have a vehicle besides my motorcycle—something I knew Andrie wouldn't dream of riding, though Alex would have jumped at the chance—we took Andrie's sensible sedan. Even with the seat all the way back, I felt closed in. In line with her sensible tan pants and light blue blouse, the car never went above the posted speed limit. Normally, I'd be volunteering to get out and push if it would get us where we were going faster, but because it gave me more time in her company, I was content to sit back and watch the world crawl by.

"Was there anywhere in particular you wanted to see?" she asked once we'd gotten on the expressway, as if just realizing she didn't have a destination in mind.

I shrugged. The request had been a spur-of-the-moment thought, a reason to be with her for a few more hours at least. "Other than yours and Vik's houses, the bar, and the club's headquarters, I haven't seen much of the city. Not enough to really feel like I know where anything is," I said sheepishly. "You know, closest grocery store, best places to eat, backways around traffic, that sort of thing."

She nodded animatedly. "I totally understand. I've been here for years, and I still find myself turned around sometimes. I mean, not that the city is even a fraction as big as Houston or even San Antonio, but we're still sprawled out enough that I lose track of where I am in relation to other places every once in a while."

I grunted, not about to admit I'd reviewed enough aerial photos and map overlays of the city, with key land markers noted, that I'd always know exactly where I was. But I hadn't lied about the restaurants and the like. Besides, I wanted to see Andrie in her environment. What places did she like? Who did she go out of her way to see? Would she point out movie theaters and malls or favor the zoo and local parks?

Vik hadn't been wrong in pointing out that we'd all changed. And while my love for this woman was as strong as it had been all those years ago, I wasn't blind to the fact that I needed to allow my view of her to move past the girl I knew and get to know the woman next to me.

Looking down, Andrie noted the time on the car's dashboard. "Well, it's early enough to start with the farmer's market. There's a great one just a few miles from here."

We spent the morning at the farmer's market, and then, after passing by the grocery store, home improvement, and other basic need-to-knows, I cajoled her into going to the aquarium instead of an art museum. Keeping the banter between us light and casual, I watched throughout the day as Andrie forgot to be prim and proper and fell into the knowledge-thirsty woman I'd known. She watched two manatees —rescues from Florida currently being rehabilitated with the hope of releasing them back after they recovered—with childlike wonder and peppered an employee with questions about boat safety and habitat preservation before pulling me to another part of the aquarium that housed jellyfish, spending as much time watching them as she had the mammals.

Unable to stop myself, I asked if she minded going to the zoo next, offering a story about never living it down with the guys if they found out I wanted to go. Her smile at my request had my heart stuttering. It amazed me just how much Alex was left in Andrie—when she forgot to keep her locked away. I imagined it was easy in her everyday … same routine, same requirements for emotion. Her patients weren't talking about rainbows and unicorns, after all, so Andrie the psychiatrist was needed not just for them but for herself as well. But days like this, out of her normal environment, it was clear the other side of her wanted to be set free.

The entire day, I kept my hand in hers as we walked. I was thrilled when, after her initial surprise and hesitation, she'd accepted and even reached for mine by the time we'd gotten to the zoo. We'd been the center of quite a few stares, me looking like I'd just stepped off the set as an extra for *Sons of Anarchy* in my black jeans, boots, black t-shirt, and leather vest with the Iron Wraiths logo on the back, and her looking like a college professor. But she ignored the attention and whispers after I joked I needed a keeper or my biker ass would likely be kicked out—she knew I wasn't far off.

At the zoo, Andrie, even more beautiful when she forgot restraint, actually pulled me over to the tiger exhibit when she saw the animal preparing to play in the water, too excited to wait on my slower pace. Enthralled in watching her light up as she studied every plaque and poster and the way she'd carefully look for each and every animal in their exhibit, I found I was having fun just watching the world through her eyes.

She even giggled—a sound that still played in my dreams—when I bought her a stuffed tiger at the gift shop on our way out. I'd just helped her into the driver's seat and was walking around the vehicle, trying to think of what to offer to do next, when a text came through from Vik.

VIK: WHERE ARE YOU?

ME: WITH ANDRIE. DO YOU NEED ME?

VIK: LOCATION?

I told him, wondering if something was wrong, when his reply came through.

VIK: YOU'LL WANT TO GO OUT FOR ICE CREAM NEXT. BRING ME BACK A TUB OF ROCKY ROAD.

I smiled, pocketing my phone. "So, what's the best place to get an ice cream cone around here?" I asked as I opened my door and got inside.

Andrie's smile, which had gotten more and more care-free throughout the day, widened.

"Let me introduce you to the best ice cream in the state," she said, putting the car into gear. I didn't care about the ice cream or the cryptic message orchestrating the move.

I had my girl, smiling, happy, and all to myself. It was as close to heaven as I'd ever get on earth.

Chapter 12

XANDER

My senses went on alert before we even got out of the car. I wasn't sure what was going on, but we were definitely being watched. Unlike the police the night before, I knew these were trained operatives because even two casual sweeps of the area yielded me no clue to their location or even how many of them there were.

But because I knew Vik wouldn't send me into hostile territory without a warning, I tried to stay relaxed and focused on Andrie.

Andrie, unaware and still wrapped up in our day, rattled on about a new exhibit opening up at the science museum the following weekend that she was excited to see as we walked down the sidewalk to the cute little shop, our hands entwined.

Businesses lined each side of the street, all nicely kept and welcoming—a far cry from the neighborhood around the bar. Unlike Vik's mostly boarded-up windows, these gleamed in the sunlight, bright flowers spilling out of window planters. Sidewalks were clean, with no visible cracks or tripping hazards, and children could be heard playing in the background—the sounds coming from a park down the street.

It said volumes about my upbringing that I felt more comfortable and at home at Vik's bar than I did on this quaint little street.

"Here it is," Andrie said as we came to a shop with a sign above the door that read, Sweet Nothings. I inhaled, breathing in the sweet smell of sugar, cake cones, chocolate, and coffee. I wasn't a sugar person—I'd take a bottle of good quality vodka over anything sweet any day of the week, but even I had to admit the combination had my mouth watering.

Opening the door for her, I let Andrie step inside first, scanning the street one more time before spotting Lessia and her man, Brody, leaning against a building, almost out of sight. The two looked like lovers forgetting themselves in a romantic embrace, but when my eyes met hers, I realized Lessia and her boyfriend were the source of my unease. I relaxed, reading the ease in Lessia's expression. Whatever she was there for, it wasn't because Andrie and I might be in danger. More comfortable now, I turned my attention back to Andrie and followed her inside, coming to a stop just inside the door.

The blonde behind the counter stopped in mid-greeting, wide-eyed when she saw me come in behind Andrie. Knowing my appearance already was out of place and likely unwanted in an establishment such as this, I forced my most pleasant and non-threatening smile, hoping she wouldn't throw us out. Seeing as she'd been one of the women dancing at Vik's two nights ago, I knew the biker image wasn't off-putting to her, but private life versus business interests didn't always line up.

"Hello," I said, keeping my voice low as well, wincing at how rough it was, no matter how hard I tried to smooth it out.

Andrie either didn't see the look on the woman's face or decided to ignore it. "Hey, Claire. Please tell me you still have my favorite still in stock?" she asked hopefully.

The woman blinked again, then shook her head as if pulling herself from her thoughts. "Hi, Dr. Andrie. It just so happens I made a batch today. There are some cartons of it in the cooler, too, if you want to take some home to stock up. I'm afraid with summer coming to an end in a few weeks, I'll start moving into our fall menu." The woman moved around competently as she spoke, spooning a large scoop of yellow ice cream into a bowl. "Do you want blueberry compote on it today?"

"Yes, please," Andrie said politely. "Claire, this is Xander. He's new to town, and I'm showing him around today."

I braced for the judging glare, but she only smiled brightly at me. "I think I saw you at Vik's the other day," she said, wiping a hand before extending it to shake mine. "But I'll admit the night's a little blurry."

I chuckled as the door opened, a bell alerting us to the presence of another customer. "I heard it was an engagement celebration. I'm surprised you remember much at all with Lessia pouring the drinks."

"You've got that right," a voice said behind me. Claire's friendly smile turned less professional and more natural, telling me she knew the man stepping up beside us.

"I'm surprised all y'all were able to get out of bed the next day." Everything from his sharp stare, conditioned body, and confidence screamed military—or at least former. He didn't have my rough down-and-dirty life experiences, but this man had seen combat. I saw him size me up as quickly as I had him, but just like Claire, he stuck out his hand despite the tell-tale signs of my biker ties.

"Boone Accardi," he introduced. "I saw you talking to Lessia that night. Friend of hers?"

He asked it casually, but the knowledge in his eye betrayed his curiosity. "A bit of one," I said easily without elaborating. I never volunteered information that wasn't needed, and I hated unnecessary chit-chat.

Claire laughed from her place behind the counter. "I'm learning that most people in town know Lessia."

Andrie and I shared a wry smile, knowing that, at least when it came to the people who ran the city, she likely did. When she'd been in Europe, I'd learned her network had rivaled my family's—and not just the rich and famous. Of course, it made sense now that I knew about her true purpose living overseas, but back then, I'd been regularly surprised when I'd found out about her knowing the true movers and shakers because most weren't on the social scene, eating expensive meals and drinking champagne. They'd been the ones at the clubs downtown, surrounded by bodyguards and unafraid to open-carry their weapons.

"I think it's safe to say she's both beloved—and feared—by a large amount of the local population," Andrie said diplomatically before changing the subject. "Would you like to join us?" she asked Boone.

Before he could answer, Claire pointed to a large table in the corner. "Actually, you might want to grab that one. I know Royce should be here shortly, and I'm sure Lessia and Brody will be in, too. I'm not sure about Gideon and Gia, but it wouldn't surprise me to see all y'all."

She turned back to me, "What can I get for you?" After I ordered and we got our ice cream, we took our seats at the large table in the corner.

Andrie, looking shyer now than she'd been at the bar surrounding my MC members, kept her eyes on her ice cream. Her bright smile from the day was dimming, and I could see her pulling back into herself despite Boone and Claire's attempts to draw her into their conversation.

I was about to make up some excuse for us to leave, not wanting to subject her to feeling pressured to stay, even if I didn't understand why she was uncertain, when movement by the door caught my eye.

Unable to stop myself from freezing at the sight, I saw a familiar face walk through the door. Looking like the former model she was, Kasia stepped inside, her smile bright as she strutted in. She wore a pale-yellow skirt, white silk blouse, and a trendy chunky green necklace that matched her sky-high heels. A massive shoulder bag completed the look.

The clothes, carefully applied makeup, and flawlessly done-up hair was classic Kasia. She never stepped outside without being completely put together. But the expression on her face, almost pure happiness as she looked at our table, caused my heart to jump. First in fear ... had someone told her about me, or did she recognize me somehow? But following her gaze, I realized she was looking at Boone. Familial protectiveness mixed with a hint of dismay, but I pushed it aside. It wasn't my right any longer. Never had been. After all, I'd never been able to reveal what I was to her—what she was to me. And as far as I knew, she didn't even know I ever had a connection to her. Besides, I was sure there were worse men to fall in love with than an Accardi.

"Kassie," Boone called, rising to his feet as she approached, pulling out a chair for her and kissing her cheek. "This is Xander. He's a friend of Dr. Demming's."

Kasia—Kassie—reached out to shake my hand, and as I enveloped her hand with mine, I couldn't help holding it for a second longer than a stranger should, almost not believing she was in front of me, safe and happy. I'd seen her briefly at Vik's, but I'd been so wrapped up in seeing Vik and Andrie again that I didn't have the opportunity to really focus on her.

Kassie pulled her hand back innocently, not seeming to notice my lapse, but Boone certainly had. His eyes narrowed, and I could see him looking between Andrie and me as if trying to decide if I had designs on his girlfriend or not.

Leaning closer to Andrie, I looked down, my mouth moving up into a smile before hesitating when I saw her assessing look. Boone wasn't the only one who sensed the undercurrents swirling inside me. Deciding I was better off owning up to it than shrugging it off, I gave Andrie a wink, letting her know without words that I wasn't hiding what had happened, but I wasn't about to talk about it either. I leaned down to her ear, whispering as if it were a secret for her ears only, "Are you going to try to stab me with that spoon if I try your ice cream?"

She raised an eyebrow, and I saw the second she decided to let the matter drop. "Are you going to trade me for a bite of yours?" she challenged.

Not about to waste the opportunity, I scooped up some of my ice cream and raised my spoon to her lips. Her mouth opened in surprise, and I could see her about to take the spoon from my hand, but the challenge in my eye paused the movement. She took a breath, as if gathering herself, then leaned forward.

She hummed at the taste of my toffee fudge ice cream, her tongue coming out to lick her lips, and I resisted the urge to groan. Boone saw my expression, and his hard gaze softened as he realized I had no designs on his girlfriend.

She flushed when she saw me looking down at her expectantly but gamely raised her spoon for me. The tartness of the lemon, paired with the sweetness of the blueberry, had my eyes widening in appreciation. It was such an unexpected choice in ice cream yet so Andrie. She'd never been one to do average things, and I was pleased she still had hints of that rebel beneath the surface.

"You're so cute together." Kassie beamed from her place across the table.

Andrie opened her mouth to set her straight, but I was faster. "Thank you. Have you two been dating long?" I redirected, knowing Andrie would want the attention away from her, and this way, I could get some details about how Kassie had come to be in Texas. I'd known Lessia had gotten her away safely—I'd been told that much—but I'd never gotten the full story.

By the time Kassie was finished with what I assumed was a highly edited version of how she and Boone came together, Claire's boyfriend Royce had joined us.

"Hey, honey," Claire said, giving him a quick kiss as she set down what looked like a mini peach cobbler with a scoop of ice cream on top. "Long day?"

Royce smiled up at her tiredly, but he looked pleased. "I just left the hospital. I had a meeting with the administration regarding Ava. It looks like she's being accepted as a candidate for surgery, and between insurance and the Foundation, we'll have the entire operation covered."

The women all gasped, and Claire hugged him in excitement.

"Ava is Gretchen's little girl. She works at Accardi Tactical and is Matteo's girlfriend," Andrie explained in a low tone. "Ava was born with some sort of hearing disability. She's completely deaf. They think, with this new surgery, they'll be able to restore most, if not all, of her hearing, but since it's still in trials, the insurance company was dragging their feet. Ava's only a few months old, so from what I understand, it'll still be a little while before they do the operation, but they don't want to wait too long because childhood development is so rapid at that age."

I nodded, putting the pieces together. "That was nice of the Accardi's to help out."

Andrie pushed the now-empty bowl away and reached for a glass of water. "They would for any employee, but it helps that Lessia sees Ava as her adopted niece. She and

Matteo have been friends for years, and I think they see each other as extended family. Plus, Royce runs the Accardi Foundation. They raise money for various charities and causes. He was only too happy to make some calls."

Everyone knew Accardi Tactical was one of the best tactical schools in the country, if not the world. Their reputation for teaching spy-craft, black-ops tactics, and overall advanced warfare tactics and principles fitted for Tier One operatives had anyone who was anyone signing up for anything offered. I'd heard their waitlist for some classes were over eighteen months long while others were via invitation only. But despite their wealth, connections, and former military background, they seemed like a normal family.

Boone and Royce teased each other, their banter about Royce's suit versus Boone's tactical pants and shirt illustrating just how different the two men were, but their affection for one another was clear for anyone to see. And no one blinked an eye at Andrie or I joining in with the rest of the family.

"So, Xander, was it? How do you know Dr. Demming?" Boone finally said after I'd been lulled into a sense of security.

Andrie tensed, but I put a hand on her knee under the table, and she relaxed slightly. "My brother's been friends of Andrie's for years, and I'm happy to say we're rapidly becoming good friends as well. Why is it your girlfriend—and everyone else at the table as well—calls her Andrie, but you call her by her last name, if you don't mind my asking?"

Boone's jaw clenched slightly at my vague answer, but he kept the same pleasant expression on his face, playing along with my change in subject. "I'm afraid I was in a bit of a mood the first time Dr. Demming and I met," he said, giving Andrie an apologetic smile. "And I was a bit snarky with her when she introduced herself."

Andrie gave him an amused twitch of her lips. "Snarky was one word for it."

Kassie giggled. "I can imagine."

Boone gave her a mock-pout, then continued. "Anyway, when I told her we wouldn't be friends, she told me only friends could call her Andrie, so I'd have to stick to Dr. Demming, and while I'd like to think we're friends now, it's now a mini joke between us."

"Oh, that reminds me," Kassie said suddenly. "Congratulations! Lessia told me about you taking a part time job at Accardi Tactical and that you'd be getting an office somewhere in the building. It'll be nice to be able to just pop down a few floors to see you instead of going to your office on the way to work in the morning."

Boone nodded, a flash of wariness I didn't quite understand quickly replaced with a pleased smile. "And it gives me another excuse to visit the office to see you," he said to her, getting a kiss for his words.

Claire, who'd been pulled onto Royce's lap at some point after she'd served her customers, admonished her boyfriend. "You didn't tell me Andrie was going to start working for A.T."

Andrie pipped up. "As an independent contractor. I'll have an office in the building and will see a few patients who work for y'all. But I'll still have my own clients, both at that office and my current one. Mainly, I'll be going through files for the HR department and some of the more specialized classes."

Claire and Kassie exchanged a confused look, but when Andrie didn't offer up an explanation, Royce added, "Gideon wants a second set of eyes for any potential new hires. After what happened with Gia, he's just being cautious. We've always relied on the military or police departments' assessments of their personnel, and that experience let us know that those reports aren't infallible."

He gave Andrie an apologetic look, but she only nodded. "Everyone's human," she said softly. "Even us therapists."

"Besides," Boone added. "It's a good idea to have someone outside the military review files for some of these men and women who we're turning into the next generation of super-soldier badasses."

Royce threw his napkin at his brother. "You need to stop listening to our sister. Your head is big enough without you boasting about what your job is."

"Hey, someone has to turn people into all they can be," Boone shot back.

"Just remember," Kassie said sweetly, "those who can't do, teach."

The entire table cracked up into laughter, Boone included.

The sound of a cell phone ringing caused Andrie to jump, and it took a second to realize the ringtone was mine. I frowned when I saw Vik's name on the display. Even if he hadn't known where I was and who I was with, he generally didn't call if something could wait until he saw me in person. "Yeah?" I answered.

But he didn't even wait for me to stop talking before he grimly ordered, "I need you to grab Andrie and meet us at HQ. Now."

I hung up on him as I rose, not bothering to ask for details that didn't matter at this exact moment. If Vik needed us there, we were going. Andrie was a little slower to rise than I was, but she'd clued into what was necessary and made our excuses as I nodded at the table.

"It was nice to meet you," I managed to get out, not wanting to appear rude to both friends of Andrie's, and people that I'd actually liked. "But we have to go."

"Need any help?" Boone asked, surprising me with the offer.

"Family drama. You know how that is," I replied, already hustling Andrie halfway across the room. "We'll have to do this again sometime, though," I called out, seeing Boone's half-smile right before we walked out the door.

"What's wrong?" Andrie asked as she half-jogged in an attempt to keep up with my longer strides.

I slowed down slightly. "Not sure. But Vik wouldn't have called if it wasn't urgent, and he said we were needed at the clubhouse." I opened the car for her on the passenger side, the manners I'd seen in movies becoming more and more natural throughout the day, and waited for her to get settled before rushing around to get in. Andrie never said a word about me taking over the wheel, quietly giving me directions, though I didn't need them.

I made the drive in half the time it should have taken, noting Andrie becoming more and more tense. The gate to the lot opened as soon as we came into view, and I flew past the gatehouse, not bothering to see who'd been manning the entrance. Andrie took several deep breaths before plastering on her most professional and unruffled expression.

"Are you ready?" I asked, as I shut off the vehicle.

The look she shot back at me spoke volumes. "Are you?"

Chapter 13

ANDRIE

The familiar calm that washed over me as I strode into the Iron Wraiths' clubhouse was both a blessing and a curse. It numbed my emotions, knowing what I was about to encounter. But while the disconnect was what I needed in order to do the most good, I always paid for it later.

Sobbing, and the occasional scream, came from behind the heavy front doors, confirming what I already knew. Without hesitation, I pushed them open, knowing the hell I was about to step into. I still saw it in my nightmares.

It was worse than I'd expected. At least fifteen women and girls were scattered throughout the room. Some were crying, huddled against the wall, others—the ones more seriously hurt and bleeding—were fighting some of the men who were trying to staunch the worst of the wounds. On one of the tables, I saw Jasper, the MC's medic and an ER doctor at the local hospital, attempting to save a woman covered in blood, her body shaking with shock and blood loss.

Despite Xander's question about being ready, it was clear he hadn't known what we were walking into. He paused inside the door, eyes wide as he processed the chaos. I didn't so much as flinch, wading into the fray to calm down the women. I heard Jasper shouting to Grimm about needing to open up the MC's medical room, which they kept on hand when they needed their own care and couldn't or wouldn't go to the hospital. It wasn't a surgical suite, but it was better stocked than most clinics.

Despite trying to be as non-threatening and unassuming as possible, the men were still being yelled at and outright attacked by the women they were trying to help.

"Drugged?" I asked Vik as I joined him. He'd managed to pull a girl, who looked all of sixteen, into his arms, holding her in a bearhug as he let her wear herself out.

"They're higher than the Empire State building. It's just our bad luck we came across them right after their captors had given them a bad batch. Or maybe not," he said, considering his words. "Whisp might not have known what was in the truck if they hadn't started screaming."

"Mobile prostitution?" I asked, knowing outfitted trucks, hauling unwilling women instead of goods, were growing in popularity. "Tame" girls were handed off to a paying customer for the night, while the ones who hadn't been broken were sold and raped right there in the truck. Without a permanent address, and having the ability to move cities every few days, mobile units were harder to bust by local law enforcement.

Xander, breaking out of his trance, came behind the four girls Savage and Shade were trying to reason with. Taking a page from Vik's book, he grabbed two of them from behind and lifted them clear off their feet. The girls, so out of it they weren't even sure what they'd been fighting against, screeched, struggling in his firm grasp.

He backed a few feet until he was against the wall, sliding down until both women were cradled to him as he whispered to them in low, soothing tones. They quieted, practically melting against him, faces wet with tears. The matching track marks in their arms and the bruises circling their wrists spoke of their past abuse.

Grimm came back into the room, his face expressionless as he reached for the medical bag Jasper had left on the table. Seeing him pull out a vial and a handful of syringes, I came over to help. "The woman?" I asked softly, heart dropping even as I held out hope.

He said nothing, just shook his head slowly. "Jasper's cleaning up real quick before he comes back out. No use upsetting everyone again. At least she's no longer in pain."

"She died free," I reminded him, keeping my voice steady. "And that's more than she could have hoped for yesterday. She was surrounded by people who care and will continue to work to help others in her memory."

His lips thinned, but he nodded once, seeming to take a bit of peace from my words. "Let's get to it, then. As you said, there are others to help."

The sunrise greeted me when Xander, Vik, and I finally stepped outside. There were seventeen women, ranging from fifteen to twenty-two, now coherent, clean, warm, and safe. Thanks to the massive number of empty rooms due to the MC's recent move to Louisiana, each woman now had their own space, safeguarded by a steady rotation of the remaining club members, and a medical doctor staying on site for the next few days. I'd visit twice a day until they'd all either gone back to their families or were relocated.

"I take it this isn't the first time you've walked into a situation like this?" Xander asked as we piled into my car, Vik practically sprawling across the back seat.

I shared a look with Vik in the rearview mirror. Hell, we'd damn near *been* a situation like this, but I didn't want to relive the memories from that time. At least I hadn't had to deal with a forced drug habit on top of the other trauma. "Normally, we have more notice," I said, unsure if Xander was a part of what this small sub-group of MC members did.

"I thought it was just moving them," Xander said more to Vik than me. "I assumed the missions were either international or at least in bigger cities."

Vik shrugged. "Just because our main focus is helping them get a fresh start doesn't mean we turn a blind eye if something happens across our path. But Andrie's right. Normally, we get the intel, and a few members who specialize in that kind of rescue situation go in. But this was completely off our radar. If Whisp hadn't been roaming, which he has a tendency to do, we'd have never known they were here until it was too late."

Vik frowned, thinking. "Grimm's going to be out for blood. This is still Iron Wraith's territory, and not only did this crew set up shop here, but none of our contacts on the streets came to us with this information."

"Wouldn't they keep it off your radar, knowing you don't allow it, if the people coming in paid them off?" Xander wondered.

I snorted. "Grimm's going to string them up by their balls for not coming to him, probably literally."

Blinking in surprise, Xander shifted in his seat to look at me. That blood-thirsty comment was straight Alex and one he probably didn't expect to come from Andrie. He saw the wallflower, the quiet one. The woman who mediated feelings instead of expressed them. But he didn't know me, not the woman deep down.

I shrugged, not a bit repentant. "I'm a psychologist, not a saint. I've seen and experienced things that humans should never have to—even if it's through my client's eyes," I covered, not wanting to explain my own past to this near-stranger. "I fully believe there's evil in this world that will never be reformed. I also believe some people's lack of a moral compass will let them allow unspeakable things to be done without losing sleep over it. For those people, fear is the only thing keeping them in line. If Grimm has to remind the others who really controls the streets around here, he'd better do it fast before they start getting ideas."

"She's not wrong," Vik said, stretching his arms over his head as much as he could in the cramped space. "You'd better get a few hours in this afternoon because you can bet he'll have one hell of a statement for us to make come nightfall."

Xander looked pleased. "Think he'll let me help? I know I'm still getting in with the crew, but you know my stance on forced sex trade and human trafficking."

I raised an eyebrow. "You have experience with it? I didn't think Vik had. At least, not until coming here." He had mentioned losing someone that morning.

Vik had been one of the men who'd rescued me from my own hell. While we'd tried to keep our lives before that moment as pushed into the past as we could, in the early years, when I'd broken down and needed to talk about Demi, Vik would tell me stories about the two of them. While I'd always thought Vik had been truthful about those times, I now realized how odd it was that he'd never mentioned a brother. I'd always thought Vik had been an only child. He and Demi were so close that I'd seen him that way—almost like a brother-in-law—when I was with Demi in Russia. After the rescue, Vik had become my brother, our bond just as strong as the one I had for Demi though in an entirely different way.

I felt more than saw Vik stiffen behind me, but Xander only crossed his arms, his jaw tight. "Someone close to me was taken when I was younger. She was a very beautiful woman and was trafficked. By the time I was able to track her down, she was beyond my reach."

Reaching out to him, I took his hand in mine. I'd lived that life, even wished I'd been the one to die several times on my journey over to the United States. I'd spent weeks in a cargo container crossing the Atlantic, the air heavy with feces, sweat, and despair. The doors had been opened only twice a day—in the morning, when they tossed in a little food and a bucket of water to be shared among the group, and at night, when they picked a girl to sample as their evening entertainment. I'd never learned what happened to the ones taken—whether they'd been killed and thrown overboard or put into another container after they'd been used. All I'd known was that I never saw them again.

Regardless, we'd started out with twenty-six of us packed in so tightly we could barely breathe let alone move around. By the time we'd arrived in America, only fourteen remained. I'd been separated from the rest almost immediately, loaded into a small truck not unlike the women tonight had been rescued from, and driven to and was present for two auctions—though, thankfully, I hadn't been the one being sold—before I'd found myself in the basement, chained to a wall, before being rescued by Vik, Lessia, Grimm, Savage, and Charge.

"I'm sorry for your loss," I whispered, pushing back the memories that wanted to break free. My eyes burned with emotion, knowing what his friend would have gone through. He tightened his grip on mine.

"Thank you," he said quietly as if it were just for my ears.

Vik broke the solemn silence. "I think Grimm would love the extra assistance when it comes to matters like this. He did tell you to find something you'd enjoy," he said, trying to lighten the mood.

Xander's lips twitched. "I think he was referring to finding a job."

"Well, a hobby's the first step in the right direction. Besides, if you can't find something else to do, you could always use this as a way to gain a reputation. Once everyone is scared of you, you'll have an easy time finding a job as a bouncer or even personal security for some of the local mob connections."

Xander rolled his eyes, "As if I'd work for any place other than yours as a bouncer. And I'm trying to get *away* from the criminal elements, thank you very much. Current company excluded, of course."

"Hey, don't look at me," I said, not quite believing I was joking with these two after the night we'd just had. "I don't even have a speeding ticket."

Vik snorted. "Yeah, 'cuz you'd actually have to *go* over the speed limit. You regularly get passed by old people."

"Doesn't hurt to drive carefully," I sniffed, needling him. "I take pride in the fact I've never even been pulled over."

"You get flicked off more often than I do," he shot back, much to Xander's amusement. "And the cops are probably afraid to pull you over for fear you'll start in on their driving. Hell, you and I can't even ride together to get groceries without you freaking out on me or me yelling at you. You literally called out every traffic sign the last time we rode together."

"I was afraid you hadn't seen them. You know, with your going twenty-miles over the speed limit and not stopping at a single stop sign," I retorted. "Maybe you need glasses. I should make you an appointment."

Xander's laughter filled the car, shaking it as I came to a stop in my driveway. "You two really are like brother and sister."

"Are not," we replied in unison, succeeding in making Xander laugh even harder.

"Come on, let's get inside. It's barely even morning, and something tells me the day isn't going to get any easier."

Chapter 14

ANDRIE

I'd splurged on the way into work, running through a drive thru and getting jumbo iced coffee and blueberry bagel with cream cheese. Anything to try to keep my energy level up and boost my mood. I was grateful I hadn't had time to sleep. For the last two weeks, I'd spent every waking moment not in my office with the women the MC had rescued. And what little time I had in between, I'd spent with Xander. Despite my attempts to keep him at arm's length, he was always ... around. And heaven help me, I *enjoyed* his company. So much so, that time and time again, I'd let him talk his way into my days. Though, so far, I'd managed to keep him out of my nights.

I couldn't seem to help myself from letting him talk me into spending time with him. Xander wasn't just sexy; he was caring and sweet and made me laugh. I had fun with him, which I hadn't had for so long. We'd gone back to the zoo—he proclaimed I couldn't have spent enough time to learn all there was to know—and he'd surprised me with an animal encounter with some Fennec foxes and a feeding experience with a giraffe. We'd also gone to the opening of a new exhibit at the science museum, and to the art museum too. Despite his grumbling about dead painters, he'd been as engrossed in some of the pieces as I'd been, and I'd seen him sneak a copy of the museum's schedule of events for the rest of the year.

Deep down, I knew I was being a coward. I was letting Xander distract me. Talking with the rescued women—listening to their stories—dragged up so many of my own memories. The rapes, the terror, all came tumbling back. With my choice of job and specialty in trauma studies, I often came across people with backgrounds that had threads in common with mine, but rarely did I see so many women, day after day, hour after hour, mirroring encounters I knew all too well. My gut tried to make me fall back, to close into myself, but my brain knew better. And if that meant allowing myself to use Xander as a crutch, to let him steamroll me into getting out of my head and spend even a few minutes forgetting about everything else, well, who could blame me?

While I was grateful I'd been keeping busy, my nights weren't restful. I might have allowed the distraction during the day, but I wasn't going to let things go too far, and taking Xander to bed, when I knew he wanted more than I could give him, was crossing a line. *If you were completely honest with yourself*, my internal voice chided, *you'd admit it wasn't your morals keeping you to your promise to Demi. It's guilt.* I promised him forever, and there I was spending time with the very man I'd broken that vow with. No wonder my dreams were filled with mixtures of my patients' retellings, my memories, and Demi.

I woke that morning tangled in sheets and damn near another panic attack only to see Xander had messaged me about plans for the day. I knew then I had to stop it. It wasn't fair to either of us, me using him this way. I wasn't sure why or what he saw in me, but it was clear he was getting the wrong idea. *Friends*, I kept telling him. But could I fault him when I was sure I was giving off mixed signals? Ignoring the pang in my heart at the thought, I'd texted him that I was going to be extraordinarily busy for the next few days, and I'd check in with him when I had the chance. We both needed some time apart. Xander needed to settle into his new life without his neighbor constantly at his side, and I needed to remind myself that I was a professional who could handle her shit. After I pressed send, I called my gym and signed up for two of their hardest classes after work—back-to-back. With any luck, I'd be so tired after putting in yet another full day, plus two hours of hardcore exercise, that I'd crash without nightmares for at least a few hours.

My first few appointments were the easiest of my bunch—more of a checkup than actually needing to work through any real trauma. Which was fortunate because, even with the extra help, I was dragging and struggled to keep my mind on the person in front of me when I was worrying about the women. It was their last few days before being moved, and they would either return home to loved ones or be absorbed into other cities for a fresh start.

I knew Grimm and the rest of the men would make sure they had clothes and food and would reassure them about their safety. But it would be hard for the women to be around that many intimidating men during the move, with what they'd gone through, and none of the MC members had girlfriends or wives to help.

Looking covertly at my watch, I tried to mentally account for traffic to see if I had time to sneak over to the club's headquarters during my hour-long lunch break. Sure, I'd only be able to stay twenty minutes, but a friendly face—and reminder I'd be back in the evening—might soothe some of their nerves.

Mind made up, I grabbed my purse as my patient and I stood, intending to lock up right behind the Special Forces' wife and rush over, when I drew up short.

"Hardy," I said, surprised to see him in my waiting room.

Hardy, my military contact, worked for the Pentagon. I'd never gotten his rank, let alone his first name, but it didn't matter. As he'd rudely told me the first time we met, it wasn't information I needed to know. Still, other than checking in from time to time and getting routine emails about personnel concerns regarding my active military patients, I barely saw him.

Resisting the urge to curse over my now-ruined lunch plans, I pasted on a neutral smile as Janice, my patient, rushed out after seeing the typical suck-lemon's expression on Hardy's face and deciding it was in her best interest to clear out quickly.

"Dr. Demming," he said when we were alone. "We need to talk." He bit out the words as if it pained him to even speak to me, turning to brush past me to take the seat across from my desk.

Rolling my eyes behind his back, I took a steeling breath. I wasn't about to let Hardy get the satisfaction of upsetting me, even if I had a sinking feeling he was going to try to do just that.

"Please come in," I said dryly, my voice almost monotone. "You didn't have an appointment, so I'm assuming there's a time-sensitive issue you need my assistance with?"

He snorted, his back still ramrod straight. "Time sensitive is one way of putting it. Tell me, Dr. Demming, do you take your job seriously? Do you think your security clearance—which is crucial for you to get me to sign off on your military patients—is a joke?"

I wanted to lean back, stunned at his accusation, but I wasn't about to give him an inch. "Are these rhetorical questions, or are you accusing me of something, Hardy?"

"Are you or are you not dating a convicted felon? A man who was released from prison barely a month ago after serving time for murder? And why the hell am I hearing you want to move offices? Do you have any idea how much work goes into vetting a new location? And what for, because you want a change of scenery? The answer to that request is an unequivocal no."

I sighed, partly for show, partly because I was tired, and partly because I hated that Hardy, while being my contact for my active military patients, did not have the clearances for my black-ops clients, let alone the rest of my undercovers. He wasn't even aware I saw anyone aside from those he cleared, their families, and my pro-bono human trafficking victims. If he had, he'd have been well aware that Xander was as much a murderer as the SEAL

I'd counseled earlier that day. And I hadn't told Hardy I wanted another office location yet. I'd just saved a drafted email that morning, planning to inform him I was looking at renting an office at A.T., leaving out that it was so I could expand my client-base and that it had been requested I change locations for my government-contracted patients. But I hadn't sent it yet, more because I'd assumed I'd get a rather obnoxious phone call, and I hadn't been in the mood to listen to the man yell. Had I known putting the email off would have brought the man here in person, I would have sent it last week.

"No." I sat back, crossing my arms and legs, looking bored and unaffected, though I wanted to be pissed. The only way Hardy could have known about Xander was if he had me under surveillance.

"No, what?" he asked suspiciously.

"No to your first two questions, to start. I am not dating anyone, let alone a felon. And the man you are referring to was not convicted of murder, but manslaughter. At least, before he was exonerated. He's also my neighbor. Some-one in your line of work really ought to do their research before taking the time out of their busy schedule to fly all the way down here with the intention of reprimanding a contractor. If you'd have bothered to fact-check, you could have saved yourself the trip. And regarding the sec-ond office, it was requested by another branch. Surely, as my handler, that request would be passed around to y'all before it would come down to me. If you have an issue with it, you'll have to go through your counterparts." I played dumb, pretending that last bit in the hopes it would keep his attitude to a minimum if he thought it came from another military office. Especially since it was kind of true.

His face rivaled the color of a tomato, but I continued before he spoke. "I think the more interesting question is who you had surveilling me and why they did such a piss-poor job? After all, a quick web search would have given you better information."

If he'd been upset before, he was practically apoplectic now. He rose, fists clenched, mouth open, and I braced for the yelling I was sure to be subjected to when the door to my office—the one I'd locked—opened.

"Dr. Andrie, are you—oh, I'm sorry, I didn't realize you were with a patient." Lessia looked completely clueless and apologetic before glancing down at her watch, her forehead wrinkled in a state of confusion. "Didn't you say we were on for lunch and office shopping?"

Apparently, I had more than one person watching me, or she'd bugged my office building. Either way, unlike Hardy, Lessia was a welcome sight and so was her lifeline.

I raised an eyebrow at Hardy, but before either of us could speak, Lessia strutted toward him, hand extended. "Lessia Accardi. Again, I'm so sorry." She batted her eyelashes as she spoke, making me want to laugh at Hardy, who was half in awe of the powerhouse beauty and half steamrolled by her. "As you might have heard, Dr. Andrie will be opening up a second office in our building soon. You simply must insist on having all of your future appointments there. It's so nice to see a man still wearing a uniform ..." she continued to flirt as she walked him out of my office and into the lobby.

Before I could blink, Lessia was back, looking quite pleased with herself.

"What? Did you shove him out the door?" I asked dryly.

"Hey, now." Her normal, no-nonsense demeanor back in place. "You're lucky I didn't kick him out of it. What was Hardly doing here?"

I snorted at the nickname. "Hardly?"

"As in, 'Hardly worth the uniform.' He might take pride in being the latest in however many generations to have served, but the man has never seen a single second of combat and takes more pride in bullying those around him than being effective in his job. If it weren't for his father pulling strings, he would've been reassigned to counting paper clips or filing papers a long time ago."

Following the wave of her hand, I went to grab my purse, then froze. Seeing my face, she held a finger up in the air, rummaging around in her own purse before coming up with a small metal box. Pressing the side of it, she waited while it turned on and began pulsing green.

"We're clear. Even if Hardly bugged your office, this baby will scramble any listening device permanently unless he brought in the really high-grade stuff. What's up?"

"Hardy knew about Xander. And he's pissed about the second office, though I'm surprised he flew here to talk about it. But I sweep for surveillance equipment daily, so there's no way he should have heard us talking about it at any point, nor about Xander at all."

She nodded. "Chances are he's bugged you somewhere else. Either your car or home. But I think he learned about the second office just through Pentagon gossip. After all,

Gideon's efficient and likely made calls right after you agreed so he could get everything above-board, as did our 'other' boss. Still." She paused, taking stock of the room around us, and put her hands on her hips. "I would do a few unscheduled sweeps over the next week or so. Just in case."

After throwing the little device into my bag, which was laying open on the desk, she motioned to the door hurriedly. "Keep that with you for a few days, and it'll kill any device in the vicinity until it runs out of batteries. I'll get it from you later. Now, come on. If we don't hurry, we won't have time to actually eat anything, and I'm starving."

"Lessia, I wasn't actually planning on going to lunch with you, you know. But speaking of lunch breaks, how did you know I had an unexpected guest crash mine?" I narrowed my eyes at her, but she didn't look concerned.

"A little birdy told me about Hardly's travel plans, and when he didn't show up at Gideon's office, I assumed he was coming here. And being a good friend, I figured I could pick you up. I know where you're planning on going," she said over me when I tried to speak. "It just so happens I'm heading there as well. Plus, knowing the men's culinary skills, I decided a catered lunch for everyone was the best option."

"How are you going to explain your presence there? Even if you weren't famous, it's not like you fit the mold of hanging out with an MC." We stepped into the elevator, pausing our conversation when a man got on from a different office.

"I'm not a part of the MC," she said once we were in my car. "But I am a woman who just recently—and publicly—announced a passion for helping victims of sex trafficking. As far as they know, I don't know the MC at all, just heard about what happened and am a do-gooder wanting to help."

"And if they ask how you came to hear about their rescue, especially considering it was done off police radar?" I wanted to know.

She shrugged, not looking concerned at all. "Good news," she said, changing the subject. "We aren't being tailed."

"Yay," I deadpanned.

Lessia cracked a smile. "I heard you and Xander had quite the date two weeks ago. Any others I should know about? And, *please* tell me you let that man take you to bed at least a few times since then. He looks like he could loosen up anyone, no matter how uptight they think they are."

The word "date" had me bolting upright. "I did not have a date with Xander. I don't date. You know that. I simply showed the man around town. You know, being neighborly." I wasn't about to tell her just how right she was about Xander's prowess, nor that he'd spent almost every day with me since he'd arrived in Texas. She'd read too much into it.

"Girl, you two shared ice cream. Literally fed each other. Kassie said it was swoon worthy, how cute y'all were."

"We traded a taste of each other's ice cream. It's not like I kissed the guy. We *aren't* dating," I emphasized, crossing my arms in front of me.

"If you say so," Lessia agreed blithely.

"You know why we'll only be casual," I said quietly, not letting myself feel the pang of regret that wanted to twist inside me. As if anyone could replace my Demi. *Xander could,* the little voice inside me said. *Not replace, but love you just the same. If you'd let him.* Ruthlessly, I pushed the thought aside, not wanting to examine that fact anytime soon. Never would be better.

I anticipated Lessia rolling her eyes and lecturing me about moving on and forgetting the past, but instead, she braked for a red light, turning her entire body to study me. "Just because you don't want to lose loving one person, doesn't mean we don't have room in our hearts for another," she said quietly. Floored, I could only stare at her, mouth slightly open. "You only have one life to live, Andrie. He did as well. If he'd have lived, would you really expect and *want* him to have lived it alone?"

"Of course not," I said automatically.

"Then why do you think you need to in order to prove your love for him?"

Chapter 15

Xander

Andrie was avoiding me. I knew I'd been pushing too hard. But I couldn't seem to help myself. Still, I'd expected her to kick me out for a day or two when she needed space, not outright vanish for almost a week. I knew she saw the rescued women, meeting with them one on one and in groups until, one by one, they'd moved on—either back to their homes or to other places for a fresh start. She likely needed time to recover from taking care of them as best she could and listening to their shared trauma.

Plus, she was working on getting her new office at Accardi Tactical ready for clients, moving patient files, making sure each of her clients knew where they were going and if they even felt comfortable moving offices or wanted to remain at the current location.

But when she started turning off her lights before eight, well before I got home from helping Vik, I knew I wasn't imagining things, and I could no longer use the excuse that she was simply busy. It was almost comical how she waited until the last possible minute in the morning to leave, bolting out the door, waving when I tried to intercept her and citing patient appointments.

I couldn't go to her office—I'd stick out like a sore thumb—and breaking into her house wouldn't win me any points. Not to mention, I had no doubt she'd call the cops on me just to reiterate her unspoken statement to leave her be.

Regardless, not seeing her for so long made me restless. I missed her. Grimm had pointed my energy to good use, letting me have my way with a few street thugs who'd thought they could grab territory after the main chapter of the Iron Wraiths had moved out of the city. And it had taken some time for us to find each and every person who'd known—or sampled—the women from the truck. Some people just didn't deserve the life they were given. Others needed to be taught their place in it.

It was just as well I didn't see Andrie some of those nights after taking part in things she'd no doubt disapprove of, despite her words the other day. Even though I cleaned up before returning home, I still felt covered in filth, the encounters too close to my past life. Not that I'd opt out—those women deserved to know everyone who was involved or could have done something to help and decided not to had paid for their crimes.

What made everything different was that it had been my choice to participate. Demi would have faced severe consequences, if not outright death, if he hadn't done as ordered. Here, Grimm and the others had made sure I'd known I had the option of participating as much or as little as I wanted. And I had brother-in-arms who supported that decision and gathered as a group after each of our "outings" to decompress.

As odd as it would sound to an outsider, securing—and enforcing—Grimm's rule over the streets had brought me closer to these men than I'd been to anyone besides Vik. I learned Savage and Shade were the jokers of the group, but while Savage was happy to participate in any sort of devious behavior, Shade was more apt to sit back and watch. I knew the blood and other bodily fluids didn't bother him—the man owned a crime scene and industrial cleaning franchise and was the go-to guy for any cleanup necessary. Whisp didn't have an issue when it came to killing or torture, but he wasn't one to play either, preferring to get right to the point. Wyck was happy to provide the muscle but stayed out of anything other than punching and the odd bone-break. Jasper, who was the MC's medic and an actual doctor, didn't go on these runs of ours. I wasn't sure if that was because he worked nights or if it was too many steps past his Hippocratic oath. I knew there were a few more men who made up the MC, but their whereabouts hadn't been mentioned, and I wasn't about to ask.

Vik had taken to the assignment with more gusto than I'd remembered him having in our past lives. But one questioning glance from me only had him shaking his head, muttering about having seen horrors worse than what we'd seen the other night and exorcising memories.

Thinking of Andrie and what she might have experienced had me only too happy to help Vik work through his demons. Anyone who thought forcing themselves on another person or forcing someone to perform sexual acts against their will was okay deserved that mental and physical anguish turned back onto them.

"What are you going to do about her?" Vik asked, handing me a beer as we sat in his living room. It was after seven in the morning, the sun was just starting to rise in the sky, but to us, it wasn't even time for bed yet.

Taking a swig of my beer, I gave into the urge to look at the darkened house next door. To anyone else, I would've bluffed my way through it. But this was my brother. "Not a damned clue."

"You know she's running from you? Metaphorically, speaking, of course. She's really hung up on an old boyfriend," he said wryly. "Swore to love him forever. He was her one and only. The sentimental fucker was just as wrapped up in her."

I grunted. "A childish fantasy, thinking you'll always get your happily ever after." *But one I still clung to, just as hard as Andrie was.*

"Instead, you damn near mirrored Romeo and Juliet. Except for the suicide." Vik cocked his head. "Well, you're not entirely far off from the suicide, orchestrating your own death and all."

I flipped him off, causing him to grin. "How did you get her to fall in love with you the first time?" he asked curiously. "If it worked once ..."

Shrugging, I took another sip. "Honestly, I'm not sure. I was a cold bastard; that's for certain. She was all sweetness and light. I didn't want to sully that sort of innocence by having her anywhere near me."

"Not for long. You two were gone on each other faster than I could blink. After one look, she claimed you as hers," he remembered. "She just put herself into your life, and you welcomed her as your personal angel. One you tried to keep safe from the world we lived in."

"I took care of her the best I could in private. I hated going out, having to pretend she didn't matter when we were in public." It had never bothered her, staying in. I'd cooked her favorite meals, we'd watched American movies, and we'd just talked. I'd shown Alex the parts of me I'd kept hidden, even from myself. I loved taking care of her, showing her how much she meant to me.

But Vik had me thinking. Setting down my beer, I ignored his confused expression as I got up and headed for the door. By the time I was down the porch steps I had moved into a jog toward her house. Pausing at her door just long enough to take a steadying breath, I didn't let myself think too hard about what I was doing as I raised a hand to knock.

I heard the faint sound of shuffling inside and, half-afraid she was going to pretend she didn't hear me, I pounded again, harder that time.

The sound of locks being thrown finally had me stopping, and I resisted the urge to smile at Andrie's exasperated expression as she yanked open the door, toothbrush dangling from her mouth.

"Good morning, su-sunshine," I quickly caught myself from using her old nickname. Without waiting for an invitation that might never come to pass, I sidled by her, heading straight to her kitchen as if I owned it. "I know we've been missing each other the last few days, so I figured I'd at least make you breakfast while you finish getting ready."

Andrie went to try to speak around the toothbrush, but I casually looked at my wrist. "Though, I guess I'd better hurry. It looks like you're already running late."

Rolling her eyes, she rushed back to her bedroom while I took stock of her kitchen pantry. I'd learned that first day that Andrie's style was ultra-modern—European in its design and very minimalistic. The ceiling, one wall of upper cabinets, and the counters were stark white. All the lower cabinets and an accent wall that contained a double oven and microwave were painted matte dark blue. Not a single item was on the counter or could be found in the sink. The orderly nature didn't bother me because it mirrored my own style. But living with Alex had been like living in the middle of a tornado—she'd never put anything back in its place. I'd more than once tripped over clothing left all on the floor or shoes in front of the door, and dishes from dinner were always left until the next day, which inevitably was right before she needed them again.

Now, while beautiful and peaceful, her kitchen—and the rest of the house—didn't feel like Alex at all. Honestly, it didn't fit Andrie either. The order and cleanliness, absolutely, but the small touches of personality were missing. Where were the flowers, the small knick-knacks, photos on the wall?

One step at a time, I reminded myself before refocusing on the task at hand and opening the refrigerator. No time for anything fancy, which was fortunate, because she didn't have a whole lot to choose from. Still, by the time she returned, I was assembling an egg, cheese, and thin slice of tomato between a toasted bagel and had a thermos of coffee ready to go.

"Here, darling," I said as she opened her mouth, shoving the coffee cup in one hand and the bagel in the other. "I put your purse and briefcase in your car and started it so the air conditioning could start cooling things down. It's going to be a hot one today."

Ushering her out the door, I pulled her house keys from their proper place on a hook and locked the door behind us both. She looked adorable, a mixture of confusion and aggravation on her face as I steamrolled her. Opening her car door, I had to wink when she stared up at me, not getting in for a long moment.

"You're going to be late," I prompted softly.

Cursing under her breath, she ducked into her little sedan. "We're going to talk about this later," she threatened, pulling on her seatbelt.

"Absolutely," I agreed mildly, resisting the urge to grin. "What time are you home from work tonight?"

Seeing my trap too late, she narrowed her eyes at me. "Late."

"Great! Me, too. Text me when you're getting ready to leave the office. I'll get Vik to hand over your spare key and pick up something for dinner. We can talk while we eat." Not giving her a chance to tell me no, I shut her car door, stepping back to give her a little wave. "See you tonight!" I called, letting my grin free now that I'd gotten my way. I was pretty sure she flicked me off as she pulled away, but I had to be seeing things. While Alex would have without hesitation, demure Andrie likely wouldn't stoop to such behavior.

I hustled back into Vik's, surprised that, while I'd been gone, Savage had arrived. He and Vik were playing some sort of video game that was paused the second I walked in.

"Well?" Vik asked, raising an eyebrow.

"I might be in late to the bar tonight," I told him smugly. "I have a date."

Chapter 16

ANDRIE

The bastard knew exactly what he was doing, I had to give him that. I took a savage bite out of the incredibly tasty breakfast sandwich, grumbling to myself as I drove. Xander knew I'd been keeping my distance purposely, and had played me like a fiddle this morning to get what he wanted.

As much as I outwardly pitched a fit, a part of me, one I was trying to ignore, was ... relieved. I'd tried to do the right thing by staying away from him. But even though I'd claimed he was only a distraction from my professional life, I knew better. I missed him. Not because he was a fun distraction, but because I liked *him*. I'd had fun with Xander and enjoyed all the time we'd spent together. Hell, I'd been more myself with him than I'd been in years. And damn Lessia for calling me out on what I was feeling, leaving me to overthink every aspect of my life for the last week. I'd gotten so wrapped up in trying to analyze myself, I'd finally broken down and called Fink, who'd practically called me an idiot before talking things through with me long enough to calm me down. Of course, he couldn't be bothered to actually help me sort everything in my head out—he wasn't about to miss his tee-time, never mind that he was retired and golfing every damn day—but he'd promised to call soon to check in.

Maybe another friend wouldn't be such a bad thing, I mused, realizing full well I was rationalizing my desire to see him again but unable to call myself on it.

Sighing, I took a sip of my perfectly doctored coffee before freezing. How did Xander know I liked brown sugar in my coffee? It didn't seem like something Vik would have mentioned, namely because I'd switched to the white artificial sweetener that was more readily available in coffee shops years ago.

Before I could dwell on the thought, my phone rang. "Doc Andrie?" The sound of what was supposed to be my first patient of the day streamed through my car's speaker system.

"Hey, Eddie. We aren't supposed to meet for another fifteen minutes. Did you need to cancel?" I asked, looking at my clock.

"Doc, are you all right?"

I blinked. "Yes, I'm just running a few minutes behind my normal schedule. But I'll be at the office before your appointment, so—"

Eddie cut me off. "I arrived just now, and it looks like someone's already been here. Doc, the door was unlocked, and your office is trashed."

It took several hours, an entire day of rescheduled patients, three calls from Hardy, and an additional one from Gideon, before the police finally released the "crime scene," otherwise known as my office. The mess in my office had been compounded by fingerprint dust and officers rifling through what had already been thrown around or broken. Whoever had broken into my office—and the locks on my desk—apparently were searching for something. Likely patient records, though anyone thought they were kept in hard copy any longer was living in nineteen-ninety-nine. Even my rare doodles or handwritten notes were scanned and digitalized, the paper copy shredded immediately after.

The intruder had managed to find my floor safe where I stored my laptop, but in their attempt to torch it open, they'd damaged the computer they'd been trying to steal. Not that there was information stored on it anyway, but it appeared the damage had caused the thief to fly into a fit of rage, knocking off knickknacks and books from the shelves, making a gigantic mess.

They'd even torn through my two waiting areas, toppling over furniture and pulling off a painting from the wall. What I couldn't figure out was if someone had been after the files looking for information about my active military patients or my pro-bono ones, as Hardy called my human trafficking patients.

Of course, Hardy blamed me for the break in, threatening to pull my contract with the military due to security concerns. When I countered back—much to his surprise—that if a civilian patient or someone looking for them could get past his "military approved" security, then how could I expect my contracted patients to be safe? If my office was so easily broken into by a civilian, then how easily could it be accessed by someone looking for military files? Hell, he'd been the one to direct me to use this very office—something else I reminded him of. Plus, despite his initial pushback at me taking on an office at Accardi Tactical, it now seemed that he'd lost points there and would have to concede. It wasn't like anyone could say it wasn't a much more secure building.

Of course, he'd blustered and fussed but eventually relented to my unyielding calm and logic. What I couldn't tell him—and something he should have realized on his own—was that there was no way anyone besides a professional could have accessed the building and my office. The cameras for the entire building had been wiped, the twenty-four-hour security guards hadn't seen anyone, and except for the inside of my office, there wasn't a sign of anyone having been there.

Unable to reach out to Harrison or Matteo for fear whoever had broken in was also keeping me under surveillance, I'd had to rely on Gideon and Matteo's network to ensure the news of the break-in got to the right people.

I was so preoccupied, I'd totally forgotten about Xander and his promise of dinner. That was, until I walked into a house filled with a smell I hadn't encountered in too many years to count.

"You're home," Xander said, tossing me a smile over his shoulder from where he was stirring a pot at the stove.

"Is that *Solyanka*?" I asked, kicking off my shoes, too tired for once to make sure they were placed neatly in the shoe holder I had at the door.

"Yes. I hope you like it. I found myself missing home. At least, certain parts of it." That last part was softer, almost to himself. He sounded surprised, as if he hadn't thought he'd miss any part of his homeland.

"I tried making it once, but I couldn't get the balance right," I said, unable to keep the sadness from my voice. The sweet and salty soup was a staple in Russia and had been one of Demi's favorites. I'd tried to make it on his birthday—the first one Vik and I had missed after settling into our lives in Texas, but it wasn't the same. Whether it'd been due to the taste or the memories, neither of us had been able to finish our meal, and I'd thrown out the rest of it, including the pot.

"I'm afraid I had to promise Vik leftovers." He was watching me carefully as if realizing he'd somehow stepped into unhappy territory. "He never could cook worth a damn."

His attempt at lightening the mood worked, at least a little, and I felt my lips turn up in a wry smile. "He caught his kitchen on fire once. Forgot to turn off the stove after cooking some bacon for breakfast. Made the whole thing worse by throwing water on it."

He winced. "Yeah, water and grease don't really mix. I guess that explains why his kitchen is the only updated room in his house."

"The guys teased him about it for months," I recalled. "And that's why he decided not to serve food at the bar."

I let Xander take my hand, pulling me toward a dining room table I was positive I'd never actually eaten at before. He'd set it in preparation for our meal, but thankfully, he'd left off flowers or candles. Hunks of rustic sourdough bread were in a bowl in the middle of the table, a cloth napkin covering them to keep them warm, with a dish of butter. Sour cream and a small plate of lemon completed the preparations.

He'd opened a bottle of red wine before I'd gotten home, and he poured us both a glass as I took my seat, bemused at his domesticity. Looking at the man, you'd never guess he'd know how to do anything other than open a beer and cook a steak. Not that I judged on appearances. But still, it was amusing to see this huge biker putter around my kitchen, a towel slung over his shoulder, as if he were born to be there.

Putting the entire pot on the thick kitchen towel, he served us both before sitting down, not across the table, but beside me. Part of me was charmed to have him close; the other felt a little smothered.

Off balance, I took a bite of the stew, unable to prevent my eyes from closing as the flavors from the rich beef, smoked sausage, mushrooms, Kalamata olives, potatoes, and carrots hit my taste buds.

"Good?" Xander asked, taking a bite from his own bowl.

It tasted just as I remembered. Demi had liked his on the thicker side as well, with extra sausage. I kept my eyes closed a little longer, trying to force back the sting in them. "Mmm."

Keeping my focus on my bowl, I took another bite.

"Hey." He put a hand over mine, pulling my attention up to him. Staring into his deep blue eyes, I tried—and failed—not to think about another set; one that was so pale, they almost appeared to be clear pools. "What's wrong? You look ..."

I forced a smile, but his expression told me he wanted the truth. So, I gave him what I could. "This was, well, it was a favorite meal for ..." I trailed off, and his face cleared in understanding.

"Would you tell me about him?" he asked, causing my jaw to drop.

"You want me to talk to you about ... him?" My mind whirled at the thought of talking about the man I'd loved—*still loved,* I corrected myself—with the man I'd slept with.

Shrugging off my confusion, he smiled. "I told you; I lost the girl I loved a long time ago. We share that, as much as I hate to say it. The fact that we lost those we truly loved. I'd like to think that you, of all people, would understand the need to keep them in our lives. I don't want you to hide his memory any more than I plan on hiding hers. Caring for others doesn't mean we have to diminish our love for them."

His words hit me like a punch. They weren't anything I hadn't told my own patients a time or two, nor myself or Vik, for that matter. Hell, Lessia had said the same thing only days ago. But the emotion and true understanding behind his words made me really believe them for the first time.

"He was a hard man," I started. "Raised in an unforgiving world. But I could see the pain in him. The softness he guarded so closely and his desire for a different life.

We'd planned on getting away together ... but the world had other plans." His mother, more accurately. "It was my hope that we would reunite here, but I got word he died not that long ago."

"I'm sorry," he said, squeezing the hand he still held in his. "I wish I could tell you the pain goes away completely after a while, but I think it only dulls into a hollow ache."

Now, it was my turn to comfort him. "Has it been long ..." I trailed off, remembering him saying his girl had been kidnapped and then killed before he could save her.

"From what Vik tells me, before y'all even came to Texas," he confirms. I wondered if she had been one of the girls in the container with me, crossing the ocean unwillingly, thinking we knew what was in store for us and not having a clue of the horrors that had awaited.

"How was it, having to stay when she ... left?" I asked, hurting for the man who'd lost two people he obviously loved.

He stared at me for a moment, and I realized he might not know what I'd been read into. "I don't know your background or name," I rushed to explain. "But I do know you're Vik's brother—a real one—from Russia. And I know Vik was forced to leave everyone behind when he came to the United States to rescue me. Because I knew Vik from ... before ... and I'm the resource the organization you're now a part of uses when y'all need to talk to someone, I have a basic idea of your past. Though, I admit, I didn't know you existed until you showed up here."

Xander cleared his throat. "It was touch and go for a long time—trying to get out of my old life cleanly and getting here. If you know anything of the life we had in Russia, you know it was not a happy or safe existence. Losing the only two people who meant anything to me made my life ... harder in a lot of ways but easier in others."

I opened my mouth to ask, but Xander read my questioning look. "I didn't have anyone I could trust or turn to when I needed, but they were no longer a threat to be hung over me, to keep me in line, either. Very little of my past is more than pain, pretense, and blood. And it's not something I relish reliving." The blankness in his eyes echoed mine, and I thought about what he must have seen ... and been forced to be a part of. "How did you end up in Russia to begin with?" he asked, and now, it was my turn to shift uncomfortably.

"I grew up as a free spirit. My parents and I weren't close—I was a late in life baby, and they were already closing in on their golden years. They pretty much let me run wild, and I left them alone, for the most part. It worked well for all of us. They died within a few months of each other. I was twenty and had already been out on my own for a few years."

"I'm sorry," he murmured, but I just shrugged sadly.

"They both had health problems, and honestly, they probably preferred that to moving on without the other. Anyway, I drifted for a while, trying to find who I wanted to be, you know? As much as I hated school, I knew I wanted to do something with social work or kids, so I went to school part time. Anyway, one of the other students was doing a fundraiser to help them pay for a semester abroad. I ended up walking past them as they were putting up flyers, and we got to talking about it. There was an orphanage in Russia that the school had partnered with—sending students interested in teaching or early childhood development. Even some students who wanted to be nurses or doctors. You know, getting experience out in the world. Of course, that was before Russia/US relations really went down the tank," I said wryly.

"Anyway, something about it just spoke to me. One conversation, and I was all in."

"I take it you were a little impulsive when you were younger," he teased gently.

Chuckling, I took a sip of wine. "Let's just say anyone who knew me wouldn't have batted an eye. I scrimped and saved and sold off my parents' house for tuition money and the travel expenses, and pretty soon, I was flying across the Atlantic."

"And … him?" he asked.

Resisting the urge to down the entire glass, I took another sip, clearing my throat before answering. "Love at first sight. You?"

"Something like that."

We both drew in shaky breaths before Xander changed the subject, clearly ready to move onto other topics. "I hear you had an exciting day at the office. You all right?"

I waved a hand at his concern. "Whomever it was that broke in was long gone by the time I got there. The idiots managed to kill my laptop in the process of torching into my safe, so they didn't even get what they came for. I was planning on branching out and having a second office, but now, I'm wondering if I should look into moving locations for this one completely. Obviously, it isn't as secure as I'd originally thought."

"I'm supposed to tell you that all parties are aware of what happened and are looking into matters." Xander parroted, making me smile. "I know it's a secret and all," he said around another mouthful of stew. "But I wanted you to know that I'm aware of the … complexities … of your practice. And while I'm still mulling over my decisions regarding future employment, I've already mentioned to Matteo that I might need to see a different therapist when and if the time comes." He raised a hand before I could comment. "You might be able to separate your feelings from professional sessions, as you do with Vik, but I'm not sure I can. And in the name of honest communication, I'd rather tell you how I feel now rather than possibly blind-siding you in the future when you find out I'm talking with someone else."

I blinked, not sure if I was more surprised to discover Xander was debating how deep to go into the ops band of brothers he'd been adopted into, that I was connected to them, or that he'd already taken steps to ensure our personal and professional lives were protected. I was the therapist in charge of all the operatives and personnel who supported them. Without clearance from me, they didn't get back out in the field after missions. But I knew there was a work-around, another Xander could see.

"Now," he said before I could comment. "Since this dinner got way too heavy and serious, I'd like to turn matters back to normal light dinner stuff. Tell me, do you prefer mountains or the beach?"

We traded normal get-to-know-you banter as we ate, the real world dropping away as we fell into enjoying each other's company. Hours passed, neither of us seeming to want the night to end, lingering over putting away the dishes and settling onto the couch with hot tea and pastries Xander had picked up from Claire's bakery for dessert.

I was telling him about the time Savage ended up riding home buck-ass naked after losing his clothes in a game of strip poker to a group of women in their sixties when we heard the familiar sound of muscled growls of motorcycles pulling onto the street.

I'd barely registered the sound when Xander was on his feet, hand on the gun in his waistband as he strode to the front of the house.

Before he could get to the door, Shade and Whisp walked in. Their grim expressions telling me they weren't there for a social visit.

Chapter 17

XANDER

T he men didn't bother with pleasantries as they walked into the living room where Andrie was sitting, wide-eyed and braced for whatever news they brought with them.

"We took a look around your office," Shade started without preamble. "And you were right. There's no way that break-in wasn't done by a professional."

"But they torched my laptop," Andrie's protest was half-hearted.

Shade snorted. "That's because you had the smallest, thinnest floor safe I've ever seen. There's barely room for a piece of paper between that shell of a computer and the door."

Whisp, who hadn't spoken a word, simply took up a stance along the corner of the room and grunted his agreement.

"But you got it?" she asked.

My brow furrowed in confusion as Shade nodded and reached for his pocket, but she only shook her head. "Keep it at the clubhouse. I'll pick up a new one as a decoy and start bringing my daily logs home on a flash drive I can keep hidden. Vik can bring them whenever he goes."

"You could keep the daily session notes at A.T. as well," Shade pointed out. "It would keep you from having to transport them. And with the break-in, you can bet some of the important players will be going to the A.T. building anyway, sooner rather than later."

"You think they were after the military patients I have or the black ops ones?" she asked, looking between the three of us.

"Military," Whisp said. "Or a pro looking for your files for the pro-bono cases. If they did any sort of surveillance, they'd know you wouldn't have our case files in that office, assuming they realize you see operatives like us at all. Other than Lessia, or an emergency case, you see the rest of us off-site." He tilted his head as if in thought. "How many of your patients are pro-bono?" he asked, referring to her rape, trafficked, or forced prostitution cases.

"Umm." She scrunched her brow in thought. "Right now, before starting with my A.T. clients, roughly forty percent are military or their families, fifteen percent are y'all, and the rest are mostly women and children. But," she hesitated. "Some of them I only see a few times. Until they move on. Others—the ones settled in this area or live here—I see more often. But, still, depending on their comfort level and need, I might see a patient several times a week or once every few months. To give you a number on current patients is ... difficult."

"You think someone is after one of her patients?" I asked Whisp.

He shrugged, but Shade answered. "We know some-one's out there looking for one of two women who were helped out of the city by an older woman who has since died. Natural causes," he added hastily at Andrie's gasp. "But we—nor the men after them—have been able to find them. Whisp and I were talking things over and wondering if maybe someone started grasping at straws. Andrie's name is hard to find, but it's there if they know who to talk to and where to look. She takes on the tough cases and has the connections to the underground channels when it comes to getting women out of the city."

"But even my files don't always contain someone's real name. How would they even know—"

"They wouldn't know that until they get into the files," Shade interrupted. "They might have thought a quick break-in would yield the results they needed without involving you directly. But they botched the job and didn't get what they wanted."

I turned to her, cluing into what wasn't said. "You need to be careful."

At her blank expression, I elaborated. "They didn't get what they wanted doing things the easy way. Next, they might come after you."

The men left shortly after I dropped that bomb on Andrie. I lingered a little longer, but the mood had clearly been broken and, after checking all her doors and windows to ensure they were locked, I let her practically push me out of the house.

I'd planned on going to the bar that night, but I didn't feel comfortable anymore leaving her entirely. I sent Vik a quick text, letting him know I'd catch up with him when he got home, then let myself into the house.

I shouldn't have been surprised to see Grimm making himself at home, a beer dangling from his hand. "I take it you're caught up?" Walking past him, I grabbed a beer of my own.

"I stopped by to make sure you had the background on what Andrie might be in the middle of. Not that we have solid proof, mind you. We don't know the old woman's contacts, nor did we have much interaction, so we don't know anyone in her network to reach out to. Trying to track the women down using our resources has yielded nothing, and other than knowing someone's looking for them, we aren't sure what they know or even which one of the two women is in danger." His phone pinged, and he looked down at the screen, frowning.

"Come on," he said, after typing back a reply and setting his beer bottle down. "We've got a meeting at the clubhouse."

Hesitating as we walked out the door, I couldn't help but look over to Andrie's house next door. Grimm saw me pause. "Whisp has her. She'll be safe while we're gone."

I nodded, relieved he was taking it as seriously as I was, before following his bike through the streets. At the clubhouse, I waved to Jasper, who was manning the gatehouse, before he shut the gates behind us.

Without a word, Grimm strode through the clubhouse entrance. But instead of heading down the back hall to his office, he went straight to the back wall, pushing something I couldn't see and revealing a panel that contained a palm and retinal scanner in addition to what sounded like a ten-digit code.

Eyebrows up to my hairline at the thought of what might need that sort of security, I couldn't help my curiosity when, with a final push of a button, a section of the wall next to him opened. The cavernous room was easily as large as the main room we'd just left, with a bank of computers and monitors covering one section of the space. Another section of the room appeared to be an armory, and several cots and a small kitchenette were neatly tucked in another corner. As a safe room, it was barebones, but all the necessities were there.

One by one, the large screens on the wall started lighting up, but instead of a clear picture of the person on the other side, most were shadowed. Clearly, I wasn't privy to identities for all the players, but I didn't mind. I didn't care if I knew everyone's faces as long as I was allowed to hear the information they had.

Three screens stayed dark, but two flickered to reveal Lessia and Brody in what looked like an office and Matteo in a room similar to this one.

"Ares, online." Matteo said, clearly starting the meeting.

"Enyo and Mars are online." Lessia was next.

"Cyber, times three, online," a woman said from one of the shadowed screens, her bubbling personality shining through the computer-altered tone.

"Grimm and Rev are online," Grimm spoke for us both.

"Eris, online," a smoky-sounding woman's voice drifted from one of the blacked-out screens.

"Thoth, online," the last voice, which was even more gravelly than mine, sounded out from one of the blacked-out screens. "Is Revenant up to date?"

Grimm shook his head. "Only partly. He knows about the possible immediate threat, but not how the women are connected to players Cyber's looking for."

Lessia jumped in before anyone else could. "Mike Tomelson and Stan Pritchard, now deceased, both seemed to have kept women unwillingly. One we think was trafficked at some point into the United States, the other might have been born here. Both women had fake identities, which pointed back to a well-known forger who sells identities for 'bought' women and children. Unfortunately, the women were aided by someone who was well known in these circles for helping victims disappear, and she died after arranging for transport for both women."

After taking a breath, she continued, "Tomelson blamed my brother, Gideon, for the loss of not only a job opportunity into Accardi Tactical but losing his girlfriend, and he kidnapped my niece in retaliation. He didn't survive the standoff with officers." She paused, glancing somewhere on her screen, before continuing, "He was the illegitimate son of Les Stanton, who's a rival of A.T., and connected to an international human trafficking ring our organization has been trying to unravel for years. Eris is undercover in his office while we gather enough information to bring down the entire ring. Stanton was an ADA here and was killed while trying to attack Claire Harden—"

"The ice cream lady?" I asked, knowing I was interrupting but too surprised to stay quiet.

Lessia smirked. "Yes. It was her grandmother who actually transported the women, but she has no idea where they ended up, nor did she actually see or even know anyone else in that group that we could reach out to. Anyway, Stan apparently was the godson of either the leader or someone high up in that ring, and he alluded to that person having connections in several layers of government here in the United States, even though they're abroad. As Stan's father isn't known, we're having a hard time tracking down who this godfather of his could be."

"Someone besides us," the chirpy woman said, "is still looking for them. We've seen waves on the dark web and are still hearing whispers from our human contacts, but we aren't sure why or who is looking for them, nor do we know if they're looking for one in particular or if, like us, they just know they were picked up and taken out of town together and aren't sure which woman they're actually looking for."

"And you think the person looking for these women either broke in or hired someone to try to get into Andrie's patient files," I finished.

Most everyone nodded, and several of the people on the call started in on suggestions of how to narrow down the dates, seeming to understand without asking that Andrie wouldn't turn her files over to be previewed, but the thought was that, if she had more direction, she could broach the topic with the women on their next visit.

Everything stopped when the man called Thoth spoke. "You seem to have something on your mind, Enyo. Care to share?"

I hadn't noticed until the room fell silent, but Lessia had kept quiet and was biting her lip and fidgeting in her seat. "I'm not so sure we should dismiss the other possible reasons for someone to try to gain access to Andrie's files," she said finally. "I know y'all seem pretty certain this is why she was targeted, but other than the fact it's on our minds, there isn't much evidence to support this avenue of thought." I rocked back on my heels, thinking about her words as she continued, "Her military patients alone would be desirable to more than a few people, both in this country and others. Add in her work with our operatives and that laptop would appear to be a treasure trove of intel."

"You think we're going down the wrong trail," Thoth said succinctly.

"I think," she said, uncharacteristically diplomatically, "that there aren't enough facts yet for us to know. Yes, there might be a connection to what we've been looking into, but if that were the case, why not also go after people who have fewer contacts with the government and therefore be easier targets?"

"What do you mean?" Matteo asked, crossing his arms as he, too, appeared to think through her words.

"Well, Andrie isn't the only one who might have had points of contact with these two women. Yes, she *poten-*

tially might know them, but there are other people in the city who help that would be easier to track and raise less alarm. Has anyone reached out or checked with the church on Oak Street? They're known for providing for women in need of a safe place. And the old woman who died, it's rumored she has a relative who might be moving into her old house. It's possible, even though unlikely, that she left information for them somewhere. Has the house had any activity on the police radar? Theft, burglary, or even suspected trespassing? It would be far easier and less risky to break into an empty house that has more of a connection to those women than it is to get into Andrie's office building, which had not only a guard in the lobby but cameras everywhere and locks on her door."

Lessia made an excellent point, which clearly everyone else agreed with, given the silence.

"You're right," I said, surprising myself by speaking up when I'd been determined to only listen and learn. After all, it wasn't like I really had a right to be there. I'd been allowed to join more as a courtesy than anything, and I'd bet Andrie would be pissed if she'd known something like this was going on without her being included. "We don't know enough."

"Hardy—Andrie's government contact—was throwing a shit-fit today with the locals, trying to dictate how they should do their job. While bullying is his standard MO, he was a little more ... high-strung than normal," Lessia continued, giving me an appreciative glance. "I don't know whether that's because he's the one who picked out that location to start with, because he was against her branching out to open an office at A.T., or because of some other pressures from his superiors, but it certainly didn't help resolve matters today. Gideon even pulled Royce and Boone in to step in and make some calls, if only to smooth over some ruffled feathers, and it wasn't even their mess to deal with. Fortunately, a shit-ton of former military work for us, and Gideon was able to say anonymous employees asked them to look into things on Andrie's behalf. It kept the locals—and Hardy—from asking too many questions. It also took a call from a superior to keep Hardy in DC. He claimed he needed to handle this personally but couldn't explain why he'd brushed off the break-in as being unrelated patients and then insist it was important enough to warrant a second trip out in less than a week."

"I'll look into Hardy. Cyber, do a broad sweep for him and every other possible angle, instead of a deep dive on the trafficking connections like I had you do earlier," Thoth said, tapping his fingers as he spoke. "Revenant, do you think Andrie has warmed up enough to permit you to stay around to keep watch? Vik can chip in if needed, but he would raise eyebrows after a day or so. A new boyfriend who happens to be between jobs, who can help her clean her office and move, won't be as noticeable. Just dress less biker and more typical Texan to raise less suspicion," he advised.

"Andrie is cautious. She'll allow me to stay close for a few days. I don't think it's something that can drag out too long. She values her client's privacy and won't be happy to have me hanging around while they're coming and going," I finally said, thinking things through.

"Good enough for now. Grimm, I know you're feeling the pressure to keep your control over the streets. Keep up the heat—the last thing we need in the city is for an all-out fight for power to blow up in our faces. If you need more bodies than the few you have, let Matteo know. We've got some operatives in other parts of the country who might like some added excitement, even if it's only short-term."

Grimm nodded. "I can recall a few men from Louisiana, too. Hazzard offered to have more stay back, but I didn't think it was necessary at the time."

"I've got some seasoned veterans who might be interested in a fun vacation. And Raptor will be back from assignment soon. Judge, too." Matteo added. "And I'm getting ready to finish vetting a few new recruits. I can always have them placed here instead of other locations. It would give us more of a chance to train them before I turn them loose elsewhere. Speaking of Raptor." He turned to Lessia. "How much more do you have planned for the crews currently working on your pet project? We're not the only ones who need them, you know?"

Lessia shrugged casually. "The A.T. building is scheduled to be completed next week. They were able to tie in the training center building to the rest of the network that had already been started, so I'd say another month and the entire complex will be ready for Wyck's construction crews. At least, until Raptor can design and approve the next phase. I'll likely need them on and off for a few years yet."

"Are you ready to let the cat out of the bag and actually tell the class what the hell you've been working on?"

Grimm wanted to know. "Or is this one of those things you leave us in suspense about until you deem the timing right?"

Brody, who hadn't said a word the entire time, finally grinned, looking down proudly at his girlfriend. "You going to tell them?" he asked softly.

Lessia matched his smile with one of her own. "The man who had owned the land Gia was held on by Tomelson finally agreed to sell. Bull and Gideon have been trying to get him to part with that property for years, but I caught him at a weak moment. That parcel connects the A.T. training grounds to Matteo's farm and branches out past both pieces. It's another ten thousand acres. In addition to the twenty thousand acres of land A.T. already owns and the hundred acres Matteo has, let's just say solitude won't be a problem. A.T. already had a government mandated no-fly zone over that land, and it has other tech that ensures spy satellites have issues getting decent images over it. It also consists of what were several different farms that had been bought out and left to rot years ago, so plenty of old large barns and other outbuildings we can renovate and repurpose like we did the warehouse in the city that operatives use as a base when they need one. Still, adding a network of tunnels and escape routes will ensure no one will be able to see a thing while connecting the existing properties. Ladies and gentlemen, in a few short months, we should have all the infrastructure we need for our own ghost-ops training site, hidden within the A.T. training umbrellas. In addition, the Cyber group, as well as some other support staff, will now have their own level under the

A.T. office building, giving them additional smokescreen and support instead of having to work solo as they are now."

Grimm whistled long and low. "You're hiding the entirety of our division—logistics, cyber, operatives, all of it—within and literally *under* Accardi Tactical?"

Her smile widened even more at his stunned expression. "What's better than hiding a needle in a haystack? Hiding it in a pile full of other needles!"

Chapter 18

ANDRIE

It took me a while to fall asleep after Xander left, tossing and turning for several hours. When I did finally fall asleep, I dreamed of Demi, gray and cold, reaching for me. No matter how hard I tried, he stayed just out of reach. Right when I thought we'd manage to touch, he turned away from me, and Xander came out of the shadows, pulling me to him. Even as I burrowed into the safety of his arms, I screamed for Demi, who was nowhere to be found.

By the time my alarm went off, I was sweating, twisted up in my sheets, and damn near falling off my mattress. Bleary-eyed, I'd barely sat up when my cell pinged with a text message. Xander, telling me—not asking—that he'd be there in ten minutes to make breakfast before *we* went to work. Before I could answer in no uncertain terms to what would and wouldn't be happening today, it rang in my hand. Steve.

Worried, I answered. This was the second time Steve had called on a day he wasn't scheduled for an appointment. The last, the morning I'd woken up with Xander in my bed, I'd been so scattered I hadn't realized until later that we hadn't touched on anything I'd have thought Steve would've deemed worthy of needing to see me for, aside from being a little nervous about seeing his old unit. I'd pushed the thought aside, realizing he must have decided he wasn't ready to share, but something must have prodded him to reach out to me again in between appointments.

"Hey, did I wake you?" he asked as I struggled to extract myself from my bed.

"No," I was quick to reassure him, "Just getting ready for the day. Did you need to see me? I thought we re-scheduled you for next week when I have a chance to move into the new office," I babbled.

His voice was rough, echoing how I felt. "Actually, my wife insisted I talk with you. I've been having some ... issues ... the last few days. I know you said my anxiety and feelings would swing around a bit, now that we're cutting back the last of the anti-anxiety meds, but this is worse than I expected."

"Can you elaborate?" I asked, frowning. For the soldier to admit he was struggling, when he'd been doing so well processing his experiences, was cause for concern. Steve knew the scars—physical and mental—wouldn't go away with time, but he'd put in the work to get through it, and I'd thought he'd be ready to get back to his unit when he and his wife returned to their base in a few weeks.

I listened to his run-down. Difficulty sleeping, feeling watched, his senses on edge, even afraid he was trailing down to paranoid when he'd driven in circles for almost thirty minutes last night after he and his wife had gone out to dinner, thinking he was being followed.

"Seriously, Doc. I feel like I'm in the middle of a war-zone," he admitted, sounding ashamed. "I can't get myself to stand down. Hell, I even slept upright in the hall in case anyone tried to break in last night. And this rental isn't in a bad part of town or anything, so rationally, I know it wasn't necessary. I was just too keyed up, you know?"

"My normal office isn't available," I told him, not elaborating why. I hadn't told any of my patients what had happened, just that I was moving offices and my window to move had changed. "Do you want me to call my new building and see if they can allow us in today, or would you feel more comfortable for me to come to you?" I didn't do house calls often, not unless they were necessary, but in cases like this, it just made sense.

There was a pregnant pause before Steve sighed. "Here. Let's do it here."

"All right," I said, keeping my voice businesslike as I heard Xander walk in—without knocking—and head down the hallway to my bedroom. "Let me grab a pen and get your address." I didn't bother asking him to text it. If he were on edge, having him send out a text on an unsecured phone to where he and his family were wouldn't go over well. After writing down the address, I strode to my closet, still ignoring Xander, who was staring at me from the doorway. "I'll be there in an hour. I'll bring over pastries for breakfast. And coffee," I added, more reverently than intended.

"Coffee would be great." His appreciation mirrored mine.

I described my car, not wanting to add to his stress, before hanging up to glare at Xander.

"You broke into my house," I accused mildly, not looking at him as I scrounged around the closet for some clothing that would both work for my morning with a patient and be comfortable enough to clean in.

"Vik gave me his key." He matched my tone carefully, his body language telling me he wasn't sure if he was about to get kicked out or not.

"I have to go to a patient this morning." Arms full, I looked up at him briefly before making my way to my bathroom. "And then I'll be cleaning up the mess in my office. I appreciate the offer to make breakfast, but I'm going to stop at Sweet Nothings on the way and grab something from Claire."

"Not going to let you dismiss me," he called out, even as I shut and locked the bathroom door. "You know as well as I do that whoever broke into your office didn't get what they were looking for. Which means you could be in danger."

"I carry a taser and pepper spray," I assured him, not wanting to rise to the bait.

"Which is pretty useless unless you see the person coming," he said dryly.

I ignored his point, letting the silence linger as I changed. I was pulling my hair up when I heard him huff.

"Let me rephrase, sunshine. I'm not about to let you go anywhere alone until the powers that be have some time to look into some things. And even if security wasn't an issue, I wouldn't allow you to spend most of the day cleaning and sorting through broken shit while I stay here and do nothing. You're lucky I was able to stave off Vik until this afternoon. That gives him a chance to get some sleep before his grumpy-ass helps do whatever you need done later on today."

Pissed from the start of this conversation, I yanked the door open. "Let me? Who the hell do you think you are, believing you have any right to decide what I can and cannot do?"

Fists clenched, nostrils flaring, he practically stomped over from where he'd still been standing near the doorway. "I haven't sacrificed my very life to get us to where we are right now only to lose you," I thought I heard him mutter. But before I could ask, he swept me up into his arms, his mouth coming down on my upturned one.

The kiss was brutally hard, claiming, and powerful. But for once, I didn't follow meekly, I gave him as good as I got, letting the fire I carefully banked and controlled for more years than I could count flare freely.

I felt more than heard his growl as his fingers burrowed into my hair, pulling it free of the half-done bun I'd been putting it into. Mine weren't idle either. My nails scratched down his back, needing him to feel that pinch of pain, of temper.

Tongues still battling for control, Xander lifted me onto the bathroom counter, stepping in between my thighs. The heat from anger was quickly being drowned out by unadulterated lust. I wasn't sure which one of us started it, but clothes went flying as both of us tore through buttons and fabric, craving skin.

No sooner had I unearthed his cock from his boxers than he speared my core with two fingers, making my head jerk back in reflex as my hips jolted in response. Andrie would have whimpered meekly, but the Alex I used to be was in full control right now. "More," I gasped, pulling him toward me.

We both cried out as he removed his fingers and positioned himself more firmly between my legs, pushing into me in one motion, impossibly deep and scorching hot. He came to a stop, either to let me adjust or to tease, I wasn't sure. Either way, I wasn't about to let him stop the sensations pulsing through me, and I growled, practically attacking his neck in bites and licks while working the muscles at my core, urging him on.

To my surprise, he chuckled even as his hands tightened onto my hips, jerking me closer to the side of the counter, angling me to get even deeper before he pulled back, only to snap his hips back to me a second later.

The angle, speed, and need hurried my climax, though I tried to starve it off, wanting more. All too soon, I could hear my own unabashed cries, so unlike me, as I plummeted off the precipice. Echoes of Xander's shout rang in my ears as we clung to each other in the aftermath.

Ultimately, I didn't have time to argue Xander's high-handedness, nor he couldn't argue my decision to visit a patient at home. Still panting, I'd registered the time and, in a panic, rushed us both out the door. Xander insisted on driving, and I called in an order to Claire as he sped down the back streets in an effort to make up time.

Claire, bless her heart, had my order ready to go when we swung through her pick-up window, and apart from a single eye-brow lift at Xander accompanying me, she didn't say a word. Though, judging by the way she was reaching for her phone before we'd even pulled away, her boyfriend was going to get an earful. I wanted to groan at the thought. Royce was sure to tell his sister, probably at Claire's direction—who would be sure to want to say something about it the next time we saw each other.

Forcing the thought aside, I focused on pulling myself together in preparation for this session. Steve deserved my full attention. My personal life would have to be shoved into a box and examined later.

When we pulled into the driveway, I placed a restraining hand on Xander's arm. "Stay here," I braced for an argument, but though he didn't look happy, he gave me a single nod.

"Yeah, I imagine he wouldn't feel comfortable opening up to a stranger who's just tagging along today," he grumbled even as he grabbed his coffee cup from the tray.

"Are you just going to stay here, or do you want me to call you when we're done?" I asked, fingers curled around the door handle.

Xander grunted, looking around at the surroundings. The house was in an older neighborhood, but everything was still nicely maintained, with mature trees and bushes. The hedges were slightly overgrown, making it impossible to see the house from where he'd parked the car in the drive, but it still had a homey feel to it that fit in with the houses surrounding it. I was a little surprised at the location—I would have pegged Steve as a condo in the city type of guy, but I also knew he was renting, and I was sure a house like this would be more affordable and easier to find than something in the city.

"Even being a bit back from the street, I'm sure someone might notice me staying in the car. If I think I'm drawing too much attention, I'll drive around a bit. Send me a text as you're wrapping up, and I'll be sure to be here. I'll stay close if I do go anywhere."

His jaw was still tight, little lines around his eyes more pronounced than they'd been earlier, and I wondered why he felt uneasy. I paused, reading into his hesitation, but unsure of the source behind it.

"I know you can't tell me much," he finally said without preamble. "But is this guy a regular of yours, and does he give you any reason to think he might become violent if he's worked up?"

I relaxed, giving him a soft smile, realizing why he was worried. "He's not a regular, just someone I've seen a few times while he's here rehabbing, but he isn't a new patient or anything. Steve's not violent, just working through some things. In fact," I paused, then decided I wasn't going too far past my own lines of confidentiality, "he's one of my Tier One military patients, so you can be sure I'll be safe from someone attacking me or anything while I'm with him."

Realizing I was about to be late, I jumped out of the car and hurried through the bushes to the front door, juggling my briefcase in one hand and the coffee and pastry bag in the other.

The door opened as I rushed up the steps, and I pasted on a smile as I saw Steve. "I've brought coffee and some sweets from one of my favorite places in the city," I assured him, noticing too late what he was holding in his other hand.

I went down before I had a chance to turn, let alone scream. The slam of the door was the only thing that registered, blocking me from view of the one person who could have saved me.

Chapter 19

XANDER

A ndrie had barely left my sight when I noticed she'd
left her cell phone on the seat. Cursing, I grabbed it
as I unbuckled, hoping I could reach her before she went
inside. I hopped out, leaving the door open, and rushed
around the car, following her path through the overgrown
bushes. Before I could push my way through them, I heard
the front door slam shut and froze.

Sure, there were several reasons for a door to slam, but
closing it after welcoming a guest you called to visit wasn't
one of them.

I stood in place for a few seconds, debating whether
or not I was overthinking and overreacting in my efforts
to protect Andrie before deciding there wasn't any harm
in doing a quick walk around the house. No doubt this
guy would feel most comfortable talking to Andrie in
the kitchen or perhaps the living room. It would be easy
enough for me to sneak around and check on her before
knocking on the front door and announcing my presence.

Decision made, I slipped her phone into my pocket and
retraced my steps, careful to keep out of view from both
the windows and street as I made my way between the side
of the detached garage and the house, mentally trying to

come up with an excuse if I was caught by the homeowner. If he were Special Forces, it was certainly possible he'd notice me, especially if he was in a twitchy mood.

I circled the house, looking into windows as I passed. A small bathroom, empty bedroom that was small enough it might have been better served as an office, and dated kitchen. I was just about to turn around, already reading myself the riot act about jumping to conclusions, when a quick glance into the dining room had me freezing mid-step.

Fear, an emotion I haven't felt since walking into my empty, ransacked apartment in Russia, flooded me, making it impossible for me to move. The world seemed to gray, and the sound of my racing heart was the only thing I could hear. That was, until I heard Andrie's small cry.

That sound might as well have been a rubber band being snapped, and the world came back into focus and, with it, my resolve. I'd died for the love of my life once; I'd damn sure kill to keep her safe.

I watched Andrie come into view. A man dragged her into the room, trying to place her in a chair, but when she kicked out at him, he touched her with something in his hand, and she went limp. He sneered at her even as he lifted her from where she lay on the floor.

As much as I wanted to storm into the room or just shoot him where he stood, I couldn't risk her. He was too close to her as he lifted her into the wooden chair, zip-tying her arms before bending down to secure her legs. Plastic lined the floor around the chair, telling me without having to guess what the man had planned.

I loathed to lose sight of her, but I needed to get into the house, and I had to do it fast if I were going to prevent any more harm to her. Slipping back around the house, I didn't bother with the kitchen window, knowing I'd make too much noise and be too vulnerable. The bathroom would've been best, but was too close to the street. I'd be at risk from a neighbor or passerby seeing me break in and calling the police.

Pulling a switchblade from my pocket and keeping my gun close at hand in the waistband of my jeans, I went to work on the small window of the empty bedroom. The door to the room was closed, so at least I didn't have to worry about being seen as I pulled the screen off with ease before using the tip of the knife to work on the window. Luckily, it was an old window, and I was able to jimmy it with the ease of someone who'd done it more than once or twice in their past.

Pulling my gun out, I waited in the now-open window, training the weapon on the door. Several long seconds passed before I slipped into the room, grateful the carpeted floor masked my entry. A trained assassin I was not, but I was grateful—for the first time in my life—for being raised the way I had. This wasn't the first time I'd broken into a building, nor would it be my first time killing. Only, this time, it was to protect someone.

"Wake up," I heard the man—Steve—say, followed by the slap of skin on skin, which made my blood boil.

Andrie didn't make a sound this time, and I wondered if she was still unconscious until I heard her soft voice drift to me. "I'm not sure what you hope to accomplish, but people know where I am. You won't be able to get away with this. It won't take ten minutes to pull your military record and track you down."

"You really think I didn't plan this?" Steve sounded amused. "Let me ask you, Doc, how do you think I ended up as your patient? After all, it's not like I could find you in the yellow pages."

"I'm supposed to believe the US government ordered you to taser me and bind me to a chair?" she asked dryly, and I had to hide a smile. Leave it to Andrie to sound completely in control of the situation, even when she was up to her eyeballs in trouble.

"Where is it?" Steve asked, turning serious.

Andrie blew out a breath, sounding as if she were tired of the subject matter already. "Where is what?"

"The list!" he practically spat out.

"My patient list? The government already has that information. It might be classified, but it's hardly a secret. After all, they are the ones who send y'all to me. It's not like it's the other way around." Her prim and proper attitude was still firmly in place, but I could sense the fear she was trying so hard to hide.

"Oh, believe me, I know the military's love of paperwork. Likely, the files are in triplicate and in some storage building somewhere. But not together. You have clearance to council all the top dogs. Navy, Army, Marine Corps, Air Force ... Even the goddamn CIA, DOJ, and NSA have you on their payroll. Do you think they read each other in? Besides, we both know if your clearance level goes that high, you have others that are so buried, they don't even have names attached to them. Hear any whispers, doc? Any ghosts in the night?" He was almost taunting her. Then he cursed. "Your fucking drive is empty. Where the hell are your patient records? They aren't in your briefcase, so they have to be at your house. Tell me where they are, and I'll kill you quickly. Trust me, I have no issues going slow and making it hurt."

"Why would you think it's at my house?" Andrie asked, her confusion evident, before she cried out, causing my hand to fist. I was slowly inching down the hall, but it was slow going. With a house as old as this one, creaky floors were inevitable, and I had to test each move before placing my weight.

"It's not on you or at your office. I know you have every-thing stored somewhere. You likely shred the paper copies we bring you as soon as you compile the information. Stop stalling. If I have to cut it out of you, I'll do it. I don't like to torture for the sake of torture, but I have no issue making a mess to get what I want. Breaking a few eggs and all that."

Andrie's voice rose, coming faster now. "You missed it in my office. I had it hidden in the bookcase. As soon as the police cleared out, I pulled the hard drive and gave it to a friend. He secured it somewhere even you can't reach." Another cry, but I didn't hear a slap that time. "Please, just let me go. You missed your chance."

"Bullshit. Why do you think I was tapped to come down here before you moved offices? Do you know how much someone will pay for that information? My partner and I already have a buyer lined up."

Andrie came into view as I finally made my way out of the hall. First, I saw her arm, tied to a chair and stained red with blood. It was slowly flowing down her arm to the tips of her fingers, dripping onto the clear plastic lining the floor. It was clearly large enough for a body, the intent spelled out for her as well as me, if the banked terror in her eyes was any indication.

She saw me almost immediately but was quick to tear her eyes back to Steve, not wanting to alert him to my presence. "I don't understand, Steve. Why do you think my patient list is anything special? I mean, yes, I have some top men and women on my lists, but I don't even have assurance the files or names they give me are real. Look at you, for instance. You call me, give me a file I assume is from whatever military branch you come from, and we start scheduling sessions. Only one branch gives me files that are mostly unredacted. Everything else has more black-out on it than words."

"You think I didn't do my own scouting around before I tried your office?" he sneered. "What kind of therapist sweeps for bugs daily? Who has state-of-the-art security in their building? And who keeps their laptop in a safe when not in use? No, you have more information than you're letting on."

"I worked with Special Forces and other Tier One operators," Andrie practically screeched as Steve came forward again with a knife coated in her blood. "My military contact picked out the office building. And the bug sweeps are in my contract—I can't afford to lose it. Who do you think showed me how to use the equipment, let alone gave it to me? And the office came with the safe. I just assumed I was supposed to use it." She was practically babbling now, I couldn't tell if it was to keep his attention on her or because the knife was coming closer and closer to her hand this time.

She fisted her hands as if to protect her fingers as the steel came into contact with her skin. I was barely five feet away now, having traded my gun for my knife as I calculated my options and opted for the one that would be the least risky for Andrie.

She must have seen or sensed me about to lunge because she screeched as I rushed forward, distracting Steve as I took two strides toward him. He whirled but wasn't able to turn all the way around before I was on him, tackling him to the ground.

Luck was on my side, and I felt my knife slide into his side as we fell, even as I lost hold of it. We tumbled to the floor in a tangle of limbs before rising to our feet. I was quicker to get up than he was, but not by much.

Never one to sit back and wait, I launched, landing several punches and an uppercut before he stumbled back and out of reach. Smiling wickedly, he slowly pulled my knife from his side, wiping it on his leg before expertly spinning it in his hand.

"Something you should know about me," Steve said, crouching in a ready-position. "I might not really be Steve Turner, but I *was* a SEAL. Before I was tossed out, anyway."

Fuck this. I wasn't a hero, and this wasn't a movie. I reached behind, intent on getting my gun. Andrie, seeing my move, leaned all her weight into her right side, rocking the chair over, toppling her into Steve.

He saw her attempt to knock into him and managed to almost sidestep her but tripped, falling next to her.

It wasn't perfect, but she'd given me enough time to grab my weapon. "Steve" rolled, ignoring Andrie, but before he could react, I pulled the trigger.

The silence in the wake of the discharge was almost deafening, but I didn't pause. I stepped up to the man and kicked away the knife before leaning down and checking for a pulse. A technicality, really. The hollow point bullet made a mess of his chest. Thankfully, there wouldn't be an exit wound, and the bulk of the blood spatter was contained to the plastic sheet.

Even as my mind went to the next step, my heart pulled me to Andrie. Turning to where she was on her side, tied to the chair, I picked the entire thing up, setting her upright. She was pale, her lips blue-tinged, eyes wide.

Recovering my knife from the floor, I cut her loose but left her sitting as I rushed to grab a towel from the kitchen. I wrapped it around her arm. Long but thankfully shallow cuts trailed down her forearm. She was bleeding like a stuck pig, but her injuries didn't appear to be life-threatening.

"Andrie," I said quietly, trying to get her to focus on me. "Sweetheart, look at me."

Keeping one hand firmly on the towel, I used the other to tuck a strand of hair behind her ear, resting my palm against her cheek. She blinked slowly, but I saw when she really registered me standing in front of her. "We've got to get you to the car. And I've got to take care of this. Who knows if someone reported that shot, and I'm not sure who you want me to call about this." I motioned to the body.

"Umm." She licked her lips, still not really focusing on the here and now.

"Okay, sweetheart." Hating that I couldn't give her time, I lifted her into my arms, cradling her against me like a child.

I put her into the car, thankful for the privacy the lot provided and the fact there didn't seem to be many people home. After getting Andrie situated in the front seat, I returned to the house, wrapping the body up in the plastic liner like a burrito before putting the entire thing into an oversized duffle bag "Steve" just so happened to have nearby. Then I carried him out and hefted him in the trunk. It was a tight fit, but thankfully, the small car had more trunk space than I'd originally given it credit for.

I didn't have time for a total clean, but I did wipe down anything that might have had my fingerprints before grabbing the man's laptop, Andrie's belongings, and the coffee and treats. Finally, I did a quick walk-through of the house, but I didn't see any signs the man actually had lived there, even short-term. No bags, clothing, nothing in the fridge, not even a damn wallet to identify him.

Locking up, I was out the door and back in the car within minutes. A glance at Andrie told me she was still in shock, but gamely, she was trying to pull herself together. Shaking, her teeth chattering, she looked around wildly. "My phone. I need to call ..." she trailed off.

Pulling it out, I ignored the hand reaching for it. "What's your passcode?" She rattled it off, not bothering to fight me. Figuring it was a toss-up between Matteo and Grimm, I thumbed through her contacts, hitting Grimm's name when it came up first.

As soon as he answered, I told him to hold on as I conferenced Matteo in. As soon as I had them both on the phone, I told them I had a matter I could use their expertise on.

Cluing into my desire to keep everything off the phone lines and the unspoken need to see them quickly, Matteo offered to have us meet him at his house. I glanced over at Andrie and considered the fact that Matteo had a woman and child living with him, and I was driving a car with a dead body in the trunk.

"Actually, I think the clubhouse might be better?" I offered, hoping Matteo wouldn't take offense to me changing his order. "Besides," I continued, "You know how us Iron Wraiths are. Where one of us goes, the others are quick to follow. It'll be easier to have us all have a beer and brainstorm where we don't have to worry about waking a kiddo from a nap."

"We did get a new pool table delivered. I'm sure the guys would love to break it in," Grimm said, not missing a beat.

"Be there in fifteen," I said before ending the call, turning my attention back to Andrie. I'd cranked the heat on full blast as soon as I'd gotten in, but she was still shivering. Placing my right hand on her leg, I rubbed gently, hoping to infuse some warmth into her. I wished I had a blanket or even a sweatshirt to wrap around her, but Andrie kept her car the way she did most of her life—utterly neat and void of any personality. The backseat looked as if nothing had been placed back there since she'd driven off the car lot.

I made short work of the drive, despite keeping to the speed limit and obeying all traffic signs. The last thing I needed was to get pulled over right now. Grimm was already there when we arrived. I still hadn't figured out if he lived in his room there or just spent most of his time at the club.

I parked the car as close to the entrance as I could, circling the hood to open Andrie's door. She tried to protest, but I picked her up again, carrying her into the building. Grimm held the door open for us before following me inside.

"Do I need to call Jasper?" he asked quietly when I placed her on the bar top.

"I don't think so," she said, even as I nodded, unwrapping the towel gently and inspecting the damage. Andrie hissed a bit as I patted the towel against the still-seeping wound.

"What happened?" he asked, after typing something on his cell phone.

"One of Andrie's patients wasn't actually a patient," I explained.

"Then who the hell was he?" Matteo walked into the room.

"Apparently, sent by someone to get Andrie's patient lists. He knew she had top operatives from just about every branch of military and alphabet soup agencies. And what the hell was he talking about, asking about 'whispers'?"

She shifted then, and the two men glanced meaningfully at each other. "Where is he now?"

I grunted. "In a makeshift body bag in the trunk."

"Any idea who he was?"

"Other than the fact he wasn't Steve Turner? A former SEAL who'd been discharged at some point. I shot him center mass, so you can still run facial rec if you want," I said, not taking my eyes from Andrie. "Can someone get a blanket and tell me what the hell he was talking about?"

"Us," Lessia said, coming from the hidden room. "He might have been talking about us."

Chapter 20

ANDRIE

I was so cold. The kind of cold that seeped into your bones, down to your very being. The blankets wrapped around me didn't so much as touch it. Jasper, the Iron Wraith's doctor, appeared in front of me, taking over from where Xander had been applying pressure to the cuts that ran down my forearm.

Xander pulled himself up onto the bar top next to me and reached his arm around my shoulders. Vik was somehow on my other side, pushing a shot of tequila into my hand.

"Really?" Xander murmured, even as he helped raise the glass to my lips.

Vik's chuckle sounded strained. "We're in Texas now, not Russia. Not everything calls for vodka."

The alcohol burned on its way down, making me sputter, but Xander wouldn't be deterred from making me drink the entire shot. Eyes watering, the heat finally spread enough to allow me to start thinking again.

Before I could say a word, though, Jasper dumped some sort of disinfectant down my arm. I hissed, trying to pull back, but he and Xander held me firmly.

"Knife wounds can be nasty," Xander said, kissing the top of my head. "Let Jasper fix it up, yeah?"

"Some butterfly bandages will be enough in most places, but I'll likely have to put in a stitch or two where he went in deeper," Jasper's soothing doctor's voice mirrored my own professional one when I was with patients, but I could see the rage in his eyes, the same way I could hear it in Vik's voice. The men were pissed I'd been hurt.

"Ready to tell us what happened?" Grimm asked from where he'd been watching us a few feet away.

Xander started. "Andrie got a call this morning from a patient who needed to see her. Because her office is still a mess, she offered to meet him at his home. I tagged along and was planning on staying in the car, but Andrie forgot her phone. I went to give it to her so she could let me know when she was done, but something didn't seem right. I cased the house and saw a man dragging Andrie onto a chair in the dining room, where he tied her up. So, I went in after her."

I took it over from there. "Steve tasered me the second I walked into the house. By the time I was back in control, he'd tied me to a chair and was going through my briefcase. I had an external hard drive in there—an empty one since I hadn't seen any patients yet and haven't had time to get my laptop replaced. He was pissed when he saw it was empty. He said he was looking for my patient files. That while each military branch had records, none would have each other's. Basically, I had a bigger, more inclusive list. And that he had a buyer already lined up for it."

"And the whispers?" Lessia asked from her seat at one of the nearby tables.

I shook my head. "I'm not sure if he meant that the way we're taking it. He mentioned something about how if I had clearance for a bunch of agencies, like the CIA and NSA, that I'd have others as well. He said something about whispers and ghosts."

"But you're not sure if he was talking about WHSPR?" Matteo asked.

"He asked if I'd heard any whispers about ghosts in the night," I recalled. "We all know beyond black ops, there are ghost operatives and WHSPR. That doesn't mean he knew what he was asking."

"You think he was fishing," Grimm commented, and I nodded.

"If he'd known for sure, I think he would have worded it differently. Yes, he'd heard the rumors, but there are plenty of people out there that have. In certain circles, anyway. A former SEAL would definitely have the access to hear such things."

"How did he become a patient of yours?" Matteo asked. "And did he mention how he tracked you down?"

Tilting my head, I struggled to think through the fog that still lapped at the edges of my focus. "Same way as the others. I get a call from them—on my secure line, the one the government provided me. I set up an appointment, and he came with his files and the release from his superior, or whoever is needed to sign off on it, to speak with me about his work. I kept the files, going through them before the first appointment. After I transferred everything to digital, I shredded the paper copies. But even those files, while supposedly complete, are often barebones or missing key details. I might have clearance and need to know certain things about a mission not typically discussed, but I don't need or receive the entire outline or description of a mission, let alone someone's past mission's list."

"Why not email them?" Xander wanted to know. "Paper seems very old-fashioned, considering the world we live in."

"I don't have internet in my office. No way of being hacked that way. In fact, Dr. Andrie Demming has no digital footprint, apart from basic information about when I graduated. There are no pictures of me anywhere online, nor a website about my practice. I have a personal email, which I use at home or on my cell if they's a need, but it contains no connection to my practice aside from Hardy's contact information. The government-assigned landline at my office is forwarded to my cell phone. One of the Cyber triplets set it up, so I have no idea on how it works, other than I'm told it's as if I take and send out calls through my office, even when I'm not there."

"And your other patients?" Grimm asked.

"The pro-bono ones have a separate phone number. It's a burner phone I picked up in Houston. I pay cash for the minutes every few months at a shop that doesn't have cameras. I check that phone once a day for messages and to call to set up times for appointments."

"And the rest of us?" Lessia asked quietly.

"You have your own phone number. Technically, it's the one all my military calls are forwarded to, but it's as secure as yours is. The triplets said the number actually routes through a proxy—or several—before it comes to me. But all y'all come to me through Matteo or Grimm. I never meet an operative alone the first time. One of you is always with them to introduce me. That's so the operative can verify who I am."

"And the files this guy wanted?" Xander still had his arm around me, but he'd turned to face me a bit more.

"Here," I said simply. "I wasn't lying when I told Steve he'd missed it when he'd broken in. There's a hidden storage area in the bookcase itself. Shade and Whisp went in and retrieved it for me."

"And you asked them to hide it here," Xander recalled.

I nodded, taking a deep breath. "Steve probably thought I was lying when I said I gave it to someone else, but I wasn't. I knew it was safe here."

"How did he get your name?" Xander asked. Everyone looked thoughtful as we tried to put the pieces together.

"My name and what I do aren't exactly secrets, even if I work with classified information. Like Steve said, I see a lot of Tier One operatives and government assets. He didn't even ask about the few people I council from WITSEC. There aren't many of us throughout the country that have the clearances I do. All it would take is one person talking ..." I trailed off, frowning. "Something he did say stood out. He knew I was about to move offices to Accardi Tactical. I hadn't called anyone yet when my office was broken into. Except for Hardy, Gideon, Harrison, and whoever they would have spoken with in DC, no one had been notified of the change yet."

"At least that narrows things down a bit," Matteo grumbled. I couldn't blame him. A leak at the top level, involving multiple agencies and military branches, would be a nightmare to investigate.

"Shade's at the house doing cleanup," Lessia said, looking at her phone. "Whisp is taking photos, DNA, and fingerprints from the dead guy before Brody and Savage get rid of him. Cyber is waiting for the photo, then they'll run it. They're already pulling together files of all SEALS discharged in the last ten years."

"I've got his laptop in the car as well," Xander was looking at Lessia, even as his hand rubbed up and down my good arm in lazy circles.

"I've got it," a tiny sprite of a woman said as she walked in, practically bouncing. Juniper might be the size of a high-schooler, complete with the backpack and sneakers—and meal preferences—but that was where the similarities ended. She was, hands-down the smartest person I'd ever met. What she lacked in people skills, she made up for with pure genius when it came to anything involving computers.

Her sisters, Jolene and Josie, trailed in after her. The "triplets" looked nothing alike, save they had similar blonde hair. Which made sense, seeing as they weren't actually blood sisters. Still, blood didn't make family, and the three were close enough to fool even those who knew better into thinking they'd been together their whole lives.

Juniper's somewhat teenage appearance was enhanced by her choice of hairstyle, which was cut short, standing up every which way on her head in a spiky mess with various faded colors of pink, green, and purple coloring most of it. Jolene's fell down her back in waves and was the darkest gold of the bunch. Josie's was pale yellow and stopped at her shoulders. Juniper was by far the shortest, while Jolene was closest to Lessia's tall height. Again, Josie fell between them.

"Always nice to see you, Junie," Grimm said, his lips twitching, as he strode to open the secured room I knew was hidden behind the back wall.

"Back 'attcha," she said, giving him a smile. "I'm starving. I don't suppose you have any chips?"

"I'm afraid we haven't stocked up lately, but I do have some cereal, if that works?" Grimm asked.

"Got any Fruit Loops?"

His smile finally broke free. "I'm sure Savage has a supply of something suitable. Anything else?"

"Mocha latte, extra-large. Double espresso, double chocolate would be great." She plopped her backpack down on a chair.

"I have dark roast coffee and chocolate milk," he offered wryly.

"No!" The rest of the room protested, cringing, even as Junie shrugged as if the two were interchangeable.

"Jolene, Josie," he greeted with a head nod, though his smile fell by the time he greeted the last sister. "Anything for y'all?"

"I thought you were waiting on us to start researching?" Matteo asked, folding his arms across his chest.

Juniper took one of the seats in front of the main computer monitor in what the Iron Wraiths called the "war room." "No need to wait. I've got things running. But it would speed things up to get an ID, and we could come here quicker than they could collect it and bring it to us."

A side door opened, and Whisp strolled through, bag in hand.

"There," Jasper said, sounding pleased. "All done."

I hadn't realized he'd been tending to the cuts this entire time. The numbing agents had done their job; I hadn't even noticed him stitching.

"I don't see anything that indicates permanent damage, but you'll be sore for a few days and likely itchy when it starts to heal. I'll check on you later this week to make sure it's still free from infection." Pulling off the gloves he was wearing, he stuffed them, along with the bandages and blood-soaked towel, into a trash bag. "I'm due at the hospital for my shift in an hour. Do you need anything else?" The last part was directed at Grimm.

He shook his head. "Get out of here. There isn't anything more you can do right now."

The two men walked into a hall after Jasper gave Xander instructions for my arm. Xander stayed glued to my side, his hand still wandering up and down my good arm. Vik was behind the bar, busying himself by cleaning bottles and wiping down surfaces. It was nothing that had to get done but was so very Vik.

An orange juice appeared next to me a moment later. "It'll help with the blood loss," he muttered when I looked at him. Reaching out, I stopped the hand wiping down the counter next to me. "Thank you," I said, knowing how worried he must've been.

He grunted. "Don't do that again, all right?"

Grimm walked back in with a sandwich on a plate in one hand, a red cereal box under his arm, and a coffee mug in his other hand. He set the sandwich next to the orange juice, giving me his own critical look, before going over to deliver Juniper's requested "brain food."

"All right," Juniper said around a mouthful of the brightly colored cereal. "Fingerprints are in and say ... Gary Smithfield. Less-than-honorably discharged three years ago. Looks to have stayed in Virginia, which is where he's from originally. I'm working through his military files, but it'll take a hot minute." Fingers flew across the keyboard as she hacked her way through the military firewall as if it were child's play.

A picture of Gary appeared on the main screen a moment later. It was definitely the same person. "He had a few drug charges and a few issues of getting too pushy with a few of the female officers. Shit hit the fan when he assaulted the base commander's daughter."

After more typing, the picture on the monitor moved to make way for another. "*This* is the real Steve Turner. He's a current SEAL but is on deployment in Syria at the moment."

"Someone pulled the name from somewhere," Josie said, leaning over her sister to look at the computer. "Any intersect between the two men?"

Juniper's hand jumped out and snagged the box of cereal just as Josie tried—and failed—to ease it backward to Jolene. "That's going to take a while. There's a lot of overlap. They've been to several of the same places in the world, trained at the same places, even crossed paths a few times." She tossed a glance over her shoulder at me. "You can go home. I promise to go as fast as I can, but I'd be shocked if I have anything before tomorrow."

Surprised that I'd managed to eat both the sandwich and juice while Juniper had been busy, I glanced around in search for my keys when a thought hit me. "I'm not getting my car back. Am I?" I asked Xander, thinking of what or, more accurately, *whom*, he'd put in the trunk.

He stared at me first, the shock of my words causing his eyes to widen. Then he chuckled. "That's a pretty safe assumption."

"Good," Lessia said, rising from her seat. "With any luck, you can convince her to replace it with something someone under eighty would actually want to drive."

"My car isn't that bad," I protested, thinking of my totally non-descript light tan sedan.

She rolled her eyes. "The only thing that car is good for is a long-term stakeout. No one ever sees the thing. It's so ... bland."

Xander gave me a boyish grin. "I hate to agree with her, but sweetheart, please, can we at least get something with a bigger engine? And more leg room," he added.

Something nagged at me even as I let the two of them help me off the bar top. "He said they already had a buyer." I whirled around to Juniper. "Gary had to have had some connection to the identity he used but also a way in to get to me. His paperwork was legit—at least in terms of what I would normally get. And he had the military release, the official one with permission to see me about active military operations as long as it tied back to 'mental healing'."

"You're right. It's another data point to add to the list," Juniper agreed, not looking at me as she continued to dig. Clearly, I was a step behind her.

"And whoever helped him get to me must also have some sort of contact with this buyer. I can't imagine Gary hatched this plan on his own. Even if he'd heard my name from another SEAL, why target me with the idea of stealing my patient files? And why enough overwhelming confidence to line up a buyer before he even has the information in his possession?"

That had everyone else in the room pausing as my words sank in. "Damn," Josie swore, grabbing a seat in front of another computer, booting it up. "Toss the info you're mining my way, Junie. I'll start sorting it out for you as you keep digging."

Lessia practically dragged me out the door, citing her need to get back to work after dropping us off. I tried to catch Vik's eye, hoping he'd offer to drive us home, but he'd disappeared somewhere in the depths of the building.

"Come on, sweetheart."

The last thing I saw before the door closed were Juniper and Josie, hard at work at their computers, with Grimm and Matteo standing behind them, watching the large monitors with information flashing over them.

Chapter 21

XANDER

To say Andrie was more patient than I was would have been a total understatement. After a brief nap, she acted as if nothing had happened, attempting to take advantage of the "downtime" and clean her house. She had me cleaning out gutters, wiping windows, and washing ceiling fans.

My reward for helping her with the domestic work included a pot of chili, two peach pies, and another night in her bed. Sleep was hard coming for both of us and not just because the sex was just as addicting as it had been in our previous lives. Even after, cuddled in each other's arms and breathing heavily, we seemed to fight letting go. I was afraid of what my nightmares might consist of, and I had a feeling Andrie's thoughts mirrored mine.

The next day, armed with a car accident story, we went car shopping. I knew Andrie well enough to know she wouldn't buy anything that large as a spur of the moment purchase, but with the help of a salesman and my input, she narrowed her options down to a larger—and only slightly—more modern version of her sedan and a sporty SUV.

While she spent more time talking with the salesman about the sedan, I hoped, based on the longing looks and price comparison searches she'd done on her phone, she'd take the plunge with the SUV.

We ate at a nearby restaurant and then met Vik at Andrie's old office. He and I made quick work of the cleanup, relegating Andrie to overseeing the packing of the lighter knick-knacks. The only piece of furniture she wanted to keep was the bookshelf. I had to admit, after seeing the hidden compartment inside what appeared to be a solid shelf, it was pretty neat. It was also a bitch to move. The entire solid piece, which was easily four feet tall and ten feet wide, with individual sections of shelves and solid wood dividers, was heavy and ungainly to move. We had to rent a moving truck in order to get it across town and to the A.T. building.

Thankfully, Boone, who was coming down as we were struggling to get it up the stairway, helped us get it to the proper floor and into the room. Kassie, the office manager for the executives, had come down to see if Andrie needed anything in way of supplies and to give her the packet IT had put together so she had the access for their computer system, which would include a secured internet connection and inter-office messaging system.

While I knew I had absolutely no say in Andrie's job choices, I loved that she'd moved into the building. Not only was it safer—the building was more secure than most embassies—but the comradery she was already being shown told me she'd no longer be alone while at the office during the day. Here, she'd have coworkers and possibly even more friends to break up the day instead of being alone and likely lonely, as she'd been in her previous location. She'd admitted, when questioned more about the old office, that she hadn't chosen it. Hardy had, and other than knowing that other people in the building were connected to government or military work, she didn't know any of them and could barely identify the people who worked in the building.

I had to say, if I had a background that wouldn't send a host of red flags up the HR ladder, I would've asked about applying myself. Not in the offices—I'd never be domesticated enough to turn into a suit—but chatting with Boone and what he and others did at their training location had me wishing I had the security clearance to look into available positions at the training grounds. The idea of taking my knowledge and using it to protect others directly instead of just stealing information and passing it on from time to time, as I'd done in the past, was appealing.

I knew that as much as I enjoyed using my skills for the Iron Wraiths, I didn't want my life filled with that much darkness in my day-to-day. Still, I made a mental note to narrow my job searches to something that would help others. Grimm and I had talked a few times about what I wanted my life to consist of, assuming Andrie was a part of it—and she would be a large part of it. I'd toyed with becoming an operative, but the thought of being away from her for large stretches while I was on assignments didn't sit right with me, and I knew she wouldn't want me to take that kind of a risk, not when she'd already lost me once. Though I'd committed to aiding the Wraiths in dismantling trafficking rings—something that was too important not to do. Still, at least with them, I'd have brothers with me to ensure my ass returned to Andrie in one piece.

I knew I wanted to find something similar to Charge. He supported the MC without question but wasn't an operative. Still, everyone knew without a doubt he would step up and do what was needed, no questions asked. And while he wasn't as far into the shady shit the MC was up to the way I wanted to be—as Vik and I had said before, everyone needed a hobby—there was something to staying below radar, the way I'd been most of my life.

Rising from where I'd been securing the bookcase to the wall, I saw Boone watching me while Kassie and Andrie talked. Vik, seeing my pointed expression, looked at Boone and then offered to take the women down to the storage room to see if anything else would be suitable for the office. Boone smoothly offered to help me finish up some paperwork that would give me access to see Andrie in the building as her "boyfriend"—something Vik and I had insisted Andrie allow, given the current situation.

I could tell Andrie knew something was up, but she let Vik lead her from the room, talking with Kassie about how far their decorating frenzy should go and Kassie's current dilemma about "refreshing" Boone's house.

Boone waited until the voices faded before closing the door. Not sure of my best move, I stood in the middle of the room, deciding to let Boone lead. On one hand, Kassie was my sister, even if she wasn't aware of it, and I had no designs on anything. I was only amazed that she, along with myself, Andrie, and Vik, had all made it to the other side of the world, safe and in one piece. However, I understood I was a strange man who couldn't help focusing on Boone's woman anytime we were in the same room. If I were him, I'd want to set me straight, too.

"I can't help but notice you watching my girlfriend," Boone said, coming around to sit in Andrie's desk chair. What surprised me was his motion for me to sit in one of the chairs across from the desk as if we were having a casual chat.

I stayed silent, still not sure what to say, as I leaned back into the surprisingly comfortable chair.

"What I can't figure out is why," Boone continued mildly. "I know you're very obviously involved with Andrie, and I don't get the straying-eye vibe from you. So, I have to ask myself, why else would Kassie draw your notice?"

It wasn't a question directed at me, but he let the silence hang. On a regular civilian, the silence might have worked, making them talk in an effort to fill it. But I wasn't a regular civilian. I let the moment stretch, not about to give in.

Boone matched me, but instead of anger or even interest, amusement sparkled in his eyes, along with a hint of respect.

"I asked Lessia about you, you know." he said finally.

Unable to help myself, I blinked, not anticipating that turn of events. "What did she have to say?" I grudgingly asked.

"That you were a protector of sorts. In another job, another life. Not one in public, but someone in the shadows. And that you kept Kassie safe, even if she had little idea she had a guardian angel."

Well, that was more poetic than I would have given Lessia credit for. But she hadn't lied, even if the details were decidedly vague. Mainly, I'd protected Kassie by staying away from her, even though I wished I hadn't had to. If any of my connections had thought I had a soft spot for the half-sister my father barely acknowledged, she would have had a neon target on her back. Still, the words warmed me enough to give him what I could. "It's just nice to see her happy. That's all. It's all I've ever wanted for her." His eyes flickered, and I feared I'd given away too much, but he hid his thoughts before I could read them clearly.

"Then I'm glad you could be here to see that what you sacrificed on her behalf was worth it." His quiet words cut me to the core.

Deciding to trade him truth for truth, I replied, "I'm happy she has you."

"Well, then." Looking as uncomfortable as I felt now that we were discussing feelings, he rose. The door opened, and the women, leading a packed-down Vik, came back into the room.

"Honey, I hope you don't mind, but I invited Xander and Andrie over to help us paint this weekend." He told his girlfriend, not missing a beat.

Andrie's attention went to me, but I only winked at her. "Boone said something about going room by room," I announced, playing a hunch on my sister going overboard.

Just because I'd stayed in the shadows, as Boone had put it, didn't mean I didn't know her. She just didn't know me.

Kassie flushed guiltily. "I'm afraid once I got started I couldn't stop redecorating. I keep telling Boone to rein me in, but—"

Boone cut her off, pulling her in for a quick kiss. "I told you, I want you to make the house yours. It's just paint and decorations, honey. I'll let you know if you're going too crazy. The house already feels more like a home, half-done and a mess, than it ever did when I lived there by myself."

As much as I loved that my sister had found a man strong enough to protect her and one who loved her enough to worship the ground she walked on, I didn't necessarily need a front row seat to him making doe-eyes at her. My phone buzzed, and grateful for the intrusion, I quickly answered it, only to find myself listening to dead air as I was hung up on almost immediately. Apparently, Juniper was a woman of few words.

"We're needed at HQ," I told Vik and Andrie. "Unless you want to spend some more time putting everything together?" I offered hastily.

Andrie shook her head. "Kassie gave me some great ideas on what I can buy to make this feel more ... comfortable. I don't suppose we can go out after your meeting?"

I heard Vik snicker behind me. Perhaps Boone wasn't the only one in the room willing to do anything for his woman. Vik knew I hated any sort of shopping with a passion, but I heard myself agreeing to go as soon as we wrapped things up, even offering to take her out to dinner if we were out that late.

I wasn't sure if Andrie actually wanted to go shopping or if she was just giving us an exit strategy, but I knew if she showed any interest in going out today, I'd be holding her purse and pushing the cart without a hint of impatience.

Within twenty minutes, we were back at the Iron Wraith's headquarters. Juniper vibrating with excitement as we walked through the door. "I found them." Her words were pure satisfaction.

"The buyer or the person who orchestrated the attempt?" I asked, grasping Andrie's hand in mine the second I felt her reach for me.

"Both. At least, I'm pretty sure about the buyer. It's not like there aren't plenty of people who would have wanted their hands on it. But first ..."

She brought up a photo of a man I didn't recognize, but Andrie gasped. "That's Hardy. He's my government contact."

"Which branch?" I asked.

"I-I don't know. He's been my handler from the beginning."

"What do you mean, your handler?" Grimm tilted his head in question.

"Having a point of contact for each military and government branch I work with would get too complicated. Instead, I was assigned one person to reach out to. He's the one who approved my office location, handled setting up my phone line—or so he thinks, considering he's unaware Matteo had it upgraded after he left—and is the one I'm supposed to call if I have any issues with security."

"How often do you see him?" Matteo asked.

"Umm ... not often. A few times. He came here recently before the break-in. He wasn't happy about me moving offices, but he didn't have a leg to stand on afterward since he's the one who picked the location."

"Why would he have an issue with moving offices?"

She shook her head. "I didn't get it. To be honest, I thought it was big-man syndrome. You know, he was mad it wasn't his idea. Lessia knows him. She called him Hardly, as in hardly does anything. He spends more time bossing people around and throwing his weight around than he does anything else. But if he were biding his time, having me accumulate more and more names, it could be he knew he wouldn't have access if I moved to Accardi Tactical."

"Ding, ding, ding," Juniper said. Even though she wasn't currently typing, her fingers—all of them—were tapping on the table, as if she were typing the words she was speaking. "At least, that's what we've been able to figure out from reading between the lines. He isn't rising in ranks any longer. His father was some sort of a bigwig four-star general, but he died last year. Hardy isn't liked by anyone, does a shitty job at whatever it is he's supposed to do, and likes the high life. Unfortunately for him, his funds are running out faster than chickens after discovering a fox in their henhouse."

"And the connection between him and Gary?" Andrie wanted to know.

"Second cousins. But their mothers were close, and they took family vacations together when the men were children." Josie rolled her eyes. "The two exchanged infrequent phone calls until a few months ago, right around the time Gary was discharged. It seems like Hardy allowed him into the plan at that point, and after almost constant contact, they had one phone call just before Gary came down here. I pulled camera footage from the airport, and Hardy actually dropped our little imposter off and handed him a packet right before they parted ways."

"And the buyer?" Vik crossed his arms across his chest.

"Irina Petrov."

"Demi's mother?"

Chapter 22

ANDRIE

There wasn't a name in the world that instilled as much fear into me as that name. Irina Petrov. As far as I was concerned, she was the devil incarnate.

I saw Jolene watching me, a sympathetic look on her face. Josie looked as if she were mentally thinking of ways to kill someone, and even Junie was staring at me.

"How do you know her?"

"S-she was the one who ..." I trailed off, unable to say anything more. But I didn't need to.

"Irina's a lieutenant for her father. She runs the entire skin trade for the Bratva in Russia. The gang's drug trafficking interests might bring in more money, but she's by far more feared," Vik stated, a coldness to his voice I didn't often hear.

"Why would she want the list?" Lessia asked, causing me to jump. I hadn't realized she'd come into the room. Or maybe she'd already been there. "Foreign operatives wouldn't be something she'd care about. Not unless they were knocking at her doorstep."

"She doesn't want it. Not for herself, anyway," Junie explained. "But from what I can gather, despite all the power she holds in Russia, she still feels slighted when it comes to respect by other players in that world. She wants a seat at the big table, and she knows the man to get her there would want it." The meaningful glances between Juniper and Matteo told me whoever the man was, he was on their radar.

"Please tell me this is enough to finally move on the bitch," Vik growled.

Xander, who'd been quiet, shook his head. "She's mine, brother."

Fear jolted through me at the thought of Xander, freshly extracted from that world, going back into it and being anywhere near that woman.

"Sorry, boys, but this one's coming to me." I shivered at Lessia's tone, completely void of emotion. As an assassin, Lessia Accardi was the best. Not only at getting the job done so cleanly she might as well have never been there, but in her execution—quite literally. Out of all the men and women I worked with, she was also so well-adjusted and able to compartmentalize it was almost scary. I'd never known anyone who could so easily put aside various parts of themselves only to pull them back out when needed. At home with her family, Lessia was loving, warm, and a powerhouse. As an assassin, she was cold, calculating almost to a fault, and without an ounce of emotion.

I'd asked her once if it bothered her to do what she did. To end a life. She'd tilted her head as if she'd never thought about it before. "No. Because I'm not ending a human life. I'm killing monsters. The men and women I eradicate gave up their souls in their quest for money or power. I'm simply allowing their body to catch up to the rest of them. Do

I respect life? Absolutely. But in the way a hunter manages their game of choice. I want the population to flourish. In order to do that, I have to remove the diseased. These people are no different. Only instead of a virus, they've been infected with their own beliefs and ideologies that they themselves are above humanity."

Blinking back to the present, I noticed Matteo didn't exactly look happy, but the resigned weariness told the room that Lessia was right.

"You're not trained for this, to start. But you're also too emotionally involved," she told Vik.

"And you aren't?" Vik challenged, crossing his arms as he glared at Lessia.

"Not as much as you are," she said, looking more amused than anything. "Besides, I'll call a favor in if I have to."

"How the hell do you have any favors left?" Grimm wanted to know. "I would have thought asking Matteo to take that shot would wipe everything clean."

"It did." She shrugged as if it didn't matter. "But I also facilitated G and Ava. And Zeke," she added.

"And that's enough to re-balance the scales?" he asked skeptically.

Lessia raised a perfectly manicured brow. "And reconciled G with her sister. I figure that tips it over the edge."

"Hey, now," I heard myself protest, amazed to hear the slightly teasing tone in my voice. "If anyone should get something for that one, it should be me. Plus, you've had me on call for the others as well. Kassie, Royce, and Boone. Does that mean you owe me?"

Grimm chuckled, but Lessia's expression didn't change. "No, that's why I got you him," she pointed at Xander. "And all of you"—she directed her finger to Vik and me before I could comment—"are why each and every one of you is staying put," she said to the men, who didn't look happy but nodded at her glare.

"So, what's the plan?" Junie asked, spinning around in her office chair.

"Jolene, Josie, and I get to planning, and you start adding whatever Irina knows about our mystery man to our list," Lessia said matter-of-factly, not waiting for Matteo to chime in.

Xander cleared his throat, his expression carefully neutral. "Actually, I might be useful in the planning. After all, I've had years to observe her habits and routine." He and Vik exchanged glances again, and for the first time, it really dawned on me that Xander, having been left behind after Vik left, had likely filled his void in the organization. Vik's main job before leaving Russia had been to guard Demi. Demi had told me Vik's family had been protecting his since his grandfather was a young man.

"I also have the codes needed to access most of their secure communications and bank accounts. I figure the communications might help track down other parts of the trafficking ring, and well, if the money dries up, it will cripple the organization. At least for a while."

Junie bounced in her chair, pulling herself over to the computer and reaching with the other hand to grab a mostly empty bag of chips. "At least now we have some cover in killing this one. I know she was off-limits for a long time, but with her trying to gain access to this list, everyone will now think the US government did it to prevent her from getting the information. They won't even look at anyone else," she said, happily typing on her keyboard, while Josie handed Xander a pad of paper on which he scribbled down line after line of meaningless numbers, letters, and symbols. When he was done, he put the papers next to Junie.

"These are her preferred passwords. She re-uses the same ones for different accounts, thinking because they're so complicated, and she moves them around so much, they won't be discovered. But because they're so hard to re-member, she keeps coming back to the same patterns. These are the passwords I know she's used in the last year. And as her father's daughter, she's listed on the majority of the main accounts for the Bratva, even if they aren't tied to trafficking. Some are legit—the companies they show to the public—but most are fronts for their drug running or other illegal activities."

Juniper practically squealed. "I love taking money from the bad guys. I always feel like Santa, giving it away to various charities and organizations once we scrub it clean."

"What about Hardy?" I asked, getting back to the issue closer to home. "And my government contracts? Am I going to lose them because of him?" I knew it wouldn't be fair, but in my experience, the government didn't care about fair. They cared about expedient and simple, and it would be far simpler to shut me down and move onto another psychologist than it would be to ensure Hardy hadn't passed my information to anyone else and compromised my practice.

"Don't worry about it." The words came from a blacked-out screen in the corner. One I hadn't realized was in use. It was computer modified, but I knew the person must've been Harrison. "I'll take care of it."

"Thank you, sir," I whispered.

"Come on," Vik wrapped an arm around my shoulders. "Xander will be a while. Let me take you out to eat."

I wanted to stay, but despite Vik's quiet words, I knew it wasn't a suggestion. He turned me around, gently leading me from the room. When I looked back, I saw Xander, staring at me from where he stood beside Junie, Matteo, and Grimm. Lessia, Josie, and Jolene were a few computer terminals down, their heads together as they looked at a computer screen.

Xander's eyes didn't leave mine. I could feel them on me even after I turned back to walk with Vik out the door.

Vik was still in ultra-protective mode an hour later, barely doing more than grunt at the wait staff and glaring as he called out our server for being "overly friendly" to me. He scared the man so badly we never saw him again. His female replacement certainly wasn't fearful of Vik's poor manners or attitude, and I had to resist rolling my eyes at her very obvious attempts at flirting.

I wasn't sure why she bothered. Objectively, I knew Vik, while grumpy and rough around the edges, was handsome in a dangerous kind of way. But his entire vibe was pissed-at-the-world and don't-give-a-damn-about-you, the rules, or anyone else.

Despite his attitude, or maybe because of it, I couldn't help poking a little on a subject that had been bothering me. "Vik," I asked hesitantly. Because, as much as I wanted to know, I knew he'd be able to sense the hurt behind my words, no matter how hard I tried to hide it from him.

He grunted, not looking up from his plate, eating as if he hadn't eaten in days.

"Why didn't you tell me about your brother? I mean, before ..." I trailed off. Yes, I was hurt he hadn't told me. But I was also off-balance by my earlier realization that Xander must have been the one to fill Vik's previous role to some degree. Did that mean he'd also stepped in as Demi's main guard? Were the two of them supposed to get out together? If so, what had happened that caused Demi's death and Xander's escape? I'd deliberately kept Demi's name out of my talks with Xander as much as possible. But had Xander known whom I was talking about this entire time?

Vik paused for a second, his fork hovering in the air over the table before he stuffed the huge helping of pasta in his mouth. "I'm sure I've spoken about him before," Vik finally replied after swallowing.

"No, you haven't."

Vik's eyes darted around the room before he gave me a fake smile. "I'm sure I have. You just might have forgotten. We can talk more about this later. At home," he said pointedly, but I couldn't quite drop it yet.

"Did Xander know him?" My miserable, pathetic, question came out of my mouth before I could regulate it.

Vik set down his fork slowly, solely focusing on me. "That's not a fair question to ask. Nor is it one you should torment yourself with, little sister. The past is the past and cannot be changed. The dead cannot be resurrected, nor anything positive come out of dredging up history. Let it go." With the finality of a man who laid down the law, he picked his fork up and dug in as if the entire brief conversation hadn't happened.

"You going to eat that?" he asked me around another mouth full of food, pointing at my grilled salmon.

I knew he was right. Nothing good could come with my line of thinking, but I couldn't let it go. I knew, as a therapist, that my obsessing over Demi hadn't been healthy. And my developing feelings for Xander was likely causing guilt to kick in—yet another reason I was trying to backtrack and lose the ground I'd gained in moving on. But despite the professional voice in my head trying to reason with me, I knew I wouldn't be able to let it go that easily.

Chapter 23

XANDER

It was late into the night before I'd finished up being grilled by Lessia, Juniper, and Matteo about everything from my mother's known favorite locales to her choice of seating, food, and even men. I wasn't exactly sure what Lessia was planning, but it was clear she dived deep when it came to researching her targets.

I knew I should feel something at the thought of knowing my mother's days were numbered and that I would help facilitate her demise, but I only felt a profound pang of loss. Not for her, but for what she should have represented. Mothers were supposed to love and support their children unconditionally, shielding them from the evils of the world. Instead, my mother was the predator in the dark. By her order, families were broken forever, children's innocence were lost, and women's cries were as familiar to me as a lullaby.

I had no illusions, even as a child, that if I didn't meet my mother's expectations, she'd not hesitate to sell me into the world she controlled. Killing me would have been a kindness, and she didn't have an ounce of that in her. Besides, as she'd boasted about more than once, there was no use in throwing away money. It wasn't until I was older—and became dangerous—that I'd known if I'd taken a wrong step she'd order my death. By then, leaving me alive would have been a risk she'd known better than to take.

I pulled my thoughts back to the present. Even though I was heartsick, the only point of warmth was the MC members who were becoming my new family. Vik had stayed with Andrie, knowing I wouldn't settle without him looking out for her. But the rest of them had made a point to come to the clubhouse, each offering some lame excuse but clearly making sure I didn't need anything and had their support if I did. Charge had come after closing down the gym he managed, his sister Bailey in tow, claimed he needed something from his room, but I noticed he never left the main room. Wyck, Shade, and Whisp sat a few tables down, pretending to enjoy a beer, but they spent more time shooting me sympathetic looks when they thought no one was looking. Jasper called from the hospital, asking me to let him know if Andrie needed any more follow up from her wound—something we'd already talked about.

Savage, who'd come in with Chinese takeout at some point for everyone, had driven me home, since Vik had taken his truck when he'd left with Andrie hours ago. As we drove, he kept shooting me looks.

"Just spit it out," I growled, tired beyond measure and out of patience.

"Fucking shit, man." He drummed his fingers on the steering wheel. "That's all."

I felt the corner of my mouth lift, a small thread of humor breaking through. *Fucking shit* was right. Providing intel that would lead to my mother's demise was shit. The fact she was the kind of person who was coded for death was shit, and that she had not only betrayed me once—at Andrie's expense—but was doing so again, even if she was unaware of it, was fucking shit.

"Yeah." I kicked my legs out as far as the seat would allow, trying to relax my tight muscles.

"You gonna be okay?"

I was grateful he didn't ask if I *was* okay. "As long as I have her, I will be," I admitted before I could snap my mouth shut.

Thankfully, Savage didn't tease me, likely realizing I wasn't kidding. "Yeah. I get that."

I raised an eyebrow. "You got a girl?"

Snorting, he shook his head. "I don't get you that much, dude. But I see that kind of thing between Lessia and her man and Matteo and G."

"I still have a ways to go before Andrie catches up."

Shrugging, he turned at a light, looking unconcerned. "She's getting there. It's just a matter of time before you two are on the same page. Likely faster than either of you realize."

"Can I ask you something?" I asked before I could change my mind.

The silent look of expectation told me I could ask, but he might not answer. "The MC. And ... the other stuff. How does it all work? I mean, most operatives have strict lines of who they can and can't eliminate. Yet y'all have been right there with us, busting knees and gutting pedophiles."

The cold, assessing gaze Savage gifted me showed me, for the first time, the assassin beneath the practical joker biker façade. I returned his stare, letting him see my curiosity wasn't nefarious, but it wasn't idle either. If I was going to be a true brother to the club, I needed to know more about how everything fit together.

"When the whole club was here, it was easier," he said slowly after a minute of contemplation. "We participated to maintain our cover, of course, but rarely, if ever, did we ever have to carry out a hit on anyone who wasn't coded ahead of time. After all, it's not like we're roughing up choir boys, and hell, we're all in this life because we know some people aren't worth the air they breathe, and we don't have a problem setting things to rights. But now, let's just say we needed to prevent a power suck. And we *did* get the green light, even if it was in an atypical way. You were on the conference call when Grimm got the directive to keep the streets in line. Our pipeline, bringing in those who need to come into the country under the radar, requires us to keep control of this territory. Even then, most of the men we've been ... interviewing ... were already on a list Grimm keeps with their exploits. Whether it makes sense or not in person, Grimm is well aware of who the truly dangerous child predators are and what men are the worst of the worst when it comes to raping and torturing women. And none of us mind slipping our leash. But we don't cut down everyone who runs across our path, nor do we allow ourselves or another in our *club* to kill as a personal vendetta. At least, not in the open."

"Is that why Lessia vetoed Vik and I?" I asked, my thoughts turning back to Irina.

Savage smirked, but it was without humor. "Partly. But it was also to stop you two from going head-to-head with Matteo over it. Neither of you is trained, though Vik has picked up enough to think he could do it. But Matteo wouldn't allow anyone less than a well-trained operative to take any mission. Especially one this high profile. And Lessia's primary focus is to keep you two on good terms with the club. With you being new and all, I think she's worried you're going to push the wrong button at the wrong time. If she took the mission, she knows you'll leave her to it, even if you're unhappy about it. If any of the rest were assigned this one, you and Vik might go rogue. With her on it, you'll back down. You both owe her too much."

I grunted, hating that he might be right. Or rather, that Lessia had us pegged. But Savage didn't know it wasn't only Lessia who would have stopped Vik and me; it was Andrie. As much as every fiber in my being wished I could avenge her that way, I knew she wouldn't want me to. Andrie would rather Vik and I stay here, safe, than risk ourselves after everything we'd sacrificed these last ten years.

I was surprised to see Andrie's lights on when Savage pulled to a stop. Before I could get out of the car, she'd yanked her front door open and practically ran down the steps. Vik stood on the porch behind her, arms crossed and jaw tight. Not a good sign. I just wasn't sure who he was mad at.

Andrie jerked to a stop in front of me, not so much as glancing at Savage's retreating car. "We need to talk."

Chapter 24

XANDER

There were few sentences that were as ominous as a woman saying "We need to talk," but damned if I'd let Andrie see me flinch. I opened my mouth to suggest we go inside first, but Vik cut me off, barking out, "Andrie. I said drop it."

His harsh tone set my back up, especially when I saw Andrie's shoulders fall even as her chin jutted out rebelliously. He must have seen it, too, because he added more gently, "Please. For me."

With a heavy sigh, she turned to walk back up her steps, stopping long enough to exchange stares with Vik before walking inside without a word and closing the door firmly behind her.

"What the hell was that?" I asked, more than a little bewildered.

Vik shook his head, practically stomping over to his own place. I cast a look at Andrie's just as she cut off the lights, clearly shutting us both out. I wondered what had the two of them at odds, but I didn't have to think hard.

Vik had already pulled out a bottle of vodka by the time I caught up with him in the kitchen. He'd poured two fingers into a glass but was studying it as if the glass held all the answers to the universe.

"You going to drink that or stare at it?" I asked in Russian. Glass shattered as he threw it against the wall. "I guess that's a third option," I said, keeping my voice mild. I grabbed the bottle to take a drink before he tossed that, too. It had been a long-ass day, and it didn't look like it was going to end anytime soon.

"She's made the connection," Vik muttered.

"She knows ..." I trailed off, but Vik shook his head before I could finish that thought.

"She realizes now you must've known Demi. She knew, on some level, that you must have been involved in the same organization, being from my family and all. But it dawned on her that if I left to track her down, my *brother* must have taken my place."

"And your place was always with him," I murmured, dread making the alcohol sit like lead in my gut.

"She's going to want you to talk about him." Vik ran a hand through his hair. "She hasn't asked about him in so long. She stopped looking for pictures and even refrained from asking Lessia direct questions when she met with her after your paths crossed. She told me it was too painful to see how much life was wearing on him, see how much time had passed. Still, she was always so damn optimistic that he'd get out alive."

Swallowing hard, I shook my head. "She had to have known that was never going to happen. She's smarter than that." *But then, Alex had always been an optimist ... and a romantic.*

Vik just grunted, turning to rifle through one of the drawers to pull out a towel.

My feet might as well have been encased in concrete as I watch him clean up the mess, thinking about his words.

"I can't lie to her," I finally said quietly. "I know I'm supposed to—that I agreed, but—"

The growl that came from Vik was animalistic and yet insulted at the same time. "Of course, you can't fucking lie to her."

"I agreed," I repeated, but there was no force in it. I meant what I'd said about lying to Andrie.

"What are they going to do? Throw your ass back to Russia?" He snorted, tossing the broken glass, towel and all, into the trash. "Still, it would be better if she doesn't ask. Do you think she's just going to accept your words with a smile, and you both live happily ever after? We'll be lucky if she doesn't turn her wrath on the entire organization when she finds out. The best case is we let things die down first—make sure Hardy's in a cage and the bitch dead and buried. At least, that way, she can process her mad without the rest of us crammed down her throat."

I raised an eyebrow. "Process her mad? You two really do spend too much time together. Soon, you're going to have to hang up your own shingle. After all, what's a bartender but a poor man's shrink?"

He raised his middle finger, but I saw his face relax slightly at seeing my amusement.

"Seriously, though, how long do you think it'll take Lessia to wrap this whole thing up? And Hardy?" I added, not about to discount the man who'd created the whole mess and had a reason to want to harm Andrie if he found out what happened to his fake Steve.

Vik shrugged. "Hardy? With the connections in DC that Thoth has, it's likely they're knocking down his door as we speak. Irina will be a while longer, but it'll likely be weeks rather than months. Lessia and company will want to use this incident as the reason Irina was eliminated. If they wait too long, the connection won't be as clear. But Lessia is methodical in her kills, even if they are bloody."

I tried to reconcile a calculated killer with the temper-prone woman I thought I knew, but I had a hard time until I remembered the dead look in her eyes when she'd told Vik and I she would take the assignment. "Well, here's to her getting in and out without fanfare before having Irina begging for it to end long before she goes," I toasted with the bottle, taking a long pull.

"It doesn't matter how long she suffers. It'll never be long enough." Vik grabbed the bottle from my grasp and downed a good bit, his eyes haunted.

"Who's on Andrie tonight?" I asked, a weird combination of bone-tired and wired. I knew no one was going to leave her unguarded until we knew she was safe.

"Shade and Charge. I've got to get to the bar, but our shifts start at three, so you should get some sleep."

"And you?"

"I'll sleep this afternoon while you're playing boyfriend. I only need a few hours."

I followed him out when he left, trying to see if I could spot the two men guarding Andrie, but I couldn't see them. Still, I could feel their eyes, and I knew she was in good hands, so I took my time showering, needing to wash away the filth. But no matter how hot the water was, I felt dirtier and dirtier as the memories I tried to repress hit me in waves. The crack in the wall I'd allowed to give Lessia the information grew wider, as if water was coming through a tiny hole in a dam.

Shutting my eyes, I tried to brace against the onslaught, but I knew it was too little, too late ...

Screams, almost inhuman, echoed down the hallway as I followed my mother down the brightly light corridor. All the books I'd read said that dungeons and bad people liked the dark, but I'd never believed it. My mother preferred white and light to dark. She said the dark was easier to hide dirt, and in her line of business, she believed in cleanliness and transparency.

I never understood what she meant, but I knew better than to ask. Children were to be seen but not heard. I'd forgotten once and couldn't walk for a week. Without Viktor bringing food and water to my room, I might've starved. Still, the sight of the girl—the housekeeper's daughter that I'd played with the week before—naked, broken and battered, crying for me to help her, while the man—

I cut off my thoughts, biting the inside of my cheek. Mother had said if I made a mistake like that again, she'd sell me with the next shipment, and I believed her. She had little patience for what she called softness in me. I'd tried to ask my father to get him to help, but he'd only shaken his head and told me to mind my mother.

"Hurry up," she snapped. Realizing I'd slowed, I jogged a few steps to catch up. She liked me exactly two steps behind her and one step to the side. Her shadow, she said in a sickly-sweet tone to the buyers who came to inspect what she called merchandise. It didn't matter what she said; I still saw them as people.

"Sorry," I said softly, trying not to wince as the crack of a whip hitting flesh could be heard as we walked past one of the rooms. I knew better than to look. The coppery smell of blood told me all I needed to know. Seeing it wouldn't help the person in there or me.

"You turn ten today."

The comment almost had me tripping, but I caught myself in time.

"Yes, Mother." I wasn't sure if it was a question or not, but not answering a question when there were so many tools at her disposal wasn't a smart move. Viktor and I already knew we needed to be smart if we were going to run away. We had to watch and wait and grow strong so one day, we could run so far she nor our families would ever find us.

"And you finally seem to be absorbing your lessons." Again, not a question. "Your father said you did well when you went with him on his business trip to France."

At least my father only made me stay long enough to introduce me to his business partners before telling me to go play in one of the other rooms of our hotel suite. He thought it was cute to show me off, telling them he was already training the "next generation," much the way mother did. I knew better than to tell either of them what I wanted to do when I grew up. They wouldn't like the answer.

Compared to my mother, my father was easy. Be polite to his guests, and stay out of his way. I didn't understand what his business was, but he traveled a lot. I tried to learn all I could about different countries so Viktor and I knew where we'd go after we ran.

"Then I guess it's time to intensify your training. After all, I can't expect you to be of any use to me if you can't instill the same fear in others that I do." She whirled around and leaned down until we were eye to eye. "But never forget, I will always be the one you're afraid of most."

She glared at me another minute, studying me up and down as if I'd grown overnight. I wished I had. I wished I'd grown as large as a man. If I were bigger than her, I wouldn't have to listen to her anymore. I wouldn't have to be afraid of her.

"Come." She was off again, going left when we came to a branch in the hallway. "Your father's picking you up after. He insisted on taking you out for your birthday, so we don't have as much time as I'd like. We'd better get started."

I shuddered at the memory, one hand going out to the cold tile to steady myself. I hadn't made it to the birthday dinner. In a rare act of mercy, he'd taken one look at me when I'd gotten in his car and had his driver take us straight to his residence. I'd barely made it inside before throwing up until I was sure every bit of food I'd had in my body was in that toilet bowl.

He'd never come up to check on me. Instead, he had a maid bring up some soup and crackers a few hours later.

The next day, he'd acted as if nothing had happened and told my mother he'd had to take a last-minute conference call, thus canceling our reservations.

The hand on the tile fisted when the next memory hit me—one I tried to keep back the most.

"Alex, solnyshkuh," *I called as I opened the door to the apartment. I stopped before I'd even walked a full step inside. Hair on the back of my neck rose, and I reached for one of several guns I was never without. It was too dark, too quiet. All the lights were off; the curtains of every room pulled. Alex always had the windows open, allowing her to hear the street below and the birds singing, even when it was cold.*

I went room by room, clearing every crevice, looking under every bed and behind the furniture, but she was nowhere to be found. And the apartment, it didn't look right. It was a mess, but it wasn't until I turned the lights on I realized what was wrong. It wasn't an Alex-nado mess; the entire apartment had been tossed.

Numb, my feet slowly brought me back to our bedroom, where we'd made love just hours before. The sheets were shredded, pillows nothing but fluff. It was completely void of Alex. Not just her, but the picture of us that she kept on the nightstand was missing. Her clothes, usually scattered everywhere, were gone.

Another glance in the bathroom and closet revealed even her damn toothbrush was missing. Apart from the mess, there wasn't a sign anyone had been here and not a single thing of Alex's remained.

I was still standing there, minutes or hours later, when Viktor let himself into the apartment, his face carved from the same stone as mine.

"Please," I begged for what was probably the first time in my life. "Tell me she finally realized she was better off without me. That she left on her own accord and got on a plane to go back to America."

The slow shake of Viktor's head tore my already dying heart in two. The pain was so visceral, I held a hand to my chest as my legs gave out. Viktor tried to catch me, but he only succeeded in toppling to the floor with me.

"I-I've got to find her. We know the—" I swallowed. "Shipping routes. If we can track down where she was sent, I can meet it before—"

Viktor's hand came to rest hard on my shoulder, squeezing until I stopped and met his gaze. "She's having you watched, Demi. One wrong step, if she even thinks you're half as hung up on this girl as she thinks you are, she'll order her killed out of spite right now. And you know she'll see your emotion as weakness."

Before he could continue, my phone chimed. My presence was required immediately.

"Steel yourself," Viktor coached, helping me up from the floor.

I paused long enough to take a few deep breaths, hoping the pain of Alex missing—of knowing exactly what she might be going through at this moment—wasn't written all over my face. I felt as if I'd swallowed glass. Internally, I was bleeding out via a thousand small cuts.

A car pulled up in front as we exited, and the driver opened the door for me. Vik shot me one last look of warning before heading to the security car behind mine.

"Mother," I said, keeping my voice monotone. There was a small cut on the side of her face, near her temple, that hadn't been there that morning. I allowed a flash of satisfaction. My Alex hadn't gone down without a fight.

"We're having an issue with the East China Sea route. It's the second time we've had difficulties with the port inspector. I'm sending you to straighten him out or eliminate him and school the replacement on expectations when it comes to working with us."

She paused, looking up at me for the first time since I'd stepped up to the car. "I'm assuming now that I have your full attention again, I won't have any more problems when it comes to your priorities and focus," she asked, her words impassive yet full of venom.

I shrugged, every bit of willpower I possessed keeping my body language casual and unaffected. "You made your point, mother. But I have to say, I'm surprised at your ... overreaction to a passing fancy." I let amusement enter my tone at her flash of temper. "What? You thought I was stuck on some American fluff?" I snorted, adding fuel to the flames. But getting a rise out of her would be the only way I could ensure Alex wouldn't take up another thought in my mother's brain. I'd do what was needed. "She was a nice diversion, though. I'll give you that."

Irina sneered. "Just keep your attention on the ones at your disposal from here on out."

I actually chuckled. "Some of us prefer our bedmates enthusiasm to come from a place other than fear of failure. But since you seem a bit ... sensitive ... to having another woman in my life, I'll keep my sex life more discreet."

She was so upset at my calling her jealous she seemed beyond words. Never before had I taunted her, too worried about toeing the line. But losing Alex meant Irina lost her biggest bargaining chip in keeping me in line. She'd played this hand wrong in her quest to keep me under control. Her second mistake was sending Viktor along with me. She might have plenty of her men accompanying us, but they couldn't keep an eye on both of us. A few days of slipping in and out of our group had them complacent of Viktor's whereabouts, and I was able to slip him on board a freight car heading for Poland.

We'd been preparing for our escape for almost our entire lives and kept several sets of documents and money ready, hidden in bags and storage lockers in various countries.

It was a risk sending Viktor so closely to Alex's kidnapping, but I couldn't bear having her in that world one more second than it would take for him to track her. Viktor and I had carefully begun placing distance between us in public for years. He was my security but didn't have much of an actual role within the organization, so his absence wasn't quickly noticed. I told the group with me at the port that I'd sent him back to oversee security in my new condo.

The condo wasn't fabricated. I knew I couldn't stay in that apartment ... our apartment ... with the memories of Alex in every room, knowing the horror of what she was going through. I'd tried to stay away from her, fearing what *would happen to her when it all came crashing down. But no matter how hard I fought, Alex not only reeled me in but seemed to completely disregard my attempts at explaining the danger around me. It was because of me that life had shattered the sunny, innocent girl I'd loved with every fiber of my being, creating a woman so much stronger yet a shadow of the woman she should have become.*

Chapter 25

ANDRIE

A warm body woke me.

"Wha—" I murmured, mostly asleep and too tired and relaxed to open my eyes. I recognized that masculine smell anywhere and just wanted to burrow in it.

"Shh," he said quietly, gathering him to me, his arms a tight band around me, barely a shade past comfortable. "Go back to sleep. I just need to hold you, all right?"

In a blink, I was fully awake. When had Xander's smell overwritten my memories of Demi's scent? Before I could focus on that thought, I realized Xander was shaking.

"What's wrong?" I asked, fighting to turn in his arms so I could look at him. He loosened his grip on me long enough for me to roll into him before wrapping me up even tighter than before.

"Nothing." He tucked my head under his chin. "I just had a really bad day and needed to feel you. To remember you're real, and I'm here, not there. If I never have to talk about that hellhole again, it will be too soon."

I bit my lip to stop myself from asking him to do that very thing. Maybe Vik was right—nothing good could come from knowing Demi's last days, weeks, or years. His thoughts or feelings wouldn't change what I'd felt for him, and whether he'd loved me still or had completely forgotten about me, it didn't change the fact that I was allowed to move on. He was dead, and nothing could change that.

Kissing Xander's chest, I extricated my arms so I could wrap them around him as best I could, stroking his back. Demi might have been my past, but Xander was here now. And the feelings I had for him were growing in a way I never thought I'd experience again. It was a slower progression this time, unlike the overnight explosion I'd had with Demi, but for the first time, I knew that if I gave my heart a chance, we'd get there. And I wasn't sure if that delighted me or terrified me to the core.

"Vik took me shopping this afternoon," I said, trying to redirect his thoughts to the here and now. "I was hoping we'd spend some time tomorrow decorating if you don't have plans. Maybe get some practice painting since you promised our help to Boone and Kassie this weekend."

I froze, realizing I'd stepped in it. It had been clear to me since their first meeting that Xander somehow knew Kassie, though she didn't have the same reaction to seeing him.

But instead of tensing at the mention of her, he relaxed a fraction, his body molding around mine before he kissed the top of my head. "Kassie was someone I tried to look out for from afar. It's just nice to see her here and happy," he explained.

Humming, I settled into the mattress, relieved I hadn't hit a nerve tonight of all nights. I'd never been jealous about his feelings, even the first time at the ice cream shop. I hadn't sensed a hint of attraction between him and Kassie—unusual, considering Kassie was a former model. Still, it was a puzzle I'd wondered about. Boone must have wondered as well, considering he'd asked me about Xander in one of our last sessions. I'd relayed the same story that I'd given them at Sweet Nothings, but he wasn't satisfied. I hoped the invitation to his house meant he'd laid his questions to rest.

"I suppose I could spend the day as your laborer." For the first time, I could hear a hint of a smile. "But I'm not cheap."

"As long as I get what I pay for," I teased, pinching his bicep. I kissed the hollow of his throat when he grunted. I could taste the salt on his skin and smell the scent that was all Xander. Unable to resist, I kissed him again, lingering this time.

"I guess I should ask for partial payment up front," he mused. "Isn't that a normal thing here?" The rumble of his voice tickled my lips, and a grin slipped out. I trailed kisses down his neck, taking my time and thoroughly enjoying turning the tables on him. Xander wasn't a passive man and certainly wasn't one to lay back and take it, but I was determined to get my way this time.

But before I could get much farther than his collarbone, he moved, rolling until I was on top of him, straddling his growing erection. Then he stood, holding me as if I weighed nothing.

"Xander," I screeched, dizzy at the sudden spinning.

"Need to wash the day off," he muttered, hiking me up higher on his waist before walking to my bathroom. "I still feel ... grimy."

I didn't comment on his already wet-hair and damp skin. God knew I'd spent more than a few nights showering until my hot water ran out.

Unable to help myself, I tensed when he looked in the direction of my bathtub, but thankfully, he turned on the shower instead.

Reminding myself to take care of him, I batted his hand away when he reached for the body soap.

"You hold me, and I'll take care of you." My words were so reminiscent of what I'd whisper to Demi as we bathed, but I pushed the memories back. I squirted some soap into my hand, then got to work on his scalp. He didn't have a hint of stubble on his head, but I relished the opportunity to rub my hands over the smooth expanse of skin.

He groaned, eyes almost rolling back in his head as I started the message. I'd done this before, a lifetime ago, but the slow, rhythmic movements came back to me as if the years hadn't passed.

I took my time, not about to be rushed, exploring every inch of his neck, shoulders, and arms. "Tell me about these tattoos." I tapped his arm, my curiosity overrunning my mouth. Every other piece of ink was meaningless swirls, but the snake on his forearm and the joker on his bicep were clear.

He shrugged. "The artist picked them out. Besides, I think they fit the 'biker persona,' don't you think?"

"You let the artist pick out something that would stay on your skin for the rest of your life?" I snorted before I could stop myself. I sounded a bit judgmental, even though I didn't mean to. I couldn't help rubbing my ring finger, where a hidden piece of ink I'd let Demi choose for me was unknown to anyone else in the world.

As if he'd read my mind, Xander raised my left hand to his lips, kissing my knuckles. "I don't know." Humor lightened his dark blue eyes. "Sometimes letting someone else take control is the best solution."

Taking that as a challenge, I wiggled until he let go of my legs, barely getting my balance before I pushed him under the spray, laughing as he sputtered. Instead of letting him step forward again, I kept the pressure on his chest and crowded into him. Another step had him pinned against the cold tile wall, the hot water running down my back.

His hands went to my body, but before they could wander, I took his wrists and drew them away from me, pinning them against the wall. "Uh-uh. My turn."

"Yes, ma'am." His smirk egged me on when my bravado would have failed me. Blindly grabbing for the bottle of body soap behind me, I dumped a healthy amount into my palms before going to work on his chest, teasing his nipples and tracing the lines of his abs until he shuddered.

The mood between us turned serious, despite the erection inches from my face when I kneeled down to wash his legs. Kneeling, my head tilted all the way back so I could see him looking down at me. It shouldn't have made me feel so ... empowered, but watching this man, his chest heaving, eyes blazing, staying so still because *I'd* told him to, made me feel like a goddess.

"Are you done?" His voice was a growl.

Reaching for the one part of him that I'd been ignoring, my lips curling in a smile when his growl turned into a groan. "Not even close."

Chapter 26

ANDRIE

I *was dreaming. I knew I was dreaming, but no matter how hard I tried, I couldn't get myself to wake up or stop and change the outcome of what was about to happen.*

I'd been soaking in the bath, knowing I had a few hours before Demi would be home. I loved our shared baths. Bathing in the tiny tub with my man varied from heart-wrenching to playful but never restful, and sometimes, a girl just needed an hour or so for some self-care. Earbuds in, music playing loud, my eyes closed against the cucumber eye mask as I laid against the towel I'd placed on the lip of the tub as a cushion, I sang along—badly, but I didn't care. These last few days—last few weeks, if I were being honest—had been magical and as close to perfect as finding the love of your life could get.

Even as I screamed at myself to open my eyes, the me in the dream never noticed the woman who slipped into the room, a large man skulking behind her. Not, at least, until the woman grabbed my wrist in a bruising grasp.

Startled, I dragged the mask away, gasping when I saw the cold, dead eyes drilling into me. Despite never having met this woman, I knew instantly who she was based on those blue irises, so pale they almost looked white. They were so similar to her son's. But Demi's were more and more often filled with love and softness. Irina Petrov was a doll in looks and soul. Despite her age, her skin was flawless, her hair shiny and perfect. But there was nothing behind those eyes.

"You are the reason my son has been shirking his responsibilities? You?" Irina sneered, not waiting for me to get over my shock. "I will never understand the impulses of men," she muttered, still speaking in Russian. "Fortunately, the fix is easy. Get up." She said the last part in English.

Demi had warned me and tried to explain just how badly this could go, but I hadn't listened—hadn't wanted to believe the woman who'd birthed the man I loved could be so monstrous as the one he described. But I believed it now.

Knowing without a doubt I couldn't let myself get taken, I didn't hesitate. I grabbed the glass of wine I'd been sipping with my free hand and hit her on the side of the head. Then I pulled her hair, yanking her down, trying to pull her into the tub with me.

She screamed, letting me go to keep her balance. Instead of reaching for her head, she reached for my throat. Instinctively I tried to claw her fingers away as my eyes bulged. Instead, I fell back into the water. Taking advantage of the momentum, she pushed my head into the bottom of the tub.

The world started to spin, darkening even as I struggled. I broke the surface once, twice, barely getting a small breath of air before I was pushed below once again. The slippery surface, the water, and Irina were too much to overcome. My body heaved once more before everything went black.

I came to slowly, realizing my hands and feet were bound, and I was slung over a man's shoulder.

"Put her in the trunk for now, then clear out that hovel. I don't want a single trace of her remaining by the time he comes back. I'll get the men at the transport to carry her in."

The man bounced me a bit as he walked down a set of stairs that I knew led to the street. Woozy, I registered the scratchy feeling of his coat against my shivering skin, and I realized I was still naked.

"You're not going to keep her? I thought you'd want to make an example—"

Irina cut him off, snapping. "This lesson isn't for her; it's for my son. As satisfying as it would be to break her into something unrecognizable, keeping her here will just lead to temptation, and his father won't be happy if something happens to him as a result of poor judgment. With the deal we're negotiating at the moment for the next shipment of American weapons, I can't afford to have him be put out with us. Besides, I've already got a buyer for this one, and he wants her ... unhandled. He's purchased quite a few to bring out to the American west. If some bikers can't tame her, they'll kill her instead. Either way, she'll no longer be my problem."

I tried to scream ... to fight ... but I knew, just like the thousands of times I'd had this dream, the worst was yet to come ...

I bolted upright so fast I almost head-butted Xander. "Easy, *solnyshkuh*. It's just me. You're safe."

On a half-sob, half-shudder, I tore at the covers, the overwhelming need to run coursing through me. Xander had other ideas, wrapping me in his arms the second I was free of the sheets and pulling me onto his lap as if I were an infant. His arms were a band of iron as I struggled to pull myself completely back to present day.

"Shh," he murmured, rocking while speaking in quiet tones, reassuring me I was safe, that he was there, and he wouldn't let anything happen to me again. At some point, I stopped fighting to get away from him and instead fought to get closer, trying to sink into him, get impossibly closer then we already were.

It wasn't until I opened my eyes that I realized he was crying, his body trembling almost as much as mine. Sweat was beaded on his brow and chest, though his skin felt cold, as if he, too, had been pulled from a nightmare.

"Hey," I said when I was able to pull myself together. "You alright? You look about as bad as I feel," I joked weakly.

He looked gutted, as if his internal light had been snuffed out. Blood running cold, I cupped his head in my hands, forcing his face closer to mine so he couldn't miss my words. "Xander, it was just a nightmare. I have them from time to time, both from what I lived through and from what my patients tell me in their sessions. It's no big—" I cut myself off, not about to lie to him.

"It's my fault," he finally said, his voice hollow.

Rolling my eyes, I retorted. "Saying Irina Petrov's name isn't like conjuring up the devil—even if she is one of his disciples. And," my voice rose over his as he tried to speak, "even if you were my Demi himself, I'd tell you the only person responsible for what happened to me was Irina, and she's about to get what's coming to her for a lot more reasons than just me. Besides, the price I paid for a love like that was well worth the nightmares."

Well, at least he was getting his emotions back, I thought as I found myself on the receiving end of an incredulous—and rage-filled—glare.

"Don't *ever* tell me that being abducted, trafficked, and sold to the skin trade is worth the price of loving—" He broke off, cursing, rocking back against the headboard. The complete one-eighty in his emotions gave me whiplash, and I struggled to keep up.

"You don't get to dictate my thoughts on the matter." My spine stiffened so fast my back cracked. How dare he.

He must have realized he pushed me too far because he stopped mid-rant, taking in several deep breaths.

"I'm sorry. No matter what my thoughts on the matter, I shouldn't yell at you. Especially when I know I'd make the same call." Well, that stopped me in my tracks.

"I don't want to fight. Not now. Come on, baby. Let's run your hot water tank dry one more time tonight."

Chapter 27

XANDER

M y phone woke us the next morning. I was up instantly, despite our rough night and the fact I'd finally fallen back asleep barely an hour ago. "Yeah?"

"Hardy is missing. Military police searched his residence, office, and even friends and family's homes. It's as if he simply walked away. Even his phone and wallet were at his house, and his car is in his garage. You're under orders to bring her to the A.T. building, and then Lessia will escort you both to another location for an update this afternoon. You'll have a shadow until you get to the office today—don't shake him. He's a friendly."

"Understood," I told Grimm as Andrie stirred next to me, her nose wrinkling adorably as if rejecting the very idea of waking. She hadn't gotten any more sleep than I had, and I imagined, if left unbothered, she quite possibly would've slept for several more hours.

Hating that I had to ruin what little peace she'd been able to find, I trailed a hand too calloused to have a right to touch her soft skin down her arm. "Are you awake yet or still working on it?" I asked quietly.

"Working on it," she replied, her eyes still closed, voice rough with the dredges of sleep.

I chuckled huskily, kissing the top of her head before getting up. "I'll get the coffee started while you 'work on it'."

It didn't take long for me to get the coffee brewing. I doctored a mug with a spoonful of brown sugar I knew Alex—Andrie—liked before pouring a mug of straight-up black for myself. Knowing we'd both need it, I put the rest in a travel mug for myself and put another pot on so I could make Andrie a fresh one before we left.

Soft singing mixed with the running water from the shower, and she greeted me with a grateful smile when I stepped in behind her. Despite, or perhaps because of, our hellish night, we seemed closer than before. Even though we didn't talk specifics, just knowing the other was there was enough.

I knew Andrie was curious—her natural nosiness as a young woman certainly couldn't have changed that much, even if she hid it under the guise of professional interest—but she knew if she were to ask about my past, she'd have to reciprocate with her own nightmare reveal.

For now, at least, I was in the clear.

We took our time getting ready, Andrie humming appreciatively as she took a sip from her mug while applying her makeup. I left her only long enough to run over to Vik's and change, leaving him to watch over the house until I returned before ordering him to sleep. He'd covered the perimeter while I stayed with Andrie, but I'd still done staggered patrols throughout the night. Fortunately, I'd only needed a few hours of sleep, and with any luck, I could get in a quick power nap while Andrie was safe in the A.T.

building with Lessia and countless other former military personnel around to protect her.

I wasn't sure what tail I was expecting, but the silver luxury sports car wasn't it. I didn't recognize the driver, either, but I trusted Grimm's directive. We arrived at the Accardi Tactical office building without incident and well ahead of the normal morning office rush.

Brody and Lessia were waiting in the lobby when we walked in. We'd had to clear two separate security checkpoints to get inside. One at the parking garage and the other at the building's entrance.

"About time y'all got here." Lessia grabbed Andrie's hand, practically dragging her to a corner of the luxurious entry that was blocked by construction plastic.

"Good morning," Brody greeted me, an indulgent smile tugging on his lips as we followed the two women at a much slower pace. "Lessia's pet project," he explained as we slipped past the opaque barrier.

I whistled, taking stock of the small, bistro-style café. It was cozy but had the upscale feel that matched the rest of the building.

"We'll start working on staffing and placing food orders shortly," Lessia was saying. "But they still have a few odds and ends to finish up on the construction side of things." She bypassed the front counter and towed Andrie down a small hallway, opening a door halfway down marked "Private."

Andrie's puzzled expression matched mine. The unimpressive utility room was lined with empty metal shelves. A small mop sink was behind the door. The entire space could barely contain us as we squeezed in so Brody could shut the door and carefully lock it.

Andrie's mouth opened, likely to question why we were all there, but shut it with an audible snap when Lessia placed her palm on the underside of one of the shelves on the side of the room. There was a responding chirp of a computer a few seconds later.

The sound of a lock being released was followed by the entire back shelving unit sliding into the wall.

I'd seen enough in my transit from Europe to the United States that I hadn't thought much—if anything—could surprise me. But even I felt my eyes widen. If I hadn't seen it, I wouldn't have thought the wall was movable, let alone could slide aside that easily. There had been absolutely no sign the room was anything other than what it appeared to be.

The space behind the wall was roughly the size of an elevator, and it matched the appearance of one. Eager now, Andrie and I stepped into this new space, waiting while the wall slid back into place.

Lessia and Brody looked at the back wall expectantly, but nothing happened. After a long few seconds, Lessia huffed and pressed a button, but the only sign something had happened was a whirling sound from the camera in the corner, which moved around until it fixated on us.

"Password?" a familiar voice asked from the intercom.

"Fuck you?" Lessia replied innocently, crossing her arms and raising an eyebrow in expectation.

"Nope! Try again," the bubbly voice said.

Andrie and I exchanged smiles, and Brody chuckled at the childish prank while Lessia cursed under her breath.

"Do you really think pissing off the person directly responsible for our new workplace and your caffeine supply is a good idea?" a distant voice asked through the intercom.

"Fine." The pout was clear in that single, drawn-out word, but the door finally opened, revealing a hacker's paradise.

"Hey, everyone! What do you think?" Juniper asked, spinning in her office chair. She whirled three times before Jolene grabbed her arm, stopping her momentum.

The room was easily twice as large as the one at the MC's headquarters and twice as tall. A theater-style screen covered the entire wall across from us, and at least fifty individual video feeds were playing. Individual desk spaces were arranged neatly throughout the room, though most were completely bare.

Andrie smiled at the perpetually happy Juniper. "What, no supercomputer?" she asked, motioning to the sleek computer on the desk in front of her.

"Oh, don't worry. She's in the basement." Juniper waved a hand in dismissal.

"Any news?" I asked before I overheard something I likely shouldn't.

Josie, who'd been over by a small kitchenette on one side of the room, came over, setting an energy drink down by Juniper with a grimace. "Nothing. Hardy didn't leave a single digital fingerprint anywhere after he left the Pentagon and went home."

"And Irina?" I asked.

Josie took a sip of her own drink. "She's in Zadar."

"Croatia?" Lessia asked. "Why?"

Josie shrugged. "I don't know. She flew in private a few days ago."

"It's a shipping port she uses for trafficking," I explained. "But she doesn't usually travel there herself."

"Does she always ship her ... wares ... via ships?" Andrie asked quietly.

My own face went carefully blank. "Most often. It's the easiest way to hide large amounts of cargo internationally. Ships are massive. Even if one were searched, it would take weeks or months if someone wanted to do a proper search of all the possible nooks and crannies. But she will occasionally take the risk of flying in a selection for a repeat, high-end buyer or use vehicles if she only needs to transport a few people across a couple hundred kilometers or over rough terrain. Hell, for a few of the more remote orders, she actually trucked them across Russia in cages."

Andrie wasn't the only one to flinch, and I immediately cut myself off and tried to switch subjects. "So, what's the plan for today?"

"Well, I say we break in this kick-ass equipment and play some video games."

The voice had all of us turning to the newcomer. A man I'd seen that morning came strolling in. He wore blue dress pants and a white button-down shirt, the matching suit jacket tossed carelessly over one shoulder. His perfectly styled brown hair and expensive haircut reeked of money, as did his tailored suit. His hazel eyes sparked with humor, brightening even more when Juniper squealed in delight and jumped out of her chair, throwing herself into the stranger's arms.

He chuckled. "Hey, little bit. It's been a long time."

"I didn't know you were back, Raptor," Jolene greeted the man, and Josie tipped her chin. Lessia and Brody welcomed him as well.

"Well, that explains why we're down here," Andrie said, her smile friendly and easygoing. "Raptor, this is Xander. He's a part of the MC and goes by Revenant. He's also Vik's brother. Xander, this is Raptor. He's been out on assignment."

We shook hands. "Nice to meet you."

"Nice car," I said.

His smile widened. "Isn't she? I love being able to open her up a bit, so I should thank you for speeding so I could hear her purr."

I chuckled. "Can't have a machine that fine wasting away in the slow lane."

Jolene shook her head as if amused at our antics. "Well, while Andrie and you debrief, Lessia, Brody, Josie, and I need to get to work."

I looked around, confused. "Aren't you already at work?" I asked her, noticing for the first time her office attire.

"Lessia has graciously created this new space for us, but we all have cover jobs in the building as well," she explained. "I'm the newest hire in Keene's office. It's easy enough to add coordinating A.T.'s travel needs since logistics are my department anyway. At least for the office staff

I don't have to worry about sneaking people in and out of countries unnoticed."

"I'm in IT," Juniper explained, finally on her own two feet again. "But the rest of the department thinks I'm in charge of network security. I have my own office in their section, but I just lock it and go through the tunnel entrance to come here."

"I'm the newest instructor, and I'll be subbing in when needed on any of the Accardi families' security detail," Josie added. "I don't know what title they've chosen for me or the class, but Lessia has me teaching how to identify credible intel from cyber dives and how to integrate that information with evidence already gathered."

"Intel instructor," Lessia said simply. "Anything else ended up being too much of a mouthful. And the classes will be called Intelligence, Search, and Sort—ISS for short."

Brody, at ease in his black tactical pants and shirt, raised an eyebrow. "Andrie and Raptor will likely be here for a while. Want to go to the shooting range? There's one in the building if you don't want to go far, but I was going to go out to the training grounds since I have to check on the most recent ammo order before my next class starts tomorrow."

The idea of blowing off some steam, not to mention seeing the training grounds, intrigued me, but I shot a glance over at Andrie to make sure. She gave me a small smile, and a pointed look at Raptor had him giving me a brief nod. He'd stay with her until I returned.

Clasping me on the back in a friendly manner, Brody smirked. "Come on, let's go shoot shit."

Chapter 28

ANDRIE

"Well, Doc. Since we both know I passed my go/no-go, can we talk about the fact you're in the middle of your own shit-show? Seriously, I know it's not exactly my place, but how are you holding up?"

Raptor was right; he had passed his evaluation. This mission, though a last-minute assignment, had been textbook, and his mental state was as solid as it had ever been.

"I'm all right. I have everyone here protecting my back."

He raised an eyebrow, a knowing smirk on his face. "And Rev guarding everything else?"

I knew my face reddened, though I tried to keep my expression casual. "Xander is new to town—as you know—and has time on his hands to help out. Plus, he's staying with Vik next door."

Raptor laughed, leaning back casually in his chair and crossing his legs at the ankles. "Doc, you need to remember you're surrounded by operatives. We're not only trained to lie but to detect them as well. What I can't figure out is if you're lying to me or yourself. That man is clearly hung up on you and not afraid to show it. I've been in his presence less than ten minutes and can tell you're just as enamored as he is."

My flush deepened. "I think we both need to focus more on the fact I was targeted for my patient list and the man who wants it hasn't been found yet."

Raptor shrugged. "Hardy will be caught soon. The man isn't inventive enough and doesn't have the nerve needed to stay low for long."

"Matteo grumbles about the MC gossiping while they're at home. I wonder if he knows it's just as bad when they're out on assignments," I complained, but there was little heat to my words, and Raptor knew it.

He rose. "Come on. Let's go see how much junk food Junie snuck into her new office space already."

I wasn't surprised to see Juniper with three extra-large coffee cups empty in her trash can in addition to the morning's energy drink. Candy wrappers littered her desk, and her feet tapped as if keeping beat to music only she could hear. Her whole body wiggled, unable to sit still with that much sugar and caffeine in her system.

"I thought you were on a strict coffee limit?" I plucked the wrappers and tossed them in the trash with the rest of the evidence, hoping like hell she'd calm down at least a little by the time her sisters came back. If she was still that ramped up after work, the other two might tie her to a chair and leave her.

"It's an emergency situation." Juniper didn't appear nearly as worried as I would have been if my heart rate was as high as hers. "I still can't find a trace of Hardy. That's the third person this year I haven't been able to track." Her words were so quick that it was hard to understand her. "I could understand if I were searching for someone in countries that aren't so tech-linked. But this is the United States of America, for crying out loud. No one, and I mean, *no one*, goes around unnoticed anymore. Not with everyone posting every minute of their lives on social media. Even elementary school kids, and I have yet to figure out why they need that in their lives. Do their parents not know how easy it is for predators to shop for their next victims when little Johnny or Jane is posting about their school, friends, sports, and favorite foods? They practically write their own map for these perverts on how to get lured away—"

"Juniper, you need to take a breath," I cautioned. Even Raptor was watching her, his eyes wide. Junie was always animated, scattered, and a little spacy at times, but she was frantic and clearly upset.

Spinning her chair, I forced her away from her computer screens, leaning down until we were eye to eye.

She nodded, practically gulping air after her run-on paragraph of words. "This is *not* on you. You are not all-knowing or all-seeing. As you said, you can't find anything on CCTV, his credit cards, phone, car, or facial recs through other people's social media accounts. If there was something for you to track, I have no doubt you'd have found it. It's not your fault there's nothing to find."

She sagged in her chair at my words, deflating. "I don't like failing," she whispered.

"You haven't failed, little bit. I have no doubt you'll find everyone you're looking for. It's just taking longer than you'd like. Patience and timing are necessary things in our world. After all, we have to adapt our plans around that of our prey. Hardy and the other two you're searching for are no different. I have no doubt they'll surface eventually. And when they do, you'll be there to find them."

Raptor's words seemed to both bolster and calm Juniper, who nodded. "You're right. I'm not beaten, I'm just waiting to pounce."

He nodded. "Like a cat waiting on a mouse to come out of their hole. Now, do you have anything else on your to-do list today?"

She shook her head. "I have my computer set to alert me if anything comes through local, federal, or military channels that might in any way be connected to Hardy. Irina's entourage is still in Croatia. I have no mission research to do today, and no one is out in the field, apart from Eris."

"Good. Now, what do you say we break in this new bat cave of yours the proper way?"

Chapter 29

XANDER

I t felt good to let off some steam. Guns had always been a part of my life, but always as a necessary tool, the way one thought of a pen or calculator. But today, with Brody, just enjoying the sunny day, the warm air holding a hint of salt from the breeze coming off the Gulf, I wasn't thinking about anything other than having fun.

"Great shot," Brody called once we both lowered our weapons. "You're better than most of my students."

I snorted. "You teach beginners, don't you? I've been shooting a handgun since I was five."

"Beginner firearms instructor doesn't mean I teach someone who's never held a gun before," Brody shot back, not looking the least bit offended. "It's just the entry-level class for anyone coming here. Considering everyone has a background in police or military—among others—I'd wager the class would be considered more than advanced at a normal gun range."

Acknowledging his point with a grunt, I loaded another clip and repositioned my ear plugs. Having spent almost all my life in cities, I found the training grounds to be a foreign world. Everything was green and rural. Unless it was mud. The training courses were put to use by men and women in tactical gear, and their loud encouragement was as polar opposite to my raising as the Texas heat was to Russia's long winters.

"Is this what you do all day?" I asked once we'd both emptied our weapons again.

"Pretty much." His Texas drawl was slow and deep as we walked down the grassy expanse to get our targets. "I help Boone out some when he needs an extra set of hands. And, of course, Lessia keeps me busy." His happiness from even mentioning her name was evident.

"You'll have to tell me about that one. How did you two end up together?" I'd first seen Brody accompanying Lessia at an event in Europe. I'd crashed the party, knowing she'd be there and needing to warn her of an impending kidnapping attempt by a wealthy German with a god complex and a firm disdain for women.

"I was hired by her brothers to keep her safe from a stalker."

I laughed, thinking of Alessia Accardi needing help protecting herself, then stopped when I realized he wasn't joking. "Really?"

He grinned. "She ended up scaring the kid—some British trust fund brat—so badly he refused to move from where he was cowering in her yard until the police came. Then she went back to making dinner."

I chuckled, having no issue picturing it. Even before I knew what Lessia's real profession consisted of, everything about Alessia Accardi spoke to her absolute confidence in herself and ability to handle anything and anyone that came her way.

"Let's just say they now know the error in their thinking." The words were innocent enough, but the weight behind them had me wondering if he meant they knew the entire story or if Lessia had just set her brothers straight. Not that it was any of my business, but I couldn't help being curious about the woman who managed to perform miracles when it came to saving victims and killing those who were thought to be untouchable. Vik had filled me in on some of her exploits, and they made for better fiction than fact.

We were packing it in when Boone joined us, looking all too happy for a man drenched in sweat in almost one-hundred-degree heat. "Hey, y'all. I was just about to stop in to see Gretchen. Do you want to check out the K-9 training grounds?"

"Stop in?" I asked suspiciously. I knew Gretchen was Matteo's woman, but I hadn't yet met her. Still, any woman who worked for Accardi Tactical and was former military likely didn't need a babysitter at work.

Boone must have seen the doubt on my face. "Kassie asked me to check in on her. Apparently, they got a surgery date for her daughter today, and it's sooner than G and Matteo expected. Which is a good thing," he explained in a rush. "But Kassie's still worried it might have thrown Gretchen off and wants me to get a read on her." He shrugged as if he didn't have a clue what he was supposed to notice but was too enamored with his girlfriend to defy a request from her.

Brody smirked. "Kassie asked you to snoop, and you want us to join you so we all get in trouble if Gretchen catches on."

Boone shrugged, not looking ashamed in the least. "I'm not just a pretty face. And I shouldn't be surprised you caught onto me. It's not like you don't strategize when it comes to my sister." He shot me a pointed look, and I blinked, realizing our little shooting match was likely Lessia's idea for me to decompress while Andrie was safe with her at the A.T. office.

"Touché." He raised his hands in defeat. "Lead on."

The kennels weren't far from the training course, and I was surprised at how quiet the building was. I'd expected the dogs to be barking, the entire place loud and smelly. But the dogs were relaxed in their kennels, and it only smelled faintly of dog, cleaner, and fresh air. We passed a few as we walked down the main hall, and I peeked in to see a solid black dog fast asleep, all four legs up in the air and a bone clutched in his jaws. He never even opened his eyes as we passed him. Eager to see more dogs, I looked into a few more rooms as I followed the other two men, but the rest were either sleeping or just stared at us as we passed. I recognized a few Malinois or German shepherds, along with some Labs and a wrinkly Bloodhound.

It wasn't until we reached the back of the building that we found a woman sitting on the ground of the kennel, eating a sandwich while a dog sat next to her, licking its lips. The Doberman Pinscher was a beautiful black and tan, her coat sleek and shiny. Judging by the swollen stomach, she was also heavily pregnant.

The dog scanned us quickly, her tail wagging once, before her entire focus went back to the food barely a foot from her face.

Gretchen looked over, jumping slightly when she saw three men outside the solid door, But then she smiled and reached over to open the kennel door. "Hey, guys."

"New friend?" Brody asked, putting a hand out to allow the dog to sniff before scratching behind her floppy ears.

"Meet Luna. She's a total sweetheart." Gretchen beamed.

"She's not a military dog, is she?" Boone asked as he got his own pets in. "I mean," he waved to her belly. "Please don't tell me we need to add an amendment to the list of requirements needed for a handler to bring their dog."

She laughed. "No, Boone. Luna isn't here as part of our K-9 program. Actually, she isn't officially here at all."

I inched into the room as the other two drifted farther inside. Boone sat on the ground next to Gretchen, who offered him a bag of chips.

"Gretchen, this is Xander. I'm not sure if y'all have met yet. He's new to the area but is friends with Grimm and Tristan," Boone explained as he opened the bag.

Gretchen smiled up at me, offering her hand, which I took. "Matteo mentioned you, I think. You're Vik's brother, right?"

Luna, who up until then had focused on the food, turned to me. I wasn't afraid of dogs—had actually wanted one as a child—but I'd never had cause to be around them much. I'd known better than to ask for one or even acknowledge any strays on the streets. My mother would have sooner killed one than allowed it to cross her path.

Crouching, I offered a hand the way the other men had. Luna sniffed, but instead of going back to Gretchen, she pushed into me, hard enough to send me onto my ass. Gretchen scolded the dog, but Luna ignored her, climbing into my lap before I'd even had a chance to fully steady myself.

"I'm so sorry," Gretchen apologized, calling for the dog, but I waved her off.

"It's no bother." I rubbed the dog in long, slow strokes. "You said she's not part of the training program?" Mentally, I wondered how Andrie would feel about getting a dog or two. Alex had routinely set out her leftover food for the strays behind our condo—something I continued after she was gone—and I had a feeling Andrie's soft spot for them hadn't changed.

"She isn't a dog here for boarding, is she?" Boone asked with a frown. "I know Gideon told you to stop allowing employees to use this facility when they go out of town. There are kennels around the city that actually cater to that sort of thing, and even with the recent expansion, you don't have the room or additional resources."

Gretchen waved him off. "In this case, you'll have to take it up with Luna's owner. I wasn't about to tell them no."

Brody groaned. "Don't tell me Lessia—"

She waved a hand in dismissal. "You're off the hook this time. This girl here actually belongs to Boone's uncle."

Boone's eyes widened. "Harrison got a dog? A pregnant dog?"

Gretchen shot a quick look at me before turning to the two men. "He asked me to watch over her while he was in DC. Luna came from Europe a few weeks ago, and I've been tapped to keep up with her training, as well as the litter, once they're born."

"He's having you train the entire litter? For what, and whom?" Brody asked.

She bit her lip, glancing between the three of us, and I realized she wasn't sure what information I was privy to. Brody must have realized it too, because he quickly added, "Xander hasn't met Harrison in person yet, but that's due to lack of time. Xander's been settling in with Tristan and his friends, and he's dating Andrie. And Harrison's had his hands full with work."

Gretchen read between the lines and nodded. Boone stayed silent, and I wondered how much Lessia's siblings were a part of this shadow world that had developed around them.

"Luna was purchased and bred with the intent for her puppies to be trained for a specific purpose. Doberman Pinschers are perceptive, smart, and loyal. They're also fearless, protective, and excellent family dogs. With early socialization and the proper training, they're completely trustworthy with anyone they see as family, including children, yet they'll protect against a threat with their lives."

"Protection dogs?" Brody asked, clearly deep in thought.

"Not in the traditional sense of the military and police dogs I train here. These puppies, once they grow up, will be going to people or places that could use dogs that are friendly with guests but would be another level of security for them."

"So, you're breeding sleeper dogs?" Boone's curiosity apparently caused his mouth to overrun his silence.

"I'm simply training dogs whose very breed was developed for purposes such as this. I'm not creating covert operatives." Her wince told me all I needed to know. Gretchen hadn't been a part of any of the meetings or gatherings we'd had, but she obviously knew of Matteo's involvement. At least, the general idea.

"Anyway, Luna is the first dog brought over, but she isn't slated to be the last. I have another—a plush-coated German shepherd that'll be coming over from the Netherlands next year, and I'm researching some breeders here in the United States as well."

"How many dogs is he trying to develop?" I couldn't help my interest, and I wondered if the pups might need a foster home-type situation when they were old enough. If Andrie wouldn't go for a full-time dog right now, maybe she'd be open to a temporary one? The thoughts I had the other day in Andrie's new office came back full force. I couldn't get a job at Accardi Tactical, but maybe I could find another way to go about helping protect people.

Luna, finally done with me, slid off my lap and stretched before returning to Gretchen's side, allowing me to stand. Gretchen fed the dog the last bite of her sandwich, smiling when the dog gingerly took it from her hand.

"As many as I can handle." She rose, snagging her mostly eaten bag of chips from Boone as she did so. "However, that won't be very many. This is a side project, and the litters are big. Plus, each dog will need considerable attention, and I can't exactly hire additional help without explaining to Gideon why he's paying for a K-9 handler who isn't actually working with the military classes. Megan, my assistant, is going through a bad break up, and while she's a sweet kid, she's not the most reliable person. Getting someone who can pass through the background check and is willing to do the shit part of the job—pun intended—as well as the glamorous stuff. Well, it's harder to come by than you think."

I wouldn't have thought much about her plight if it wasn't for Brody's stare. Boone tilted his head for a second, his attention going back and forth between us a few times, before looking over to Gretchen. Then he broke out into laughter.

"Oh, no." I shook my head as I realized I'd been set up. Jamming my hands in my pockets, I rocked back on my heels, ruthlessly pushing down the spark of interest that had kindled. "I'm hardly a good candidate. I've barely been around dogs. And I doubt my background would pass muster for Accardi Tactical."

Gretchen, catching on, whirled around to fully face me, hope on her face despite my words. "Do you like them?"

"Dogs?" I shrugged, not wanting her to see how much the idea appealed to me when I knew there wouldn't be a way to make it work. "Who doesn't? But—"

"Are you willing to learn? It's hard work and requires a lot of time and dedication. *They* require consistency, fairness, and affection."

Luna padded over to me, sitting expectantly while I slowly extracted a hand to give her the petting she clearly felt she was due. I felt myself weakening as I stroked her short silky coat. "The background—"

Brody cut me off, smirking. "Oh, I'm sure there's a way around it. After all, you were exonerated from your 'crime,' so technically, the manslaughter charge isn't on your record."

"It wasn't the only crime on there, if you care to remember," I drawled, though even I could hear the interest in my voice. I still had a litany of charges, even if none were as severe. And while most were supposedly on my juvenile record and sealed, I had no doubt the typical A .T. background search would open those in a heartbeat. I needed to blend in with the Iron Wraiths on paper without having anything severe enough to trip up Andrie's military and federal contacts. Well, not enough that it couldn't be swept under the table.

"An independent contractor or company would allow for more leniency on our part of the hiring process," Boone added helpfully. "We use them all the time for our janitorial staff and even the new café workers. After all, you wouldn't technically be an employee of ours. It also would work with getting Gideon's approval—not that I think that would be an issue to begin with. But Xander could work for this separate outfit and still have all the clearances he'd need to work here. Plus, I'm sure your 'boss' wouldn't mind you helping out the normal classes and K-9 upkeep as needed. Also, anyone with clearance would certainly have an easier time visiting the office more often, seeing as they'd be staff and all." The last part was added innocently.

I'd been slow on the uptick, but I was fully aware now. It wasn't an off-the-cuff offer that hadn't been fleshed out. Either it had come down from this Harrison—who I had a sneaking suspicion was Thoth—Lessia, or Matteo. Possibly even a mixture of the three. Matteo would get someone in the same building as his woman. Harrison got a plant who could work his pet project in plain sight of the regular staff while reporting to and working for him and him alone. And Lessia ... well, I wasn't sure what her motivation would be, but I was sure if she was involved, there was one.

Regardless of who it had originated from, it was an offer I wasn't about to reject. "It just so happens I'm looking for a more permanent job than helping out my brother at his bar," I started to say as Gretchen's smile grew. "But I'm committed to helping Andrie right now," I finished.

Undeterred, Gretchen's excitement and relief were all but tangible. I wondered how much she was taking on between the upcoming litter, expanded classes, and her assistant's split attention—not to mention her young daughter's surgery.

"It'll be a few weeks before Luna delivers—not that you have to wait that long to start. But I have a feeling your paperwork won't be finished processing until whatever you're working on with Dr. Andrie is complete."

Somehow, I thought so, too.

Chapter 30

ANDRIE

I don't know what Xander expected to find when he came back that afternoon, but the three of us, laughing and playing vintage video games on a screen bigger than a movie theater's, likely wasn't it.

"Jeez, Andrie. You're playing a game, and you're still the slowest driver on the planet. Kick it in gear and push him into the wall," Junie reprimanded me. She'd just wrecked her character's car, forcing her to restart.

"If I go any faster, I'm just going to go off course," I complained.

In less than a minute, Juniper's character passed me as if I were standing still. "If you don't pick up the pace, the entire race is going to pass you," she warned. Then she giggled manically as she shot at Raptor, causing him to curse when he was sent back to start with one less life. "The game isn't about how perfect you can drive. It's about winning and blowing up others in the process."

With that, Junie's character crossed the finish line, doing donuts to celebrate. Raptor demanded a rematch as he and the rest of the field—then myself—finished the race.

Chuckles from behind us had me turning around. "Face it, babe. Even playing a game, driving isn't your strong suit.

Unless we're trying to stay off police radar—then you're our girl."

I blushed at Xander's gentle teasing. "Did you have a good time shooting?" I asked, noting his relaxed stance.

A flicker of excitement crossed his features before he schooled his expression. "It appears as if you aren't the only new hire for Accardi Tactical. After we get everything with Hardy squared away, I'm going to be working with Gretchen Moore. She needs an apprentice, it seems."

Raptor looked over his shoulder to Xander. "Make sure you have Brody show you the new training building sometime after you start."

Narrowing my eyes at Raptor, I started to put pieces of a larger puzzle together. I knew Lessia had put Raptor—who'd been with the Army Corps of Engineers in another life—to work adding the underground infrastructure to her new land purchase. Raptor had also inspected and maintained the tunnel pathways the operatives used to get to and from a base of operations in the city. He'd even been a part of designing the escape routes for Matteo's new house. I also knew from Gretchen that the update to the training building, where the dogs had several mock scenes to train in, had been unplanned until Lessia had stepped in. Apparently, it had been decided that someone who knew more—or would soon know more—about the organization needed to be within easy reach of an entrance and exit point.

The smooth-looking operative returned my knowing stare with a wink. Clearly, he'd either known about the offer or had already reached the same conclusion.

"Do you want to join us?" He motioned to the screen. "Maybe you can defend Andrie's honor and help me put this one in her place. She's won six out of ten so far." Juniper stuck her tongue out at him.

"I'm afraid my childhood didn't leave time for games such as this. Vik has been teaching me some, but this doesn't look anything like what we've been playing at his place." Xander tilted his head, studying the screen.

"It's because it's ancient. At least, in the gaming world. But I'm not about to let anything that needs to be connected to the internet down here, and it's fun to revisit the classics," Juniper explained. "These are actually easier to play, and even if the graphics aren't as sharp as the ones today, they still require focus to keep up with what's on the screen. It's a great way to let loose for a bit." She took a breath, steeling herself, and offered her controller to him.

Xander, bless his heart, smiled down at Juniper, not realizing how big of a move it was for someone as technologically connected and socially anxious as her to give up their security blanket. But instead of taking it, he gently pushed it back into her hands. "I'd love to learn. But as I understand it, if you're the winner, then I need to be your official challenger. Raptor, if you haven't taken her down in ten games, then I'd have to say you need to hang up your dreams of an upset. Let a rookie step in and see if they can do any better."

The four of us played for another hour, Juniper wiping the floor with all of us repeatedly in a variety of games, even when the two men tried to team up against her. We'd eaten our weight in popcorn, chips, and junk food by the time Lessia, Brody, Jolene, and Josie called it a day.

"Is this fair?" Jolene asked Josie, teasingly. "We spent most of the day stuck with someone training us on the ins and outs of the office, procedure, and security protocols, and they're here playing games."

Juniper stuck out her tongue. "My department is all bent out of shape that I got hired without them even knowing there was an opening, *and* that I got my own office. They're all pouting right now and leaving me the hell alone, so I don't have to keep up appearances." That news might have her sisters backs straightening, but Junie seemed completely oblivious as she reached for her third bag of chips, protesting when Josie snatched it from her hand.

The glare the two sisters were exchanging had Jolene stepping up, preparing to referee, when a beeping interrupted. Junie scrambled to her feet, almost bumping into Brody, who steadied her before she ended up back on the floor. Not acknowledging him in the slightest, Juniper raced to her computer, her fingers typing before she'd even sat down.

"Man. Grimm's going to be so pissed," she muttered, more to herself than the rest of us as we gathered behind her. She pressed a button on her phone while typing with the other hand, never taking her eyes off the screen.

"What?" Grimm's voice sounded as Juniper's cell connected to a speaker in the room.

"One of the men you and your guys roughed up went to the police to charge you with assault. Of course, they jumped all over that once they realized your home address matched the club address. When the little weasel realized he might buy himself some goodwill with the cops if he threw you under the bus, he offered up incentive, claiming he's seen you all dealing and using drugs there. And he says you store all your black-market weapons under the floorboards. We all know he's never been there, but I'm betting he's assuming if he can get the cops in the door, they'll find something incriminating."

She rolled her eyes as Grimm cursed creatively, then continued, "They're afraid you might have a mole in the department and that's why they've never been able to pin anything on you before. Right after the warrant was signed, they started rolling your way. I'm guessing you have fifteen minutes at most."

We heard Grimm ordering someone to close the gate to the parking lot and stall and for someone else to wipe the server to the surveillance system. "We'll be ready in five. Thanks for the warning. I don't suppose you could ..."

"Almost done. Check in after." Juniper was already typing before he got the words out, and a second later, Xander's phone pinged.

"Fifty?" he asked, not understanding the code.

"Five-oh. Cops," she elaborated when it was clear he didn't understand. "It's not much of a code, but it's not supposed to be. If the police see it, it just adds to the thought that the Iron Wraiths can't be all they're hyped up to be if they're this unsophisticated. The smart cops know better, and it drives them nuts. I sent it out to everyone not at HQ right now so they don't end up showing up while it's being searched. The less people the police see or interact with, the better. Grimm will have anyone else there leave."

"Won't that just solidify their thoughts that they have a mole?" he asked, new to this game the MC had with the local police.

Juniper nodded. "Which will keep them looking at their own department. Or maybe giving the court clerks a hard look. No one would know I'm in their system."

He raised an eyebrow. "And if they do?"

She shrugged, looking unconcerned. "If the feds haven't found me crawling around in their network, you can bet the locals will never track me either. Besides," she said with a wink, "I might know their head tech consultant."

I was starting to remember why the triplets originally weren't settled in Texas when we'd been given new identities. Having Juniper and Lessia in the same state was a bad idea. If either one of them got a wild hair, the other was sure to be on board. Between the two women, I was pretty sure there wasn't anything they didn't have their hand in or could get information about.

Xander must have had a similar thought. "Just what can't you do when it comes to computers?"

Her smile was half-mischievous, half-maniacal. "Nothing, my new friend. There is *nothing* I can't do with one of these babies in my hand."

We left Accardi Tactical a while later, still no closer to finding Hardy but a lot more settled about the entire matter. When you pretty much played hooky all day in a hidden room eating junk food and laughing with friends, it was hard to stay stressed. Xander, too, seemed to be back to his normal self and not at all the fragile man who'd climbed into my bed last night.

"Would you like to go out to eat tonight?" he asked, his fingers squeezing mine as we held hands. "Or are you filled up on potato chips?"

Before I could answer, I got a text. "Vik says everyone's going to Matteo's to hang out since the clubhouse is still being searched."

"Grimm has to be loving that," Xander said.

I winced. Grimm was definitely going to be out for blood after this—even if he couldn't get to the actual man causing all the issues at this moment in time. The Iron Wraiths ran the streets in the city, but they generally kept their criminal pursuits away from where they lived to keep everything mostly peaceful and somewhat clean.

Gangs might deal a little coke or meth on the streets, but they knew better than to get too greedy or draw too much attention. The areas around MC hangouts were certainly dangerous, but only to other people like them—they didn't allow for innocents to be drawn into their business. Which kept the police without a trail, too.

This, however, wasn't something Grimm could afford to let go. Not if he meant to keep his control. Whoever had gone to the police had made a grave error. Instead of taking his licks and learning from the warning, he'd gone and publicly tried to get one over on the Iron Wraiths. Even if Grimm wanted to, his father would come back and beat his son himself if Grimm didn't respond to the threat the man had made against the club.

There were already several vehicles and motorcycles at Matteo's when we arrived. I'd made Xander stop so we could pick up some ice and soft drinks, knowing the men had covered the beer portion in spades.

Wyck, Shade, Vik, Jasper, and Whisp sat around a picnic table, while Matteo and a large black dog were by the grill. Savage came out of the house, holding baby Ava in one hand and a swing in the other. Gretchen was behind him, carrying a beer and wearing an amused expression.

"The princess is here. Now, we can get started," Savage announced, trying to set the stand for the swing up with one hand as he spoke.

Shade rose. But instead of helping with the swing, he grabbed the baby and walked off with her, talking nonsense as he did so.

"I don't know why you bothered having Tristan bring that thing out," Matteo said to his girlfriend, taking the beer from her. "It's not like any one of these guys will let her be the entire time they're here."

"I'm sure you're right," she said, shaking her head in bemusement. Despite all this time around the MC, she still wasn't used to the fact these bikers were all suckers for kids. "And that was Tristan's beer."

Matteo winked at her as Xander and I stopped next to them. "I know." He drank half of it down in a single swallow.

"We brought more ice and some drinks," I said by way of greeting. "I figured the guys had the harder stuff covered, and it always seems like y'all are prepared for an entire contingent."

Gretchen laughed. "Yeah, the guys come over at least a few times a month, sometimes even once or twice a week. We've learned to keep enough food on hand to feed everyone a few times over. Today, you're in luck—we've having steak, corn, potato salad, and two entire sheet pans of cake. The men all have a sweet tooth, so make sure you get a piece early because there won't be leftovers." She wrapped an arm through mine. "Come on, I need some girl time, and we have two cakes to frost."

I tossed a glance over to Xander as I was dragged off, but he just gave me a little wave as I stumbled up the stairs.

Chapter 31

Xander

"So, I hear congratulations are in order," Matteo said, taking the bag of ice I was holding and dumping it in a cooler by the grill.

I snagged a water before it could be buried, not about to drink anything that could slow my reaction time, even if we were among friends.

"Do I have you to thank for that or Lessia?"

He didn't answer, instead saying, "I'm sorry it was sprung on you that way. Normally, we'd at least talk before putting a plan into motion, but the timing of this one wasn't one I was watching as closely as I should have. Still, Grimm and Lessia were pretty sure you'd go for it. If you decide it's not for you, just let me know, and we can make other arrangements. All I ask is you stay with it until we can insert a replacement."

Even after being with the men these last few weeks, it still took me by surprise that I had the freedom to choose and that my feelings and opinions mattered. My entire life had consisted of being a soldier of sorts for my mother and a puppet for my father, toeing the line to keep everyone I cared about safe. Before Alex, Viktor and I were held in place by our loyalty to one another and the knowledge that we needed to be absolutely meticulous about any plans of escape. After, well, if my staying in that role was the price I needed to pay to ensure their new life was secure, it was worth it.

"I can't imagine it being anything close to as distasteful as my last job," I half-joked, still not completely comfortable telling anyone just how excited I was to get the job offer. "I'm sure I can handle it."

The dog, which had been lying patiently on a raised bed by the grill, rose. He wagged his tail hopefully but stayed on the platform, clearly waiting to be released.

Matteo made a gesture with his hand, and the dog came bounding up to me, his body almost wriggling in excitement. "This is Zeke. He's ours but was a rescue, so we're still working on obedience," he explained as Zeke tried to jump up. I leaned down instinctively, recognizing him as the goofball sleeping in his kennel earlier in the day, and gave the dog the attention he wanted.

"As I told your girlfriend, I don't know much about dogs. But I'm willing to learn." I gave the dog one more pat before he bounded off in the direction of the men.

Vik headed our way then as the others rose to start playing with a soccer ball. As they began kicking it to each other, Zeke raced into the middle of their circle, trying to catch the ball before it could reach the next person.

"How's Andrie? And yourself? I know yesterday couldn't have been fun," Matteo asked quietly as Vik came up beside us.

"We're fine. She's handling everything better than most. It helps that she's a psychologist. Her coping mechanisms are fully developed and constantly being used. And yesterday wouldn't even break the top one hundred on my bad days list." I took another sip of my water, feeling the two men evaluating my words.

"I know you don't want to rely on Andrie as your psychologist. If either of you need it, I can fly in our semi-retired one. He's the one Andrie talks to when she feels the need," Matteo said carefully.

Vik snorted. "Fink's probably chomping on the bit to come down here. The last time Andrie spoke with him, he was grumbling about the impending cold up north."

"It does get cold up in Colorado," Matteo pointed out.

"She talked to him a week or so ago. It's still summer," Vik replied.

"In Texas, maybe. But you can bet the weather's already changing up north." Matteo chuckled. "He'll be here for less than a day before he's complaining about the Texas heat."

"No question about it."

But despite the lighthearted words, Matteo's scrutiny only intensified. "Seriously, I know you haven't been here long, but you've gone through a lot in a few short months, plus settling down with Andrie. I know you've waited a long time for this and paid for it in ways I'm sure I don't even know. But I'm also sure the woman you're getting to know isn't exactly the one you've been dreaming about."

I bristled because Andrie was *exactly* the woman I'd been dreaming about. Matteo raised his hands and continued, "I'm just saying, it must be hard, reconciling all you've had to sacrifice with only a fantasy to keep yourself going.

And now that the flesh and blood woman is in front of you, I worry it's not the magical life you've been dreaming of ... that you're going to regret what you've done these past years and what we're about to do. Is this life going to be enough?"

Vik, who'd been matching my anger, clenched fist for fist, suddenly hesitated, pissing me off even more. I knew what Matteo was clumsily asking and even understood it on a basic level. I'd been existing on dreams of Alex and me for more years than I cared to count, and I could see where some would envision a future as a way to keep themselves on their mission. Even worse, Alex and I had only truly been together for weeks, barely even months, prior to her abduction. Though we'd known each other on a soulful level, we'd still been learning about each other's past and surprising each other with new facts about the other almost every day we'd been together.

But I wasn't most people. Life lessons from those around me had never led to dreams of the perfect life. I'd dreamed of a regular life ... of coming home from work, squabbling over dirty clothes and dishes, making dinner for her, and even watching television on the couch almost as often as I'd fantasized about making love to her. My life had never been normal, and that was all I'd ever wanted. Sure, normal for us might not be the typical American dream, with her list of patients and my being involved with the Iron Wraiths. But it was still going to be ours.

"I'd sacrifice another lifetime if it were to get me what I have right now," I gritted out. "And the only regret I have is not killing off Demetri Melnikoff a long time ago."

The sound of glass shattering had me spinning, realizing too late what I'd just said, and that Andrie had heard me.

Chapter 32

ANDRIE

The wine glass fell from my fingers as I stood there, dumb-struck. I couldn't have heard that right, could I?

But the guilty expression on Xander, Vik, and Matteo's faces told me otherwise. Pain ripped through me like a knife wound, hot and breath-stealing, and my hand immediately went to my chest as I bent over. The agonizing heat turning ice cold in an instant.

I heard Gretchen say something, but I only shook my head, unable to focus on anything. That was, until I saw a pair of boots in my peripheral vision. Staggering back, I slammed into the house, trying to get away, to reject the last minute of my life. Xander couldn't have ... could he?

He took another step, and I whirled, reaching blindly for the patio door and yanking it open. Xander cursed behind me as I ran headlong into a dining room chair, my legs tangling with it. I almost went down to the floor face-first when I felt hands gripping my waist. They set me on my feet and let me go before I could wrench away from his hands.

"Andrie," Xander said, his voice almost as rough as I felt, but I only shook my head, still moving, but not for long.

I ended up against the kitchen counter, one hand on the cool white and gray marble I'd just complimented Gretchen on. She and Matteo had just finished renovating the kitchen the weekend before—with a huge amount of help from Wyck and his construction crew.

Strong arms pinned me against the counter, and I went wild, turning to kick and hit blindly. My heartache turned to rage in an instant, and I welcomed the heat that flared through me, replacing that painful cold. Xander let me fight, until one of my punches connected so solidly, I heard him grunt. Apparently done letting me use him as a punching bag, he lifted me a few inches off the floor and pinned me against the gray cabinets with his body.

"Alex!" His face was inches from mine, and I prepared to snap my head forward, intending on head-butting him, when I registered the name he'd called me. How had he known my real name?

"Just listen to me, all right? What you heard was out of context, and I know it sounded bad. But do you really think the others, namely *Viktor*, would allow me to live, let alone breathe in your presence, if there wasn't more to the story?"

His Russian accent was getting heavier and heavier as he spoke, and his pronunciation of Vik's full name—had me pausing, thinking about his words.

My chin tilted up. "Let me go," I said, clearly enunciating each word.

"Do you promise not to try kicking me again?" he asked.

"No." I might as well stay truthful.

A corner of his mouth twitched. "Fair enough, *sol-nyshkuh*." I flinched at the nickname. Only one person had called me that, and, from what I'd just heard, the man in front of me was responsible for his death.

"Did you really think Demi would have been able to escape under his own name?" he whispered, his somber face an inch from mine. "That Irina and Senior would just allow their son to disappear? And when Irina was killed, or even died under mysterious circumstances, Anatoly would immediately suspect him, even if he'd supposedly been dead for years. Anatoly has never been blind to his grandson's hatred of Irina, even if she pretends otherwise, and he would bring the weight of his entire organization down on anyone he even suspected might have helped him."

I froze, feeling the blood drain from my face.

"So, you had to pretend to kill ..." I trailed off, trying to understand. Was the price of Xander's passage here faking Demi's death? And, if so, where was Demi? After all this time, had he decided he wanted a life—a love—other than with me? The second the thought crossed my mind, I rejected it.

"I didn't kill Demi, Alex. But I did arrange for his death, more than once. His exit from his old life was ... complex." The anticipation, or maybe expectation, on his face confused me. It was as if I wasn't keeping up with what he was saying.

"So, if you didn't kill Demi, where is he?" I finally blurted out when it was clear Xander wouldn't elaborate further.

His smile was a mixture of relief, delight, and apprehension. "Where else do you think he'd want to be, except in your arms?"

Blinking, I tried to understand what Xander was saying, shaking my head slowly. *No, there was no way Demi* ... I pushed against Xander, and he let me go. He took two steps back, his arms hanging to his sides, letting me look my fill.

Sure, Xander was similar in height to Demi, but that was where the similarities ended. Xander was much more muscular, easily seventy-five pounds heavier. He was bald whereas Demi had thick, pale blond hair that was almost white; a darker blond beard covered a jaw much less square than Demi's had been. His eyes, too, had been so light they were almost without color, and Xander's were definitely blue. His cheekbones were higher and more pronounced, and his nose was different. Hell, even his tattoos didn't match.

Nothing in the man's face was familiar. Nothing except the look of what I would swear was love in his eyes. He must have read my rejection of his words because he raised a hand in an unspoken command to wait before walking to the door, where I was sure everyone was eavesdropping.

"Shade, I need a black light." Xander's words might confuse everyone else, but I gasped, hope starting to rise even as I tried to reject it.

He came back with a small light, pulling the shades in the dining room and kitchen as he made his way back to me.

"We might not have exchanged our vows in a church in front of a priest," he said, reaching for my left hand. "But I considered them just as sacred, as have you." Clicking on the light, the tattoo I didn't think anyone alive knew I had fluoresced a bright blue on the side of my ring finger. I didn't need to look closely to know what it showed.

"An infinity symbol," Xander said huskily as he gently rubbed the marking. "A sign of endless possibilities. Because, even then, we knew that despite how bleak a future together looked, there was always a possibility we would get the world we wanted to live in."

I knew what else was detailed on the tattoo, the starburst of a sun on one side, and a crescent moon on the other. Because Demi had always lived in the darkness, and I was his sunshine.

When the light flashed on his own tattoo—the only one remaining of his old ones—it mirrored mine. But whereas mine was wispy and feminine, his was solid and bold.

"Demi," I breathed, scarcely hearing a phone ringing outside. A torrent of emotions burst forth—elation and joy, guilt and confusion. "I—I don't understand. How did I not know?"

"Didn't you?" he asked softly, pulling me into his arms. "You didn't so much as look at a man until I came through that door. You might not have realized it was me on a conscious level, but deep down, your subconscious knew. You wouldn't have slept with me that first night otherwise."

His smug, somewhat patronizing smile, stopped me short from melting into him. "So, you planned on running into me that night?" The lightbulb dawned ... Lessia's insistence on me joining them, our talk, and Vik's anxious behavior, his insistence on meeting his "brother." They'd orchestrated it. They'd known Xander's identity.

Furious at being played, I pushed with all my might, making Xander release me to catch his balance. "You, what, decided since you were now in the free and clear after all this time, you might as well celebrate by picking up the drunk woman who was *still mourning the loss of the person she loved* and have sex with her? After all, considering she was grieving over your 'death,' it didn't really count, did it?"

His eyes narrowed, even as he took another step back. "Considering how much time we'd both lost, I didn't want to waste another moment in starting the rest of our lives together."

"Were you ever going to tell me?" Understanding the depth of the betrayal, I balled my hands into fists, welcoming the pain of my fingernails digging into my palms.

"Of course," he said, placatingly, his voice calm and controlled as if I were being unreasonable. "When the timing was right."

"Fuck you," I shot back. "You knew I was grieving for Demi—for you. You knew I wrestled with the idea of letting go of the past so I could have a relationship with you, and for what? Some male satisfaction that you could make me fall in love with you twice?"

Not about to stand around and listen to what he had to say, I stormed from the house, coming to a stop when I came face to face with Vik, Matteo, and the rest of the men behind them—all of whom had to have known Xander's real identity.

"Andrie—" Matteo started, but I cut him off, not able to look at him or Vik.

"I'm going home." Looking around wildly, I spotted Wisp in the shadows. "You," I snapped my fingers and pointed to him. "You're taking me." I might have been beyond upset at everyone there, but I wasn't stupid enough to storm off in a huff.

"Yes, ma'am." Whisp trailed behind me as I headed to the truck Xander and I had been borrowing from Vik since I'd lost my sedan. Though I knew it likely killed him not to drive, he jumped into the passenger seat without hesitation, buckling his seatbelt when I refused to back up, eyebrow raised pointedly until he did so.

"Did you know?" I asked, already knowing the answer.

"Yes." Whisp wasn't a man to mince words or use any more than absolutely necessary.

The tears I'd been holding back started to fall. I'd thought these men were my friends. Hell, Vik was like a brother to me. For the first time since I'd met Demi, I felt totally and utterly alone. Even after Irina's man had placed me in that truck, after the rapes and moves across the United States, I'd never given up the feeling that Demi would somehow find me and rescue me from that hell. When Vik and the others had rescued us, my thoughts had been confirmed. Yes, Demi hadn't been able to come for me himself, but I understood why, and I knew he'd done everything he could—even sending me the only person in the world he trusted—to ensure my safety.

"When Hardy is found ..." I threatened.

Whisp shifted in his seat. "What?" He hesitated but ultimately decided now wasn't a good time to hold back information.

"While you and Xander were ... talking ... Matteo got a call. They found Hardy at some old cabin his cousin's grandfather owned. He's dead."

"Dead?"

Whisp shrugged. "Apparently, he took the easy way out. The locals are still processing the scene, but we'll get a full report soon."

I pulled into my driveway. "Good. Then you don't need to stay." I heard the rumble of a motorcycle in the distance. "Get out."

He shook his head, but I wasn't in the mood for another man to dictate my life. "Hardy is dead, so there's no reason for you to stick around. I don't want a single one of you hanging around my property, let alone taking a step inside my door. I'm not leaving my house for the rest of the day, and as far as I'm concerned, I just want to be left the hell alone."

Not waiting for a response, I slammed the door on the truck and disappeared inside my house, waiting pointedly at the window until Whisp reluctantly said something to Savage, who'd followed us on his motorcycle, before getting into an SUV I recognized as Shade's. The three men left, reluctantly turning back the way they'd come.

Wiping my eyes, I took a steadying breath before reaching over to put the car keys into the bowl by the door I always kept them in, and organizing my shoes neatly. No matter how much I wanted to throw everything in a heap, I refused to let my emotions get the better of me. If it killed me, I would put everything away properly before I raided my ice cream stash and crawled into bed to cry.

I was just turning around to head to the kitchen when I heard the sound of footsteps.

"Well, well. I have to admit, you weren't the woman I thought I'd be torturing tonight." I froze in fear as a woman stepped out from my spare room. She tilted her head, still speaking in Russian. "More correctly, I guess, it is the same woman, just different name. Tell me, how is it you escaped your captors and ended up here of all places?" She sneered, as if Texas were one of the last places on Earth anyone would want to live.

I couldn't answer her. My body shook too badly to be able to speak. She smirked, watching my terror. "Never mind. We can talk plenty later." Holding up a gun, she motioned for me to grab the keys I'd just put away. I grabbed them and reached for the door, wondering if the men had doubled back after making a show of leaving or if I was on my own.

Before I could even unlock the door, Irina was behind me, wrenching my arm up in a painful hold. "Don't even think about screaming or causing a scene, or I swear I will shoot every man, woman, and child I come across until I run out of bullets. Do you understand?"

I nodded, then screamed out in pain when she added more pressure. I knew if she applied even another ounce of weight, my arm would dislocate. "I understand," I managed to get out.

"Good." The grip only loosened slightly as she reached around with the hand still holding the gun to pull my phone from my purse, dropping it on the floor before unlocking the door. "You're driving."

Chapter 33

XANDER

"Fuck," I swore, running a hand over my scalp when I came out of the house a few minutes later. I'd heard Andrie leaving, and as much as I hated letting her go, I knew we were both better off cooling our tempers before I tried talking to her again.

Matteo's stony expression, paired with the men's somber glances and Gretchen's sympathetic look, told me the entire backyard had heard our discussion.

"I'm sorry," Matteo said quickly. "I shouldn't have brought that up now, and I certainly should have phrased it better. I just wanted to see where your head was at. I didn't mean to—"

I cut him off with a wave, my anger turning to weariness. "I was planning on telling her anyway. And I have a feeling it wouldn't matter how I tried to present it. She'd go to mad before settling on happy. I'd just feel better about giving her space if I knew she was safe."

"That's some good news I can give you." Matteo turned his attention back to the steaks while he filled me in about the police finding Hardy.

"You think he committed suicide?" I asked.

He shrugged. "Andrie is typically the one I'd ask. But if I had to guess, I would believe so. Hardy comes from a line of men who've served and served well. The fact that he was about to be exposed as a traitor, with nowhere to run, makes me think he might have thought this was his only option."

Because I agreed with him, I didn't comment. Instead, I zeroed in on Vik, who stood at the edge of the yard with the dog next to him. Excusing myself, I headed over to him, knowing Andrie and I weren't the only two hurting right now.

"It's going to be alright," I said when I stopped beside him, scratching the dog behind his ears. "She's beyond mad right now and hurt. But she's too logical not to understand why we all did what we did once she calms down. Besides, she cares about us both too much not to forgive us."

"I hated the way she looked through me when she left," he admitted softly. "As if she couldn't bear to see me after she realized I hadn't told her."

For the first time, I really understood the full situation Vik had been in. I might have hated lying to Andrie, but I'd been the one that had agreed to it. Vik hadn't had a say at all, and was forced to follow the orders he'd been given. He'd truly been placed between a rock and a hard place, lying to the woman he considered a sister to protect the brother of his heart.

"I never should have agreed to it," I said suddenly. "I was just so relieved when I heard you both were safe and prepared to do anything in order to ensure you stayed that way. I don't think the powers that be really believed we'd still love each other—not after only having been together those few weeks. If I'd pushed when I got here, I might have been able to change their minds on how we went about this entire mess."

Vik shook his head slowly. "Maybe. Hell, probably. But you had no way of knowing that. It's not like you've ever met Thoth in person. I'm not sure how much he even knew about y'alls feelings, and he was likely more concerned with Andrie recognizing you. After all, if you couldn't fool her, there's no way your cover would hold. There's a distinct possibility you could cross your father at some point or, even more likely, some of the people Irina forced you to traffic. You'd be surprised to hear how much some of them remember."

I winced because having to participate in that world—knowing the life I was sentencing those people to—was something I struggled to reconcile. I knew I didn't have a choice, but it didn't make me feel better to know that I'd had a hand in shoving people into a life of hell. No matter how much information I had been able to pass onto Lessia over the years in hopes of saving them and shutting the entire operation down, it would in no way ever make up for what I'd been forced to do.

Fortunately, I'd been mostly been on the outskirts of the operations my mother dictated for years. After Vik and Andrie, she'd lost most of her power over me, and seemed to know pushing me too hard would result in me turning on her, especially as the years drug on, wearing on my soul. Though I'd still been present for much of her operations, most of my work had consisted of intimidation—keeping everyone in her network in line—and securing the area around any transfer locations.

Wisp, Shade, and Savage came back in through the house. "What the hell?" I muttered to Vik, but Savage put a hand up before I could ask.

"Andrie kicked our asses to the curb. Doesn't want any one of us on her property or watching her. She said with Hardy no longer a threat, we weren't needed. She did promise to stay home, though. We called Juniper a few minutes ago to let us know if there's any movement around her house. We, uh, figured it would be best to let her have some time to cool down."

His unhappy expression told me the men felt just as uncomfortable being placed in the middle of our fight, and they possibly felt as guilty as Vik was feeling.

"It's all right," Vik reassured them. "We all know once she calms down and thinks things over, she'll get over it. Mostly." He shot me a glance, telling me I'd better make sure everything got smoothed over. "Let's give her a few hours, and then, y'all can take Rev back to my place. She might be able to kick y'all off her property, but she's not going to keep me out of my own damn house, and he can keep close to her until they get this shit sorted."

A trickle of unease ran down my spine at the idea of her being alone, even if Hardy was no longer a threat. "Juniper's got eyes on the place?" I asked, more to reassure myself than anything.

Shade nodded. "None of us wanted security cameras inside our own homes, but she's got the perimeter of all our homes and businesses wired. She's watching the cameras on her and Vik's properties. Come on." He clasped his hand on my shoulder affectionately, spotting Matteo pull the last steak off the grill. "Let's eat. We'll even be gentlemen and let you bring the leftovers to Andrie. Maybe some cake will sweeten her temper."

The men seemed to drag the meal out, every second slower than the one before it. When everyone was finally finished with their plates, I practically shot up, more than ready to leave, but Gretchen insisted on wrapping up dinner for Andrie. Unable to find a way to pass without being rude, I tried to appear appreciative despite hating the delay.

Finally, I jumped into Shade's SUV, not about to ride bitch with Vic on his bike. "I really need to get something besides my motorcycle," I grumbled, looking at the speedometer. While Shade was driving much faster than Andrie, he was still well below where I would have been had I been behind the wheel.

"I can't afford to get pulled over tonight of all nights. The last thing we need is the police to detain us to go through my vehicle due to a traffic violation. And you can bet, after not finding anything at the clubhouse, they're assuming we all have our illegal shit in our cars."

Seeing his point, I tried to settle back against the seat, only to start drumming my fingers against my thigh.

Shade raised an eyebrow but was smart enough not to comment. He shook his head, then reached for the radio, turning it down so it was only background noise. The heavy metal pounding through the speakers was completely different than Andrie's preferred classical composers and much more familiar. It also echoed my mood. I hated that Andrie was angry but, more importantly, that she was upset. I'd seen the sheen of tears in her eyes, the heartbreak at my lie. She hadn't so much as looked in Vik's direction when she'd stepped outside, something I knew cut him to the core.

I'd known she would be angry and a little hurt. But I hadn't counted on the pain. Alex and I hadn't fought during our brief time together, but I'd expected her to yell or throw things—her temper, the few times I'd seen a glimpse of it, had always been red hot. But Andrie wasn't the same person she'd once been. And she'd just realized she'd been betrayed by the people she trusted and loved most.

"She's going to forgive you, man." Shade said after a few minutes of silence. "She's loved you for ten fucking years and waited for you for almost all of it. She's not going to kick you to the curb now that y'all can actually live out your happily-ever-after together."

"You obviously have never dealt with a pissed off woman before. She's as likely to shoot me as she is to absolve me."

I cursed when I saw all the lights off in her house as we pulled down the street. Despite her warning signs, there was no way in hell I was going to go another hour before talking it out.

Shade punched the accelerator, and I flew back in the seat. "What's wrong?"

"The truck isn't here. She promised Whisp she wasn't going to leave the house."

Vik came roaring up next to us as we parked, his bike screeching to a stop. Shade pulled out his phone as it rang and put it on speaker. "What is it?" Juniper said, not waiting for him to speak. "You came barreling down the street like your tail was on fire."

"Where's Andrie? You were supposed to tell us if she left the house."

"Dude, she hasn't left. There's been absolutely no movement at the house since I pulled it up. Not so much as a stray cat through her yard."

"The fucking truck isn't here, Juniper! How the hell did you miss her pulling out of the driveway?"

Her voice was small and shaky. "Shade, there hasn't been a truck in the driveway since I queued her camera feed two hours ago."

Chapter 34

ANDRIE

"I 'm not sure whether I should start with the interrogation or torture you first so you'll be begging to talk instead." Irina sighed, tapping her gun to her chin as if deep in thought, but I knew better. Irina was like a cat who enjoyed playing with her prey before killing it. It didn't matter if I told her what she wanted to hear in the first five minutes or after five hours. She wasn't about to stop until I'd drawn my last breath. Killing wasn't the goal—the goal was to see how long she could extend the pain.

"Tell me, why would a second-rate human trafficker want a patient list from a psychiatrist no one's ever heard of?" I countered.

The flare of anger wasn't unexpected, but the punch was. I saw stars as she connected with my cheekbone. She'd stripped me naked and tied me to a chair as soon as we'd stopped. Psych 101 to make a victim feel more exposed. Unfortunately for her, I'd gone weeks without clothing at all, and while I couldn't say I enjoyed freezing my ass off, I didn't let the vulnerability get to me. The first thing she'd done after removing my clothes was crank up the AC. The house we were in was nice, if a bit remote. Irina had been quick to warn me that she'd found the house on a rental site under a shell corporation, and no one would be around for days to check on it.

Spitting out a mouthful of blood, I smiled, as if she'd done exactly what I'd predict she'd do. The more I could set her off-balance, the better. "You do realize the government pulled all of my contracts the second they realized Hardy was dirty—including confiscating my patient files. Even if I had copies, which I don't, it wouldn't do you much good. The US military and all the rest of the branches that used my services are all doing damage control right now. By tomorrow, any government asset I've ever come in contact with will have a completely new alias and background. You illegally entered the United States, kidnapped a former government employee, and are likely guilty of a list of other crimes with nothing to gain," I lied without hesitation, keeping my confidence as bolstered as I could.

Her lips thinned as I spelled everything out for her, face paling a bit as I went. But then her jaw tightened, and she sneered. "You think I did this for nothing?"

"We both know you didn't want this list for anything other than political gain in your circles. And the second you try to use it to buy yourself a seat at the big-boys table, you'll lose what little credibility you've been able to get from them. Because I can bet that each and every one of them has enough strings to vet that list before they even buy it from you, and they won't take kindly to you trying to fleece them." This time, I rolled my eyes as if annoyed that I needed to spell it out for her.

I expected irritation and cold calculation, but instead, she lashed out again, punching my stomach. At first, the move pleased me. Punches and blows were nothing compared to what Irina would do to me if she were in control of herself and wrapped up in her games. Then, the wildness in her eyes, the rage she was letting loose, registered. This was not the woman known for her love of torture and inventive ways of "playing" with her wares. This woman was panicked, reactive, and outright scared. While I didn't love the idea of an unpredictable Irina, the fact that she was out of control and not thinking clearly might work to my advantage. At least, in terms of choosing just how painful my own death would be. Fortunately for me, I knew exactly what buttons to press to get what I wanted.

"You know, Demi used to laugh about you," I wheezed. "Saying you were always drunk on power you didn't even have. Sure, everyone toed the line with you in Russia, but that was only because they were afraid of your father. Demi said it was kind of pathetic that you didn't realize the men around you were just humoring you."

Irina screamed again, this time pistol whipping me across the face. My head spun, blackness creeping into the edges of what was already narrowing sight—thanks to a swelling eye from the first hit—but I fought it back, knowing I'd be helpless if I passed out. The pain was intense, so intense I wanted to vomit, but self-preservation won out despite the cold sweat and double vision.

"How is he by the way?" I might be beyond angry at Xander right now, but no way in hell would I put him in jeopardy. "I always regretted not being able to thank him for a good time, even if it did cost me a hell of a lot."

Internally, I winced, I'd meant to keep her focus on Russia and her problems, not me. "He's dead." The lack of emotion would have been surprising if I hadn't heard stories from Demi about growing up with her. He'd warned me when we'd first been together that his mother was capable of murdering not only me but him as well if she felt he was becoming more trouble than he was worth. Even though she hadn't been the one to kill him, she probably hadn't shed a tear over the loss of her only child.

"I hadn't heard," I lied again, my eyes wanting to cross as the world faded from focus before I forced my attention back to the woman in front of me. "I would've sent flowers."

Undeterred, Irina tilted her head, her anger cooling as her curiosity got the better of her. "How did you escape your fate? Sex slaves have such a short expiration date. I honestly didn't peg you as being able to survive the trip across the Atlantic, let alone live out the rest of the year."

"Raid. Right place at the right time," I tried to match her blasé tone. Were my words slurring? I couldn't tell. "I can't say the trip was fun, but I made it out with only a few scars, so all in all, I chalked it up to a learning experience and moved on."

"A ... learning experience?" For once I'd shocked her.

I shrugged. "You date men in dangerous jobs, you're likely to end up in just as much danger as they surround themselves with."

"So, you became a boring therapist in the suburbs?" she asked, a little skeptical, as if trying to reconcile what little she'd know about the woman her son had been briefly living with all those years ago with the straight-laced woman in front of her.

"Not totally boring. I did have all those government contracts," I pointed out. "Until my handler betrayed me and tried to have his goon get my patient list, that is. How did he track you down?"

"The dark web. I saw his ad listing and, as you already guessed, thought that might be of use to some." Putting the gun into the small of her back, she grabbed a butcher knife from a nearby counter. "I'm afraid I had more confidence in his ... reliability ... than I should have." She tapped the knife blade to her lips. "He did make the entire thing sound so simple. A lesson for next time, I suppose. What's the American expression? Don't count your chickens before they hatch? Well, I suppose it's a good thing I was able to track the list back to the original source. After all, it's always better to get the information first hand."

I didn't like that glint in her eye, the mask settling over her face. I was losing her, and I knew what that meant for me.

Chapter 35

XANDER

I wanted to jump in Shade's car and head in the direction the camera had seen her and a woman in black go. A woman who looked suspiciously like my mother.

Instead, he'd all but muscled Vik and me into the back of the car before tearing back for Matteo's underground communications room. Everyone was gathered by the time we arrived. The triplets, Juniper, Josie, and Jolene, were front and center in the large monitor. Judging by the background, the three hadn't left Accardi Tactical and were still in the room we'd spent so much time in earlier in the day.

"The truck left less than two minutes after y'all did," Josie explained as Juniper typed frantically on her keyboard. "And her phone's GPS is still pinging from her wi-fi, so I'm assuming she left it somewhere in the house."

"Isn't she chipped?" Savage wanted to know. "I thought y'all just had to pull up the satellite data to track us."

Jolene shook her head. "Operatives are the only ones with permanent trackers. The rest of y'all's MC circle had the option, but most rejected them. Support staff wouldn't have a reason to be tracked, and it's not like these things aren't pricey. I hate to say they're cost prohibitive, but honestly, it's not like we're outfitted with bullet proof vehicles the way the head honchos are, either."

"They took my truck. Can't you track the GPS?" Vik asked, pacing behind me.

"Working on it," Juniper said, not taking her attention away from her screen. "But it looks like someone had a jammer in their bag of tricks, and it's interfering with the signal. Let me see something else ..."

She trailed off, and the screen split. "I'm pulling up traffic cameras. We know the plate number, but a dark blue pickup in Texas isn't exactly hard to come by, and there isn't CCTV covering even half of the roads they could have taken. With traffic, trying to see all the numbers won't be easy."

"There," I pointed to one of the feeds on the screen. Junie had played back the few that were near the house at the time Andrie had left. "You see that. She stopped for four seconds at the stop sign."

"The angle isn't right to see a plate ... the car behind them is too close. Are you sure?"

"Positive." All of us sounded off at once. Only Andrie would abide by all traffic laws while being held at gunpoint.

Sure enough, as Juniper followed the truck onto the main highway, then quickly onto the interstate, she was able to keep tabs on the truck until it made its way out of the city. Again, only Andrie's diligence in keeping to the exact speed limit let us know we were watching the correct truck. We were able to speed up the process by doing the math and anticipating when she'd be passing the next camera.

Irina—if I was correct—had Andrie double-back several times, clearly suspicious of a tail, but eventually, they ended up in a suburb. They turned down a road that had several offshoots into large neighborhoods, with yet a few more roads past them that were larger private residences.

"Fuck," I swore when Juniper stopped and sat back, clearly at the end of that avenue of tracking.

"Don't give it up yet," Grimm said, coming to stand next to me. His confidence was something I greatly needed at the moment. Every second Andrie was in the presence of the monster who birthed me was another step closer to her end, and I knew it.

"Anyone of note with property in that area?" he asked. "There's no way she could have snuck out of Europe and had the time to hunt down a vacant property."

"No," Jolene shook her head, looking over Juniper's shoulder to look at her screen.

Josie tapped the screen. "But look at this. What do you think the odds are she booked a house through a website?" she asked almost absentmindedly.

"There are only two listings." Junie started typing vigorously at her keyboard again. "Let me hack into their security cameras. It'll be faster than me breaking into the site's records."

It took a few minutes, but Juniper was finally able to pull up the security cameras for the first house. The outside camera showed several vehicles, making hope rise that we'd found them, but a quick look at the interior ones showed a kid must have "borrowed" a parents' credit card in order to book it because a full party of underage and over-imbibed teens filled every screen.

She cut the feed and switched to hacking into the other house while Josie made an anonymous call to the local police station to report the rave.

Seconds ticked by, with Vik pacing behind me, while I stood frozen, unable to move. I knew more than anyone what Irina was capable of, and the thousands of scenarios racing through my head weren't possibilities; they were past experiences. I'd watched her knock out teeth with a hammer—one at a time. She'd taken ears, tongues, fingers, toes. Once, I'd watched her castrate a man after he'd been forced to rape another victim of her games. Electrocution, waterboarding, hanging a person on a wall using nothing but hooks through their own skin ... she'd done them all.

I'd realized before I'd even hit puberty that Irina got off on torture, not sex. She didn't care about age, race, or gender either. Other people didn't matter to her. The only person I'd seen evoke even a hint of emotion was my grandfather. And even then, I wasn't sure how far down her affection for him went, though he loved his only child blindly, only laughing at her exploits and killing anyone who dared say anything negative about her.

"Here we go," Juniper said, pulling me from my thoughts.

My eyes went back to the screen, relief almost making me sag when I saw her, alive and breathing, before horror had me freezing again.

She was bound to a chair, naked, though she sat as regal as a queen. Irina's back was to the camera, but there was no mistaking it was her.

Not waiting for a second longer, Vik and I ran from the room, ignoring the shouts to stop. We could call on the way if needed, but no way in hell were we waiting now that we had a location.

Chapter 36

ANDRIE

"**A**nd that's how they should've done it the first time," I heard over my screams. Irina sounded as impassive now as I'd been earlier. I'd tried to keep my responses contained, but I'd lost the battle when she'd decided to show me the *right way* to cut someone up with a knife.

She'd scoffed when she'd seen the healing lines on my arm, insisting only an amateur would have started off that way. Her attitude was that of a salon stylist looking at the work of a four-year-old let loose with scissors.

Using the butcher knife, she'd meticulously filleted almost the entire skin of the top of my forearm, peeling it from my body as she went. After that, she'd cut out what she declared was fat, before revealing the muscles, which I could see trembling through the blood seeping from the open wound.

Jasper won't be happy about this, I thought sarcastically as I tried to calm my breathing through my adrenaline-induced panic. He'd insisted on scheduling a checkup for tomorrow to see how my arm had been healing.

"Now, onto the hand," Irina said. The only emotion I saw from her was a flicker of excitement in her eyes. "We'll start with the fingernails," she started to say, pulling out a pair of pliers from a drawer in the kitchen that I assumed the owners used as a junk drawer. "After, we'll move on to asking about those patient names."

Even knowing it was futile, I tried to jerk my hand from her when she reached for it, forcibly outstretching my pinky and laying an arm across my hand so I couldn't move it away from her. Before she could position the pliers, the sound of a door being kicked in had both of us jerking toward the door.

Xander, gun in hand, stepped into the kitchen before she could react. "I wouldn't do that," he said in Russian when she began to reach to her waistband for her own weapon. I knew he couldn't shoot her, not with her still crouched like she was in front of me. Irina must have already come to that conclusion because even though her hand paused, she smirked.

"Or what?" she practically purred.

Footsteps behind me echoed down the hall, telling us that Xander hadn't come alone.

"Or one of us will shoot you." Vik came into view as he slowly came around me, his gun drawn.

Her eyes widened when she locked in on him, ignoring her son completely as she recognized his old best friend.

"Well, well. I guess I should have assumed my son sent you after this one." I squeaked despite myself when the pliers tightened ever so slightly. "But I have to say, it's pathetic to think you've spent all this time still following orders. You never did have an original thought. Are you going to spend the rest of your life stuck in limbo, waiting for the next directive that will never come?"

Vik smiled, taking a page from my earlier playbook and needling the older woman before lifting his head to Xander. "I wouldn't say *never.*"

Irina couldn't hide her surprise that time, spinning on her heel to look at Xander straight on. There was a pause, then a snort. "Who the hell are you?"

Vik chuckled then, while Xander gave her a patronizing smirk. "You don't recognize him?" I asked, relief coursing through me at the idea that even his own mother didn't know who he was. After all this time, all this effort, he was *safe.*

It hit me then. That he was truly here. After all these years and despite all our time apart and everything we'd both gone through, he still loved me as much as I loved him—both the Demi of the past and the Xander of the future.

"I love you," I told him, ignoring Irina. The sting of tears in my eyes had nothing to do with the pounding headache or pain in my arm; it had everything to do with the emotions running through me.

For the first time since he stepped into the room, Xander's attention came to rest on me. His expression softened, his eyes filling with a warmth that hadn't been there a moment ago. "I love you, too, *solnyshkuh.*"

"You'd better," I told him, smiling despite my situation. "Because if you didn't, after all we've been through, I'd unleash Lessia on you."

"Did someone mention me?" Alessia practically melted into view on my other side.

"Where the hell did you come from?" Vik wanted to know.

Lessia ignored him, focusing on Irina. And for good reason.

Irina, seeing she was boxed in and trying to take advantage of the surprise Lessia's arrival had caused, spun as she reached for the gun at her back, rising as she did so.

Before I could blink, several shots rang out, seeming to come from every direction. Instinctively, I closed my eyes and tried to hunch down as best I could.

My eyes were still shut, ears ringing, when someone grabbed my hand. Unable to help myself, I let out an undignified squeak, pulling back momentarily before recognizing Xander's touch and trying to launch myself to him.

I kept myself focused on his beautiful, blurry blue eyes, even as Vik procured a bedspread to toss around my shoulders and Xander pulled me free of the restraints and into his arms, careful of my injury.

"Xander," I breathed into his neck. I wasn't sure if I was shaking or he was.

"I've got you." He lifted me off my feet, cradling me against him as if I were a small child. Finally feeling safe, I didn't fight the darkness when it overtook me, knowing Xander was there.

Chapter 37

XANDER

"How's she doing?" Grimm asked, his voice rough. I know it had to be hard on him and the rest of the MC not being able to be with us at the hospital, but we all knew it was for the best.

After Andrie scared the ever-loving fuck out of me by passing out in my arms, Thoth and Lessia had jumped into action—making calls that led to Vik, Andrie, and I catching a ride in a medical life-flight to Brooke Army Medical Center. It was there the doctors had discovered one of the hits to the face Andrie had received had caused a brain bleed that required emergency surgery. Once she'd stabilized, they'd performed another procedure for her arm and took a skin graft from her leg to help close the wound.

I'd hoped that we were out of the woods, and she'd wake up, but an infection had set in, and the meds had her confused and lethargic the few times she'd opened her eyes.

Vik and I hadn't left her side. Thoth had to have worked some magic because none of the doctors or nurses had batted an eye at us ignoring visitor hours, made us produce IDs, or even asked our names—even Andrie's.

"Her fever finally broke." I wiped a hand down my face. I was sitting in the uncomfortable-as-fuck chair next to her bed, having sent Vik to get some food and a break. "Her last scan showed her swelling is resolving, and doctors are hopeful she'll wake up sometime today." If there were a God, I hope he allowed her to wake today. Seeing her so small and pale in that hospital bed was killing me. "They think she'll make a full recovery but can't promise anything until she's awake."

Even as I spoke, I kept a careful eye on the monitors and listened to the ever-present sound of her heartbeat. I knew, without a doubt, there wasn't anything we couldn't do together, but damn, hadn't she been through enough? Lived through enough?

"Do you want us there?" Grimm asked immediately. "We can make it happen—"

I cut him off, my voice rough with gratitude. "We're alright for now, man. But I appreciate the offer. I just wish ..." *Wish I could hear her voice ... see her beautiful eyes ... tell her how much I love her.*

"I know," he said simply. "And if it helps, she knows it, too. Andrie might have been mad and a little hurt, but she knows what your feelings are for her. Knows what you've both lived through to get to this point. She's not going to toss your ass to the curb."

The corners of my mouth twisted up. "She might kick it a time or two."

"Nothing we don't all deserve," he assured me, and I let out a low chuckle.

"Now, that's a sound I missed hearing." The soft, drowsy voice almost had me dropping the phone.

"Hey, sunshine." Hanging up on Grimm, I dropped the phone and immediately took the hand not attached to the IV drip, unashamed that my eyes turned glassy.

"I like it better when you call me *solnyshkuh.*"

"Noted," I said, leaning down to kiss her knuckles, relieved as fuck that she was finally awake and coherent. "How do you feel?"

Grimacing, she shifted. "Like I have a headache from hell, and my arm is sore. But all in all, not nearly as bad as I could be. What's the damage? Where are we, and is there going to be a cop in here anytime soon that I need to have a story ready for?"

I smiled. How like Andrie to immediately organize the important points.

"You had a bleed in your brain that required surgery to release the pressure. You ended up with an infection, likely due to the knife wounds, and have been out of it for a while. We're at BAMC."

"Brooke Army Med Center?" she asked, looking surprised.

I nodded. "Someone pulled some strings. We haven't been asked any questions, but I'm not sure if that's a permanent or temporary reprieve."

"Who's we?" Andrie asked, struggling to sit up.

I pressed the button on the controls for her bed, raising it until she nodded. "Vik and I came with you. Everyone else—and I mean everyone—has been checking in at least twice a day, even though we've been sending updates." At my words, I grabbed my dropped phone, texting one-handed to let Vik know she was awake. I couldn't seem to let her go.

"Sweetheart," I started, unable to wait a second longer, even knowing I should call the nurses and save the heavy discussions for later. "I am so sorry for what I put you through. Both in the past, with my keeping secrets," I said, not wanting to get too personal, even though we should be perfectly safe. "And with what happened to put you in that bed. I *never* meant—"

I cut off when her eyes narrowed. Though, she immediately winced. "Xander," Andrie started to scold, then grinned. "Alexander. I should have realized," she murmured, almost to herself. Her smile grew. "You took my name, and I took yours."

Smiling, too, I rubbed her ring finger gently. "We did vow to honor and love each other for as long as we both lived. I can't think of a better way to honor each other, even if we did have to remain apart for most of it."

"But never again," she finished, her hand turning to grasp mine.

"Never again." I promised, leaning down to kiss her.

My lips had just brushed hers when the door flung open hard enough to slam against the wall. "Andrie," Vik said before stopping short when he realized he was interrupting. His hesitation lasted only a second before he continued his stride, ignoring me completely as he came around the bed to take up the empty chair next to me. "How are you feeling, honey?"

I felt her lips curve into a smile against mine again, and as much as I wanted to curse, I found myself smiling, too.

All I'd ever wanted was the love of my life and my brother at my side. And now, despite everything, it looked as if all of my dreams were coming true.

Chapter 38

EPILOGUE—GIDEON

"Oh, good. You're still here."

Biting back a sigh at my sister's words, I wondered if she'd go away if I pretended I didn't hear her. I wasn't *supposed* to be there this late. I'd planned on being out of the office an hour ago so I could get dinner started before Gia got home from school. It was the first week back from summer break, and as much as I wanted to take her to and from school, she'd insisted on all things being normal, despite what had happened just a few months ago.

Sure, both drivers were PSOs—personal security officers—assigned to keep her safe. But they weren't me, and they hadn't been enough before. Wasn't a father's first and primary responsibility to protect his children? I was in a never-ending battle of what seemed like a war with no winner—either love my child enough to let her go, even knowing the dangers she could face, or smother her.

Andrie—Dr. Andrie Demming—had assured me that what I was feeling was perfectly normal. As was Gia's rather fast bounce back to her mostly-normal self after her abduction. Still, after yet another round of arguing that morning with my daughter, I couldn't help the sense of failure. I'd failed my daughter. I hadn't been there to protect her when she'd been taken and her guards shot. I'd failed her again when I'd let my sister confront the man holding my little girl hostage and do what needed to be done to ensure her safety. And ... apparently ... I was still failing when it came to my resolve to stop working so much and spend more quality time with Gia while I still had her. How was it that my little girl was almost a teenager when it was just yesterday I'd brought a motherless, tiny newborn home from the hospital?

"Did you have a chance to look over our proposal?"

Well, shit. Turning from where I'd been poised to press the button to the elevator and wishing I'd been ten seconds faster coming down the hall, I turned to face the only woman in my life I always had the urge to hug or throttle, sometimes at the same time.

Lessia was my baby sister and a ballbuster. She could be—hell, *was*—a handful on her worst day. I'd been smart enough to double our legal fund the second I'd known Lessia was retiring from her jet-setting days in Europe and settling back home, knowing trouble didn't just follow her ... she cultivated it.

And sure enough, she'd blown through that account in less than six months. Despite the headaches, extra work-load, and chaos she caused, she was also our favorite. All four brothers admitted it—just not to her directly.

"The one ..." I trailed off when I zeroed in on the woman Lessia was practically dragging behind her. "Jesus, Lessia, slow down before you pull the poor woman off her feet," I scolded, slamming a door on my body's reaction to seeing

Madison Harris struggling to keep up with Lessia's much longer stride. As a former model, Lessia towered over most women, and her legs were certainly longer than Madison's, who was at least six inches shorter.

"Sorry, we just wanted to catch you before you left for the day." Despite her words, she didn't slow a bit until the women reached me in the alcove in front of the door.

"I'm already late," I tried, not wanting to do this now and in front of an audience, but Lessia talked right over me.

"The one I emailed you with the subject telling you to read it immediately." Rolling her eyes, she gave Madison a pointed look as if she was the one responsible for keeping me in line.

Bristling, I punched the button again, not caring if I was being rude. "You know all proposals go through Legal, not me. I have plenty of work that *can't* be handed off to others, so I'm not in the habit of taking on extra just because you don't like following protocol, Lessia."

Madison's gorgeous jade-green eyes fell to the ground, her body slumping as if she could melt into the floor. Immediately calling myself an ass, I apologized. "I promise I know exactly who the blame lies with, and none of it is with you, Miss Harris." I was quick to assure her, not wanting her to think I was upset with her in any way.

Madison's mouth dropped open, but before she could speak, Lessia jumped in, with her hands on her hips and a smirk on her lips. "If you'd bother to read it, like you were *supposed* to," she said pointedly. "You'd have known that this was a personal idea. One Maddy offered to help me with on her own time. And because it's personal, I can't send it through our legal department. In addition," she raised her voice when I started to speak, "I wanted *your* opinion because not only do I value your thoughts and expertise, I had the crazy idea this would be something you'd want to volunteer your time toward, especially since Boone and Keene both already offered."

Eyes blazing now, she took a step back as the elevator door chimed and opened—right on time for my sister and two minutes too late to prevent me from making a fool of myself. "But don't worry, I'll take note that you don't have the time or inclination to be a part of anything of this nature in the future. Tell Gia I'll see her tomorrow."

Not waiting for a reply, she grabbed Madison again, towing her back down the hallway.

"Is he always like that?" I overheard Madison whisper as they walked away. I felt those words, the incredulity and disgust behind them like a stab to the gut. Because, though Madison had no clue who I was, we knew each other inside and out and had spent months learning almost everything there was to know about the other. Damn it, I loved her. And didn't that just fuck all, considering she didn't realize the man she'd been talking to over the phone for months—the man who'd broken up with her with a sorry-ass excuse—had just been standing in front of her.

AFTERWORD

Thank you so much for reading *Captivating Beauty*. If you loved this book as much as I enjoyed writing it, please take the time to leave a review. The Accardi Tactical series is my first foray into the writing world, and I treasure hearing your thoughts. *Fierce Beauty* is already underway, and I promise to get it to you as soon as it's ready to be shared.

As a side note, everything I write is written 100% by me—absolutely no AI software is or ever will be used to create my books. In addition, all my covers and graphics are designed by human creators. AI has its uses, but not in my writing world.

ABOUT THE AUTHOR

K.C. is the alter ego of a thirty-something dreamer who lives in the heart of small-town USA. Seriously, cows outnumber people four to one and she has to drive almost an hour to visit the grocery store! Business owner and farm girl by day and writer by night, she keeps herself busy. When she's not working or writing, she's playing with her countless dogs, riding her horses, or reading books by her favorite authors. She writes what she loves to read—primarily protector romance and romantic suspense. You can count on her to provide entertaining stories filled with strong women, hot alpha men, and love forever after.

She loves to hear from her readers! Please reach out at authork.c.ramsey@gmail.com, and check out K.C. Ramsey's Readers on Facebook for upcoming releases, book signings, giveaways, and bonus content.

Made in the USA
Monee, IL
16 July 2025

21238712R00204